I0695109

PAMELA G. BAKER

Chasing Time

By

Pamela G. Baker

CHAPTER ONE

I maintained a death grip on my steering wheel all the way from the Atlanta airport to I-20. I'd always believed bumper-to-bumper eighty-mile-an-hour traffic was an exaggeration—until today. When traffic thinned, my heart rate lowered to normal, only to increase again when I neared my hometown.

Main Street in New Hope, Georgia, hadn't changed in the three and a half years since I'd graduated from college and moved away, but I had. Ma would be disappointed. I squared my shoulders and concentrated on what I saw with my eyes and not my mind. No point in dredging up memories from my childhood.

Then I passed New Hope General Store, which had been restored to the original facade from the 1800s, and unwanted memories flooded back. In 1870, wooden walkways flanked the front of the store and church. I'd either be driving a wagon or riding a horse side-saddle down the dirt road. Hitching posts stood every several yards, more in front of the livery. Funny, a gas station now stood on the corner where the livery had been.

The LED snowmen, snowflakes, and Christmas trees hanging from the light poles looked garish compared to the greenery and bows from my childhood. I shuddered. Why get wistful for the old days, now? I had purposefully banished it from my mind when Todd brought me to 2010 and hadn't thought of it much in the nearly ten years since. Too painful.

I left Main Street and drove through several commercial areas and subdivisions before I reached Bridger Street. Todd had seemed delighted I'd accepted his invitation to spend Christmas with him and his wife, Chantal. Despite the yearly invite, this would be my first Christmas with them since I'd moved to Seattle. Did he suspect there was a hidden motive behind my last-minute acceptance? I took a deep breath and glanced at the long suburban street that contained both Todd's residence and his wife's business.

The neighborhood felt serene compared to Atlanta, less than an hour's drive away. Kids ran around in front of immaculate middle-class houses, most with Christmas lights, blowup snowmen, and a few nativities. Several homeowners waved from their front porches. Cousin Nate's house stood sentinel at the end of the street. Except for the bed and breakfast sign, it looked like it had when he'd built it.

A vision of the house when it was new competed in my mind with the B&B, though the main differences were the surroundings. Now, there were fewer and larger trees, and no outhouse. A wooded area still stood in the distance, but most of the vast acreage had been parceled off for commercial and residential purposes. Todd had bought the house from Nate's great-grandson soon after I'd moved away, but he hadn't decided what to do with it until Chantal decided for him. I'd always thought he would make it into a museum like it had been before Cassie traveled back. Marriage had a habit of changing things, though. Relationships in general alter people. I needed to find a partner, unlike my current boyfriend, who would allow me to evolve for the better.

My shoulders tensed as I pulled around the cul-de-sac and parked. Nate's house. I glanced back toward Todd's home, three doors down, built in 2000, more than a hundred years later than this one. That's where Cassie's story began.

Cassie, Todd's former girlfriend, had activated his time machine and landed in the field where Todd's house stood now. In 1870, the only residence nearby was the one I shared with my parents, brother, sister-in-law, Lera, and her son, Caleb. We lived a mile away, down a path behind Nate's. Now that area is a subdivision with starter homes.

I left my small carry-on in the trunk and walked toward the No-Vacancy sign. I'd probably be staying in their guest room down the street instead of the room I'd requested. Would Chantal want help running the place for the week I'd be here? They'd had it open as a bed and breakfast for about eight months, so they must have enough staff. Good, because I didn't know the first thing about running a hospitality business. I glanced down at my old sneakers, ripped jeans, and Hogwarts hoodie. On top of that, I'd tied my hair into a messy ponytail and hadn't bothered with makeup. Chantal may not want me inside her establishment until I changed clothes, but she'd have to lend me something.

I sighed as I climbed the porch steps. This was as much like coming home as possible, without a time machine.

The front door opened. An average height, brown blur squealed and ran toward me. Chantal wrapped her long, bony arms around me and squeezed. "Lydia! I am so happy to see you." She backed away, held me at arm's length, and clicked her tongue at me. "Girl, you need to get some meat on those bones!" She let go and waved her arm downward to punctuate her sentence.

"Look who's talking." I poked her skin-and-bones upper arm. "Merry Christmas."

She laughed and ushered me inside. Then she stopped in the foyer and looked me up and down. "Where's your baggage? I mean the physical kind." She squinted and smoothed her relaxed shoulder-length hair. "Your emotional baggage is on full display. You look even paler than normal." She flicked her finger. "Let's get you a nice cup of tea, and you can tell me all about it."

That eerie Deja vu feeling descended as I followed her through the small parlor and dining room, furnished similarly to when Nate first built it. The grandfather clock in the corner resembled Nate's. Either Chantal had done a great job restoring the house, or Nate's descendants hadn't changed much. When we reached the kitchen, I relaxed, impressed with the commercial appliances and workspaces Todd had installed in the room that was originally a mudroom and pantry. I gazed out the back window, surprised to see the detached kitchen.

"That old kitchen is empty." She sighed. "I sure wish they'd kept the wood stove."

I coughed to cover a gasp. "How'd you know there was one?"

She waved toward the window. "Well, there had to have been once upon a time."

I didn't plan to spill all my problems to Chantal, but I

relished a cup of tea, so I sat at the butcher block table and waited for the water to boil.

Chantal placed a plate of gingerbread cookies on the table, then brought the kettle over and poured water into the teapot. How many times had my mother or Lera done the same thing? Probably thousands. The teapot even looked similar—white porcelain with rosebuds and vines painted on it. This place brought back too many memories. Good thing, I only planned to stay a week.

Chantal smiled and sat opposite me at the small kitchen table.

I drummed my fingers on the wood. "I hope I'm not keeping you from anything."

She shook her head, swishing her hair. "No guests right now. Just you. My brother arrives tomorrow." She leaned forward, placing both palms on the table. "Now, tell Mama what's the problem." Her dark brown eyes bore into mine.

How did she know? I'd told Todd I'd accepted their yearly invitation to spend Christmas with them, so I could see what they'd done with the place. I pulled my ponytail over my shoulder and twirled it. "What are you, about nine years older than me?"

She raised her eyebrows. "Almost ten, and that doesn't make much difference. It's all about attitude. Plus, when I started dating Todd, you were what, eighteen?"

I nodded.

She pursed her lips. "I took on the mom role for you then, and I haven't let it go."

I held my hands up. "If I remember correctly, you took on that role for Jamal, too. Why's he waiting until Christmas Eve? Is he working?"

She snorted. "Little bro always got some angle going, but nothing you and I would call work." She peered at me. "And don't change the subject."

I smiled and lowered my shoulders, trying to appear relaxed. "I wanted to see you and Todd for Christmas. That's all. You're the closest thing to family I have."

She patted my hand on the table. "I know. Too bad the state wouldn't allow you to live with Todd. I hate it that you ended up in the foster system." She shook her head and frowned.

I squinted at her. "Is that what he told you?"

She tilted her head. "You don't remember how I met Todd?"

I shrugged.

"I worked at social services at the time of the accident."

My breath hitched, but I covered by clearing my throat. "I don't remember you before you started dating Todd."

"I wasn't your case worker, but I helped make the decision. Todd didn't fit our profile of a foster parent." She glanced at the ceiling. "It was a strange case. I didn't believe him about the accident at first. He said he'd seen you in the car with three hoodlums and had followed. When the car crashed into a tree, he got you out and brought you to the hospital instead of calling 911. Said the boys were already dead." She set down her cup. "Then, when I asked him where your family was, he told us they were overseas and you were staying with him." She whistled a long, low tone. "What a legal nightmare. He had nothing in writing from your parents."

What would Chantal think if she knew my accident happened in 1870 while fighting a fire, and Todd brought me to the future to save my life? Todd had to come up with some kind of cover story, and had found an unwitnessed accident that happened out in the country. He'd explained the absence of my family by saying they were overseas missionaries who had let me stay with him. His boss had found someone to get me a birth certificate and fake evidence that a Gardner family had died in a fire in Africa. Todd's boss would have done anything to cover up the existence of the time machine because one of their engineers used it and never returned.

Chantal lowered her head. "I wish I could go back and change it. Advocate for him, now that I know. . ."

"What?" I sat up straight. Could she know about the time machine?

"How good a parent he'd be." She patted her belly. "Well, will be."

My eyes went wide. "Are you?"

She smiled. "Not yet, but we're trying."

My shoulders lowered. "Cool."

She bit her lip. "But I still feel bad about you getting shuffled between foster homes."

"I survived." I pressed my lips together.

She leaned over the table and locked gazes with me. "This is the first Christmas you've visited us since your last year at Tech. Why are you really here?"

I pressed my fingers into my temples. "Austin and I have been fighting."

She sat up, sliding her palms on the table. "I knew it!" Then she clamped her mouth shut and rolled her hand, indicating I should continue.

"Thank you for not saying, I told you so." I groaned. "It's escalated so much, I don't even feel comfortable at work."

She gasped. "Oh wow." As if tea would cure me, she poured some into my cup. "How long have you felt like that?"

"A while."

She nodded. "Thought so."

"How'd you know?"

"Good guess?" She poured her own cup and sipped.

I rolled my eyes. How could this woman know me so well when we hadn't spent more than a few days at a time together since we met seven years ago? I took a deep breath. "It started last summer with creative differences on the latest version of the software."

"Which game again?"

"*Warlords and Dragons*." I cleared my throat. "Since it's his company, he went with his idea."

"Of course he did." She mimed zipping her lip. "Go on."

"I thought everything was fine until fall, when his idea didn't pan out like he'd thought. Turned out, our customers wanted more dragons and fewer human battles." I tightened my grip on the teacup handle. "Austin blamed all the programmers, even me."

"Does he ever accept responsibility for his mistakes?"

"Of course." I fixed my gaze on the commercial oven, trying to recall an instance where he took the blame for something.

She cradled her cup in both hands and peered at me. "Can you think of an example?"

I blew out a breath as I frantically searched my memory. Nothing. I'd been so busy trying to be the perfect girlfriend, I'd missed it, and probably other red flags as well. Was I in love with the real Austin or my ideal one? "You know, I can't at the moment, but I've been stressed." Why couldn't I admit my mistake to Chantal? Had Austin rubbed off on me? I set down my cup and slumped against the chairback. "And I'm exhausted."

She covered my cold hand with her warm one. "So did he continue to treat you the same outside the office?"

I swallowed hard. "He moved out of our apartment in September. I had to find a roommate in order to make rent." Another reason I tried not to think about Ma. I hoped she couldn't see me from heaven, or wherever she was.

Chantal's brow furrowed, and she leaned back. "What happened yesterday?"

I squinted. "How'd you...Oh, I accepted your invitation yesterday." I sat up straight. "He called me asking why I wasn't at work." My face heated. "I told him it was Sunday. Then he said my work was sub-par." My voice rose a notch. "He accused me of sabotaging his business."

She set down her cup, still holding it with both hands. "By not working on Sunday?"

I shook my head. "He claimed I had deliberately inserted bugs in the latest game."

Her mouth dropped open.

"Exactly. I had no reason to do that." I jumped up and paced the length of the counter. "I was furious. I told him I wanted time to look for another job. He told me to go ahead."

She leaned forward. "He fired you?"

I stopped and clasped my hands together. "Not technically. He told me to take two weeks off and we'd re-evaluate, whatever that means."

Chantal sat back and clicked her tongue. "You could use

the break anyway. When was the last time you had a vacation?"

"After the last release." I tapped my fingers with my thumb, counting the months. "A year and a half?"

"You're welcome to stay as long as you like." She took another sip of tea and smiled. "I've even made up the room you requested."

I tilted my head. "Didn't I see a No-Vacancy sign?"

She grinned. "It's Christmas. I want it to be only family."

"You know, if you keep doing this, you won't make any money."

She flicked her wrist as if finances were the farthest thing from her mind. Chantal was the kindest person I knew. Was that how she'd uncovered almost everything I'd wanted to hide?

~

Nostalgia crept over me as I carried my small suitcase upstairs and u-turned at the landing. The view appeared the same as the last time I'd been here, the day before Lera's harvest ball. At the top of the stairs, two doors stood across the hallway. The one on the left had been mine and Cassie's when we'd stayed with Nate, and Nate had used the one on the right. Farther down from my room was the door to the water closet. The hallway wrapped around the staircase, showing two doors on the perpendicular wall to my right, and one for Cassie and Nate's master bedroom on the left. Behind me, at the back of the house, were two walk-in closets opposite a stairway that continued up to the playroom on the third floor.

I took a deep breath as I crossed to the door on the left. Other than the brass number 2 at eye-level, it looked the same. I entered the room and gaped. Somehow, the bed and dresser had remained here since 1870. I blinked to make sure I wasn't just seeing what I expected. The quilt looked new and was manufactured, not hand-sewn like the one Cassie and I had used a hundred and fifty years ago.

I placed my suitcase on the bed, walked to the window, and opened the curtain. The room lit up, revealing a new door on the side wall closer to the water closet. Curious, I strode over and turned the knob half expecting it to be locked. To my surprise, it opened into the original bathroom, complete with a clawfoot tub but with a modern shower.

"Huh." I glanced across the bathroom. The original door into the hallway had been plastered over. "I guess I have a private bath." The rest of the rooms probably did also. My room was the smallest, so it made sense to incorporate the original bathroom into it and add new ones to the others. But the primary bedroom was just around the corner. I would have connected the bathroom to it and made that a historic suite. I shrugged. Chantal was the hospitality expert, not me. Wait. Hadn't I seen the bathroom door from the stairs? I charged into the hall. Yep. The door frame was there, but it didn't have a knob. She must have kept it to maintain the symmetry.

Back inside my room, I sat in the rocking chair—not the original but similar—next to the window and gazed down the suburban street. When this house was a museum, Cassie had gazed out this window at a similar view. Could she have seen this suburban street in her mind when we gazed out that window in the spring of 1870? I shuddered. It must have been so hard for her. Why was this the first time I'd ever thought about that, even right after Todd had brought me here? In my defense, I'd been fifteen at the time, and fighting to survive.

After I recovered, I jumped into this life of freedom to learn and become whatever I wanted. At times, I'd been a little too enthusiastic, entering every science fair possible. One foster mother complained that she couldn't keep up with me. The others thought I was weird, or they didn't like my relationship with Todd. He was the only person who knew my secret, and that gave us a unique bond. Though I loved my family, even Pa told me I belonged in this time. I'd never once entertained the idea of going back, and purposely had not researched anything about them. To me, it was as if they'd died in the present, and finding out what happened to them felt like cheating. So why were thoughts of home bombarding me today? Was it this place, or my state of mind? Maybe I was ready to find out how my family had fared.

No. I was only trying to avoid a tough decision. I couldn't continue working with Austin.

CHAPTER TWO

My body unpacked my suitcase as my mind listed bullet statements on my resume. Three years of programming for a mildly successful game developer probably wasn't the exact experience an employer would seek. Then again, Todd might have some contacts, and my Georgia Tech degree in computer engineering would be an asset. Maybe I should come back to Atlanta. Seattle was overrated.

By the time I skipped down the stairs for dinner, my resume was on the cloud, ready to be printed or e-mailed, and I felt a weight lifted. I could take the next few days off and start the job hunt in earnest after the holiday.

As I hurried through the small parlor, voices emanated from the dining room. I stopped short of the closed door.

"Any idea what's wrong?" Todd sounded tense.

My shoulders tightened. Why didn't I want him to know about Austin and me?

"Why does there have to be something wrong?" Chantal asked.

Whew. She didn't spill my plight.

"Because I know your brother. It's the only time Jamal

visits."

My shoulders relaxed. I guess everything isn't always about me. I pushed open the door and stood in the entrance pretending I hadn't heard them. "Is it dinnertime? I'm starving."

They jumped and whirled around.

I stepped back. "I didn't mean to startle you."

Chantal glanced at the grandfather clock in the corner. "It is, in fact, time for supper." She trotted through the rear door.

"Hi, Lydia." Todd walked over with his hand out to shake. I opened my arms, and he offered me a one-armed side hug. Why was it still so awkward between us? "It's been a few years," he said in answer to my unasked question.

"Sorry about that." I looked at the floor, then glanced around the room. "Did you find original pictures to restore this place?"

He shook his head. "Some, but not for this room. I used Cassie's diaries."

I leaned toward him. "I didn't know she left them. I want to see!"

"They're all in the closet upstairs."

"Where I found Pa's journal?"

He nodded.

"It's time for dinner." Chantal held the door open for me. "We'll eat in the kitchen."

I sat at the butcher block table, and Chantal loaded my plate with chicken pot pie and spinach salad.

"Why the sudden interest in your family?" Todd asked.

"That was rude." Chantal slapped him on the upper arm.

I smiled. "It was blunt." I took a bite of chicken and tried to formulate an answer. My reaction to the diaries had surprised me. "Never knew about the diaries." As Todd opened his mouth, I raised my hand. "I know that's not an excuse. I was fifteen when I got out of the hospital, and all I wanted was to fit in here. Keep the past in the past." I stopped short and looked at Todd. "Does she know?"

He cleared his throat. "Of course, she knows. You're a descendant of the man who built this house. That's why I was so interested in purchasing it."

"Oh, right." How could I keep Chantal from suspecting I was hiding something?

She pointed her fork at me. "You know, the more you find out about your ancestors, it might help you feel like you fit in."

I squinted, considering.

"Well, anyway." She scooped a bite of salad. "I guess everyone has problems fitting in from time to time."

I cocked my head. It wasn't just me?

Todd changed the subject, and we finished supper, catching up on the last few years since I'd moved to Seattle. For me, there wasn't much to tell—other than release dates and awards. At least I had some money to show for it, though not as much as Austin.

Todd accompanied me into the dining room and glanced behind. "Did you think I told Chantal our secret?"

I nodded. "For a split second. When you brought up my family."

"I would never tell." He scowled at me. "We got lucky tonight. Please be careful."

"Why don't you tell Chantal?"

He rubbed the back of his neck. "I wanted to, but I didn't

think she'd believe me. Now, it's too late."

"She'd be mad?"

"Yeah." He glanced toward the kitchen door. "Have you ever told anyone?"

I snorted. "Of course not."

He grimaced. "Then why do you think I should?"

"I'm not married." I flounced out, hurried through the small parlor, and upstairs. Instead of going to my room, I walked around the corner past the master bedroom to the back side of the house. I opened the door on the left, noting the ladder leading up to the second-story portion of the closet. I'd always wondered why Nate had put that in, since there was a door into it from the playroom on the next floor. Todd had indicated the diaries were on this level, so I perused the shelves to my right and found several journals stacked at about waist height. I started to thumb through them, but the closeness of the tiny room suffocated me. I grabbed the whole stack, several books of varying thickness, and hurried to my room.

My hands full, I managed to open my door without dropping any books, but nearly fell. Good thing I only had to take three strides to get to the bed. I collapsed onto it, and the journals slid out of my hands and spread out on the quilt.

They were all dated on the front, except for the smallest one, which was my father's. Five were dated before I was born in May 1855—not the 1995 listed on my current birth certificate—and two were dated in the early 1870s. I reached for the 1871 journal first. From the opening line about Nate, it had to be Cassie's. I leaned against the pillows heaped in front of the headboard and settled in to read.

The first journal spanned January 1871 to March 1872,

and the second, April 1872 to June 1873. The entries ranged from every day to a few weeks apart, and most were short. I flipped to the middle of the first one and lingered on a pencil sketch of Ma. Cassie had captured her twinkling eyes and upturned mouth. Her salt and pepper hair was pulled back in her normal style, and she looked as if she could jump off the page and nag me about reading my Bible. I chuckled and shook my head. Ma never would give up. I turned the page and gazed at a sketch of Pa. His intense eyes peered off the yellowed paper, his brow furrowed enough to show he was serious, but his lips turned up in a slight smile.

I wiped a tear from my eye. "Thank you, Cassie, for including these."

Of course, several sketches of Nate appeared throughout both volumes, and I found myself wishing Cassie had done at least one self-portrait.

The memories washed over me, and for the first time in a decade, I let them. Ma taking care of me when I was sick, and taking care of everyone else, including half the town. Pa working long days with Nate, and then finding time to do experiments in his workshop with me and later Caleb. My brother Mark teasing me endlessly about always having my nose stuck in a book and not even looking at the boys in school. I used to snark back at him about how girls were the only thing he thought about, especially Emily.

Lera and Caleb moved in with us after my oldest brother, John, died. I smirked at the memory of Lera's deal with Ma that sent her snooping on Nate instead of us. I shared a room with my sister Sarah until she married and moved away, shortly before Cassie arrived.

I smiled, remembering how awkward Cassie had been

at first, and now I understood why. I couldn't imagine traveling the opposite direction. She must have a strong love for Nate to decide to stay. My breath hitched. Wrong tense. She must have *had* a strong love. They were all dead now. Long gone. I balanced the journal in my palm. This was my only connection to them, unless... no. The time machine was gone. Todd regretted changing the timeline and decided to keep it from happening again.

A knock on the door startled me. I hesitated. "Who is it?"

"Me," Todd said.

I almost said, "me who," but wasn't feeling like myself. "Come in."

He entered and glanced at me, then at the journals on the bed. "I see you didn't waste any time."

"Have you read them?" I couldn't object if he had. They were now historical documents, and Cassie was his former girlfriend.

He threw me a sheepish grin and nodded.

Had he told me about the journals as a general interest, or was there something specific? "Anything you wanted me to see?"

"I thought you might want to know how they fared." He nodded toward the journal in my hand. "At least for a few years."

"Any indication of why she stopped writing?"

"I assumed she got busy." He shrugged, sat on the end of the bed, and turned toward me. "Isn't that why most people stop writing in journals?"

"Yeah, but Cassie isn't most people." My mouth dried out. "And, I can tell she wrote this for our benefit." I bit my lip.

He gazed at me and put his right hand up. "Maybe there are more journals somewhere. "Anything could have happened. This house was passed down through at least three generations before I bought it."

I leaned back and let him think I accepted his theory. "Well, I've just started this one, so...."

"I can take a hint." He stood and headed out. "Email me your resume. I have a friend looking for a research assistant." He hesitated at the threshold. "If you're interested."

I'd never thought about doing anything like that. "I'll consider it. Thanks."

"No problem." Todd blinked. "Oh, wait. Don't hurry. I won't be able to talk to my friend until next week."

I grinned. "Yep. Gotta love the holidays."

Todd waved and backed out of my room, closing the door.

I read through the first half of 1871, mostly about having Lera and Simon as house guests while their new house was being built. Cassie was encouraged that the house would be completed around November because it would only be half the size and not as grand as their original mansion. Lera had no intentions of throwing any more grand balls.

After the fire, the night I was injured and traveled here, I could understand why. If it were anyone other than Lera. Almost losing Simon must have changed her more than losing my brother, John.

Back to the journal. Lera gave birth to Simon Jr in May at Nate's house. Cassie wrote that it would be good practice for her to help Lera care for a baby before she had one of her own. No mention of when that would be, though. I skimmed through entries about the baby, tutoring Caleb, preparations for Mark and Emily's wedding, and the wonderful day when Lera and Simon moved into their own home. I leaned back, part of me wishing I'd been there and part of me glad I wasn't. I loved my family, but living here had major advantages. I plopped the books on the nightstand and pushed off the bed to change into one of Austin's old t-shirts. After using the bathroom, I climbed into bed, turned off the lamp, and drifted off.

My phone chimed. I sat up and squinted against the sun streaming through the window. I covered my eyes with my arm and flopped back onto the pillow. Why hadn't I closed the curtains last night? My phone chimed again. I groaned and reached to the nightstand for it. When I picked it up, I knocked the pile of journals off. Great. My phone chimed yet again. Who was texting me repeatedly?

Chantal had written, "Happy Christmas Eve...Come join us in the festivities...The kitchen smells heavenly."

I hauled myself out of bed and dressed in a fresh pair of jeans and a light sweatshirt. Before I left the room, I retrieved the journals from the floor and stacked them on the nightstand. A newspaper clipping had fallen out of one of them and lay on the rug. I retrieved the folded news sheet containing several ads and placed it on top. Why would an ad page be in the journal? Wait. Bridger Cotton. That was Nate's business, but why keep an ad? I checked for the date, flipping the paper and turning it right-side-up. Nov 12, 1873. These journals didn't cover that time period. Weird.

~

I slid the last pan of gingerbread men into the oven and shucked the oven mitts. "Fifteen minutes to completion."

"Not so fast." Chantal piped icing onto one of over a dozen cookies laid out on the worktable. "We still have to decorate."

I smirked. "I'm the baker. Not creative enough to do that."

A bell chimed.

Chantal dropped her piping bag and hurried out of the kitchen. "That's Jamal!"

I checked my watch in case I didn't hear the timer and followed her, eager to meet this brother I'd heard so much about.

When we entered the parlor, a medium-height, lean, light-skinned man, clad in a smart gray suit and open overcoat, dropped a large pack and sauntered toward his sister.

Chantal ran into his open arms and bear hugged him. Then she stepped back and eyed his threads and the bundle next to him. "Come into some cash?"

Jamal lifted his chin and grinned. "You know it." He opened the satchel and placed several brightly-wrapped packages under the tree.

Chantal waved her arm at the packages. "And how did you come by it?"

"New business venture." Jamal emptied the pack and raised his hands, palms toward his sister. "Strictly legit."

"Mm hmm." Chantal took a deep breath.

"Really." Jamal smiled. "My partner and I are flipping houses. We sold one and made a bundle last week."

Chantal waved him off. "What do you know about

remodeling houses?"

Jamal shook his head. "Don't have to. I just hire people to do the work."

Chantal rolled her eyes, headed to the kitchen, and stopped short when she passed me. She touched my shoulder. "Where are my manners? Lydia, this is baby brother, Jamal."

Jamal extended his hand. "Pleased to meet you."

"Likewise." I gave him a firm handshake. Pa would be proud.

Chantal tapped her brother on the shoulder, then strode toward the kitchen. "Well, come on back and you can help out. That is if you want to eat."

Jamal chuckled and followed her.

I stayed behind and studied the tree. I hadn't even noticed all the gifts that had been under it before Jamal added to them. My name appeared on a few of the tags. How could I have come for Christmas and forgotten to bring gifts?

I raced through the dining room to the kitchen. "Chantal, do you mind if I go out for a while? Those cookies need to come out in a few."

Chantal smirked at her brother. "I'll put this guy to work. Have fun."

I trotted upstairs to get my wallet, phone, and hoodie, then down to the front drive where I'd left my rental car. The shops would close for Christmas Eve in about four hours.

After a five-minute drive, I parked the black Jetta and meandered down Main Street. The stores were somewhat different from when I'd left three years ago. A shop devoted to olive oil occupied a building that had been a convenience store. The general store occupied the same location as in my childhood, minus a small section now housing a candle shop. The storefront had been made to look more old-fashioned than when I'd left in 1870. I jaywalked across the street and entered. More people milled around inside than I'd seen on the street.

"More last-minute shoppers." A teenage girl stood behind the register and sneered at me.

I stifled a giggle. She reminded me of myself at that age. Apart from the counter area in the same place, and the attempt at period furnishings, the store looked completely different. I shook my head to clear it. Instead of comparing my surroundings to the past, I needed to shop for three people I didn't know anymore. Strike that. Two. One, I'd just met.

I headed to the seasonal area, checking out the edibles. Chocolate or munchies would probably be safe. As I rounded a corner, I saw the soda fountain, installed decades before I arrived in 2010. Todd sat on one of the stools, talking with a woman I'd never seen. Was he cheating on Chantal? I stepped back and peered around the shelving unit. She was large for a woman, close to the same size as Todd, stocky but not fat. Her shoulder-length, dirty-blonde hair hung limp, and her face seemed plain. She scowled. Since Todd was mostly in profile, I couldn't get a good look at his expression, but his body was rigid, and he leaned away from her. I let out a breath. Most likely not a sexual liaison. I edged closer so I could hear.

The woman huffed. "If you're not going to pursue it, I don't understand why you won't give me your research."

"You'll have to take that up with my boss." Todd stood and angled away from her. "And don't bother me outside of work again." He stomped off.

The woman balled her hands into fists and stalked off in the opposite direction.

What was that about? Should I go after Todd? No. He strode toward the exit, and I had shopping to do.

After perusing the edibles, I grabbed a hot cocoa set, a coffee collection, and a box of chocolate. At least I'd have something to put under the tree.

The bag wasn't too heavy to carry, so I ambled down the street in search of better gifts. My mind replayed the scene I'd witnessed. Cassie had told me Todd was a genius and he'd always had people interested in his work, but he'd told me that since destroying the time machine, he'd backed off on anything cutting edge. He'd concentrated on robots in the last several years. Could that woman want his robot research? Or could she be talking about the time machine? I sucked in air. That would explain Todd's coldness.

I stopped in the middle of the sidewalk. The time machine was a secret. No way this woman could have found out about it.

~

I sat across the card table from Jamal, Chantal to my left, and Todd to my right, and stared at the full house I held. Too bad we weren't playing poker.

Jamal, my partner, laid down three tens, starting a new pile, and not helping me to play any of the cards in my hand. It didn't matter, though, who won or lost. I enjoyed the Christmas music in the background and the occasional chatter while we played. Also, the cup of hot chocolate Chantal made tasted delicious.

I had picked up two cards when my ring tone sounded. "I'll get that later."

Chantal leaned over and peeked at my phone. "It's Austin. I'll refill the hot chocolate and bring out the gingerbread." She pushed her chair back and hurried into the kitchen.

I rolled my eyes, picked up my phone, and wandered toward the front door, hoping he'd give up before I answered. No such luck. I touched the 'answer-with-video' icon. "Hi, Austin."

He held his phone too close to his face. "Hey, babe, what took you so long?"

"I wanted privacy." I opened the front door and stepped onto the porch.

"Where are you anyway?" He moved the phone so I could see more of him, plus the couch in his office. He'd pulled his sandy hair into a man-bun and hadn't shaved in a few days.

I pointed my phone outward, circled to the cul-de-sac and street, then showed him the front door. "I'm at Todd's B&B." I sat on the wooden porch swing. "What's this about? I thought we were on a break."

"Oh, that." He lowered his eyes and showed me his charming grin. "I shouldn't have said those things. Can you come over tonight? I don't want to spend Christmas Eve without you."

My jaw dropped. He was serious. I shook my head and laughed. "Didn't you hear me? I'm at Todd's."

He shrugged. "Yeah, so?"

"In Georgia. I can't come over tonight." My jaw tightened at the exasperated tone in my voice.

He blinked. "So, who's Todd?"

"I've told you many times." I gritted my teeth to keep from screaming at him. "Is there anything else you wanted to tell me?"

"Uh, yeah. Design meeting on Friday. At the office."

I tightened my grip on the phone. "Did you forget? I'm on leave, possibly for good."

He huffed. "You know I didn't mean it. I was just blowing off steam."

I hesitated, then forced a smile. "I'll think about it. Merry Christmas." I lowered the phone.

"Wait!" Austin lurched forward. "Are you seeing Todd?"

"No." Why did I answer so quickly? I raised the phone to my face and forced myself to slow down. "Why do you care? You moved out, and I haven't seen you since, other than at work."

"I've been stressed." He raised his arms, causing the picture to blur. "I didn't move anywhere. I've been staying at the office. Can I come home?"

I should have known, but I hadn't wasted any mental energy on where he was living.

"Well, I have a roommate, so..." Did I want him to move back? He did look cute at the moment. I'd always been drawn to his light blue eyes.

"No problem." He stuck up his index finger. "I promise to keep myself in our room and stay away from hers."

I blew out a breath. "Fine. Use my apartment until I get back. We'll talk then."

"Friday."

"We'll see." I hit end and slumped on the swing.

So much for a simple, old-fashioned Christmas Eve.

~

My stomach full, I leaned back in the wingback chair next to the fireplace. Mounds of shredded and wadded wrapping paper littered the floor, while unwrapped presents lay stacked in four piles. Chantal and Todd reclined on the sofa, and Jamal sprawled in the recliner.

I glanced at Chantal. "We should clean up some of this stuff."

"Maybe later." Chantal smiled and patted her belly. "I want to savor the quiet and time with family for a while longer."

Todd snored with his mouth open.

Jamal yawned and closed his eyes.

"Okay." I leaned back and let my mind drift. "I'll help you clean up before I continue reading Cassie's diaries, though."

"Who's Cassie?" Chantal asked.

"Uh." I almost said she was Todd's ex-girlfriend. "She's Nate Bridger's wife. Todd found her journals. You didn't know that?" I leaned forward and gazed at her. "Todd said he used them to remodel the house."

"He didn't mention who wrote them. I never read them. Thought they were decor journals from the way he used them."

I chuckled. "Cassie wrote about a little bit of everything. It's a good history of life here in the early 1870s."

"Sounds interesting," Jamal said, his eyes still closed.

Chantal scooted to the edge of the couch and snapped her fingers. "That sounds like fun. You should read them to us."

"Uh, maybe some time." I wanted to skim them first.

"What a perfect thing to do on our first Christmas here." Chantal stood, animated all of a sudden. "Where are they?"

I hauled myself out of the chair. "My room. I'll get them." I plodded up the steps, trying to come up with a good reason not to read them to her. Except I felt eager to get back to them. Maybe reading them aloud would motivate Chantal to find the rest.

When I returned, Todd sat upright, slid his hands up and down his thighs, and nodded at me. He must trust me to read only the entries that won't make Chantal more suspicious.

I settled into my chair and skimmed through a few short entries. "This looks good. Sunday, April 7, 1872." I glanced up at three sets of eyes glued to me and began to read.

> Interesting afternoon. We finally got to meet the young man who had attended church then vanished, each Sunday of the past three weeks. Nate left the service during the last prayer and caught him on his way out. He invited Lucas home for dinner here, instead of at Aunt Mattie's. I'm surprised she hasn't been here or sent Ed to get the scoop.
>
> Lucas is an interesting character. He hardly said anything until after he'd wolfed down the stew I'd had ready for our supper, having expected to eat Sunday dinner at Mattie's.
>
> Nate asked him if he would be interested in a job.
>
> "Yes." Lucas raised his eyebrows. "With you?"
>
> Nate nodded and explained how Ed wanted to spend more time working on the equipment and

needed to back off the heavy labor.

Lucas grinned. "I can plow, and hay, and do anything else you need."

Nate chuckled. "Good. Can you start tomorrow?"

Lucas smiled wide. "Yes, sir." He stood and shook Nate's hand.

"Where are you staying?" Nate asked. We'd been wondering where this young guy was hiding out. Church was the only place anyone had seen him, and no one had talked to him.

He gazed at the floor and shifted from foot to foot. "Other side of town."

Nate narrowed his eyes and glanced at me. "If this works out, I can help you build a place closer."

Lucas snapped his head up, his eyes wide. "I'll work hard." He started out the back door.

"Dawn tomorrow," Nate called.

Lucas tipped his hat and left.

I touched Nate's shoulder. "I know you and Ed have been talking about Ed cutting back, but you never said anything about hiring anyone."

"Hadn't thought that far, until church this morning." Nate tapped his chest. "Felt a conviction when I locked eyes with Lucas. That young man needs work, and he needs family."

I smiled and raised an eyebrow. "And you wanted to beat Aunt Mattie to it."

He guffawed.

"That's what she wrote." I pointed at the journal, then turned the page and sucked in a breath. "She sketched

Lucas." A pencil drawing of a man with wavy, collar-length hair, tender eyes, a slender nose, and full, upturned lips peered off the page.

"Stop ogling it." Chantal nudged my shoulder. "He's been gone over a hundred years."

I scowled. "I'm not ogling. I'm admiring Cassie's talent."

Todd snorted. "Uh huh." He leaned in. "Her sketches improved with practice."

Jamal yawned. "Why are you guys so fascinated?"

Chantal reached over and whacked her brother on the shoulder. "It's interesting. It's written differently than most journals, too. Those things happened in this house. It gives me shivers thinking about it."

Todd and I exchanged a glance. If she only knew.

Chantal settled against the sofa-back. "Read another entry. I want to find out who this Lucas is."

I smiled and began reading.

> Friday, April 12, 1872. This week went by in a blur. Well, it was the first week of planting. I'm so glad Nate had help. Lucas has been worth every penny of his salary, at least to hear Nate talk. The two of them, plus several others hired only for this week, kept me busy making breakfast and lunch. Mattie wasn't here because she had to help Emily feed Mark's crew. Lera brought Caleb to work with Nate, and she worked with me most mornings, but she could only stay about an hour, because their nanny is sick and Simon wouldn't watch the baby any longer.

I glanced up. "She drew a smiley face here."

"Huh." Chantal furrowed her brow. "They used emojis back then?"

I buried my face in the book to hide my guilty expression.

Todd cleared his throat. "I'm sure Cassie wouldn't have called it that, but it's a pretty generic symbol."

"Anyway." I pointed to the page.

"Wait." Chantal peered at Todd. "Wasn't your ex-girlfriend's name Cassandra?"

Todd shrugged. "Yeah."

Chantal furrowed her brow. "She went missing, right?"

He shook his head. "I thought so at first. Turns out she moved to D.C. and didn't leave a forwarding address. Her brother told me months later."

"That is some coincidence." Chantal frowned and pointed to the book. "Cassie is a nickname for Cassandra."

"And there are loads of both, throughout history." Todd pulled her into his embrace.

Chantal exhaled. "Yeah, you're right." She shook her head. "These journals feel so modern. It's weird."

I shrugged to cover my cringe. "Well, people don't really change."

"I guess." Chantal wrinkled her nose.

"I'll put this away and come back down to clean up." I jumped up and hustled toward the stairway with the journal. Could I make it any more obvious that I wanted to change the subject?

CHAPTER THREE

Boxing Day dawned cloudy and cool, a good day for visiting friends. Too bad I didn't have any in the area. Jamal had gone back to Atlanta until New Year's Eve. Todd and Chantal had invited me to tag along with them on their visit with Chantal's best friend, but I'd declined.

Instead, I spent the day by myself. Wandering around the neighborhood brought back too many unwanted memories, so I returned to my room at the B&B and buried myself online surfing for jobs all over the country and scrolling social media. Maybe I'd connect with old college friends this week.

Why couldn't I stop glancing at the journals? Even if I could go home, I didn't want to.

The registration bell dinged, rousing me from my computer. I hopped off my chair and raced downstairs. Chantal hadn't mentioned any guests. Who could it be?

Chantal stood at the counter behind her open laptop, one hand on the mouse and her phone against her cheek. "Yes. We'll be ready tomorrow." She set down her phone and peered at me, biting her lip.

"You rang?" I placed my hand on my hip.

Chantal inhaled. "The only guests I had registered for this weekend just added three rooms to their reservation. They're having an impromptu family reunion."

"Starting tomorrow?" My jaw dropped.

She nodded. "I know you planned to take off on Sunday, but could you stay and help?"

"You didn't rent my room, did you?"

"No. Just Jamal's." She grinned. "But if he comes back sooner than he expected, he can stay with us. If you stay, I'll be glad to have someone I trust here with this crowd. We'll have several young teens and a set of ten-year-old twins."

I deadpanned. "Goody."

She clasped her hands together in a prayer pose. "Please? Todd will help in the kitchen, but he's useless with the guests."

"I've noticed." He'd always been introverted, especially right after getting back from 1870. "Okay. I'll change my return flight to after New Year's. What do you need help with?"

She applauded. "That was quick. I thought I'd have to beg."

"I guess I wasn't looking forward to going back so soon." I imagined the expression on Austin's face when I missed his Friday meeting, and stifled a chuckle. Weird. My stomach felt more settled than it had all day.

"You know you're welcome to stay indefinitely." Chantal led me to the kitchen as she detailed all the cleaning that needed to be done by tomorrow. Oh joy, I'd get to clean four bathrooms. At least they weren't outhouses.

~

Four days later, I cleaned up the breakfast dishes while Chantal checked the guests out, all twelve of them. When she returned to the kitchen, she plopped into a chair and flung her arm across her forehead. "Glad that's over. Thank you, Lydia. I couldn't have managed without you."

I closed the dishwasher and sat next to her. "You're going to have to hire someone."

She let her arm flop onto the table. "At least for weekends like that one. Whew."

"Those ten-year-old twins were something." I'd followed them around all weekend, confiscating knick-knacks and putting them back before they broke. I poured tea into Chantal's cup.

"Bless you." She took a sip.

We chatted and drank tea for a few minutes, then Chantal pushed up from the table. "Better get those rooms cleaned up today. I want to spend a peaceful New Year's."

"No big New Year's Eve party?" I peered at her over my cup.

She scowled. "I wanted to have one, but Todd nixed the idea. Now, I'm glad. I plan to do what we did on Christmas Eve." She snapped her fingers. "I almost forgot. You haven't read us the rest of those journals."

I grimaced and set down my cup. "We'll see."

She narrowed her eyes. "Why did you all-of-a-sudden cool toward those?"

"Not sure." What could I say? It reminded me too much of home. I didn't want to see those sketches of Ma and Pa again. Too bad the images kept floating into my mind.

Chantal clicked her tongue. "Tell me when you figure it out."

~

Late that afternoon, Chantal prepared a light supper while I set the kitchen table.

Todd ushered Jamal in the back door. "Look who I found outside."

"Hey, little Bro. Just in time. Dinner's about ready, and all the work's been done."

Jamal grinned. "Perfect timing."

I rolled my eyes.

As we finished dinner, my phone chimed.

Chantal peeked at it. "It's Austin. You might want to take it."

Steeling myself, I strode to the foyer, grabbed my jacket, and exited to the front porch. What did he want? And what would I answer? I took a deep breath and accepted the Facetime call. "Hi, Austin."

He sat on the sofa in his office. "Hey, babe. You missed a great meeting."

"Sorry, I had to stay and help Chantal." Why did I apologize? I'd sent an excuse for missing the meeting, even though I was still on leave.

"Where are you?"

"At Todd's. Well, at the B&B." I rotated my phone and showed him the area. "Exactly where I was last week."

"I really want you to come home tonight. I cut you slack for the meeting, but, babe, it's New Year's Eve." He puffed out his lower lip as he frowned. How had I thought that expression was cute?

"So?"

"So, we always kiss at midnight. I don't want to miss

that."

I snorted. He missed kissing at midnight. Like he needed me for that. I clenched my jaw. "You'll have to miss it this time. Even if I wanted to come, I couldn't make it."

"Yes, you could. It's only three-thirty."

"I'm still in Georgia!" I stopped short because a man at the nearest house stood on his porch and watched me.

Austin rubbed his stubbled chin. "I do remember, but it's only a five-hour flight. You could totally make it."

"You want me to leave this minute, drive an hour to the airport, wait at least an hour, if not more, to make it in the nick of time just to kiss you at midnight?"

He grinned. "Romantic, isn't it?"

Maybe a year ago, or two. My face heated, and I could practically feel the steam coming out of my ears. "Here's a thought. Why don't you do it?"

He scoffed. "I couldn't make it. The time difference."

I folded my lips together and pressed hard, then resumed breathing. "Austin." My voice shook. "Take my name off the apartment lease, and send my last paycheck."

He ran his hand through his long hair. "Babe. No."

"Don't babe me. I'm not coming back." The waver gone from my tone, I ended the call and plopped onto the swing. My phone buzzed in my hand. I sucked in air and answered. "We're through."

"Don't say that," Austin whined.

"Thank you, Austin. You made my decision easy." I tapped "end" and shut off my phone. Then I marched upstairs, opened my laptop, and canceled my return flight. I'd start my Atlanta job search for real on Monday.

~

A tap sounded on my bedroom door. "Lydia?" Chantal said.

I shut my laptop. "You can come in."

The door opened a crack, and Chantal poked her head in. "You all right?"

I took a deep breath and released it as I stood. "Yeah." My shoulders lowered, and the queasy feeling in my gut subsided. "I canceled my flight home. I mean, back to Seattle."

Her eyes widened. She rushed to me and held me at arm's length, peering into my soul. "You're staying for good?"

I chuckled. "Not in this room, but in the area. If I can get a good job."

"Of course you'll get a job. I'm so happy you're staying." She stepped into the hallway but stopped and turned toward me. "What about Austin?"

"For the life of me, I can't remember what I ever saw in him." I shuddered. "How stupid was I?"

"No more stupid than any college-aged girl. Most of our mistakes at that age have to do with men, or should I say, boys?"

"You got that right, where Austin is concerned anyway."

"Please come down. It's almost time to ring in the new year."

Did I dare hope this would be a better year than last? I followed her downstairs and into the small parlor.

Jamal and Todd watched *Dick Clark's New Years Rockin' Eve* on TV. Todd opened a bottle of sparkling cider, poured it into a wine glass, and handed it to Chantal.

"Thank you, sweetie." Chantal took a small sip. "No alcohol for now."

I side-eyed her. "Already?"

"Maybe. We won't know for sure until next week." Her last word sounded squeaky.

Jamal lifted a bottle of Veuve Clicquot toward me.

"Yes, please." I knew for a fact I wasn't pregnant, and that suited me fine.

While Jamal popped the cork and poured champagne for the rest of us, Chantal cuddled next to Todd. "Ah. This is nice. Just the family for the holiday."

I accepted my glass. "When are guests arriving?"

Chantal sipped. "Day after tomorrow. I plan on sleeping in, so you're on your own for breakfast in the morning."

Jamal sank into one of the cushy chairs near the fireplace. "Fine with me."

Chantal set her glass on the coffee table. "Tomorrow afternoon, maybe we can play cards." She clapped her hands together. "Or Lydia can read more of the journals."

I blinked. We'd been so busy, I hadn't thought about them, but last week, I purposely set them aside. They dredged up too many memories. And it was getting harder to keep Chantal from guessing how well I knew the people mentioned in them.

Jamal sat up straight. "I'd rather play cards or go on a hike."

Todd chuckled. "You? Go on a hike? Those journals must have bored you to tears."

Jamal focused on the television. "The ball's dropping."

Chantal sat up straight. "Oh, it's midnight."

The illuminated ball in Times Square slowly traveled to the ground, and then *Auld Lang Syne* played.

Chantal planted a kiss on Todd's lips while Jamal and I shifted in our seats. When they broke away, she lifted her glass and faced me. "Here's to new beginnings." She swiveled toward Jamal. "Good fortune." Then made moon eyes at Todd. "And Love."

Jamal raised his glass. "To 2020. Come what may."

CHAPTER FOUR

I closed the journal, pushed back from my desk, and gazed out the window of my room. Fields and trees flanked the dirt road. I squeezed my eyes shut and pinched the bridge of my nose. When I looked out again, the paved road, lined with medium-sized modern houses, extended straight out from the cul-de-sac. I shook my head. Why had I allowed Chantal to cajole me into opening the journals again? Spending so much time reading Cassie's words had transported me back, if only in my mind. I needed fresh air.

On my way downstairs, I passed a yuppie couple, each hauling an overnight case. The guy could have carried both, but the woman, tall and lean with dark blonde hair tied back in a no-nonsense bun, probably wouldn't let him carry hers.

I cocked my head as I approached Chantal, seated behind the counter in front of the pocket door to the large parlor.

Chantal lowered her voice. "Brian and Allison Whitney. Here for the weekend, but I don't think it's a vacation."

I raised one eyebrow. "How do you know?"

She smiled. "They asked if Richard Harker had arrived yet."

I shrugged. "So. They're meeting a friend."

"He's a history professor in Atlanta, doing research here for a client." She nodded toward the empty staircase. "Since we only have one other couple and they got in yesterday, I assume Brian or Allison is the client."

"You have a point." I turned toward the front door.

She reached over the desk and placed a hand on my shoulder. "Stop. I require more information from Cassie's diary." Chantal smirked, her eyes flashing.

I chuckled. "I wasn't aware you had a moment to spare."

She emerged from behind the desk and motioned for me to follow her through the large parlor to the back hallway. "Come and regale me while I start supper."

I'd come downstairs to get away from the journals, but I followed her. Maybe if I updated her, I'd process them.

We walked down the short hallway into the gleaming kitchen.

Chantal pulled a cookbook out of a high cabinet and flipped it open. "So, what have you learned?"

I took a seat at the counter. "You'll be happy to know that Lucas was still working for Nate in the summer of 1873. That's the end of the last journal."

She glanced over her shoulder as she opened the fridge. "Have you searched the house for more?"

I drummed my fingers on the granite. "Yes, and I can't find any." I blew out a breath. "Cassie's pregnant, and I want to make sure the baby's okay." Shoot. I sounded afraid for them.

Chantal giggled as she pulled a large blue glass bowl out of her cupboard. "You sound like it's happening now. Easy to get caught up in other people's stories, isn't it?"

She shouldn't learn that I had such a personal stake. I flashed her a sheepish grin. "Yeah. Guess I need to concentrate on someone else at the moment, and not my own life."

Chantal peered at me as she measured flour into the bowl. "Any idea what you want to do next?"

No, but at least she changed the subject. I blew a long breath, letting my lips flutter. "I sent out several resumes to Todd's contacts. Hopefully, I'll find a job soon and then I can get out of your hair."

"Don't worry about that. If I book your room, you can stay with me and Todd."

"At least you aren't going to turn down money to let me stay."

She laughed. "You could help renovate the old kitchen or the attic. We're thinking of turning them into suites."

I nodded, hoping it wouldn't come to that.

"Okay, don't let me get off topic." Chantal pointed a wooden spoon at me. "Any more news in the journals?"

"Lucas has become like one of the family. Nate's Aunt Mattie has been matchmaking for Lucas, but he doesn't appreciate it."

She chuckled. "Most people don't. I know Jamal doesn't."

I glanced toward the dining room door. "Where is Jamal, anyway?"

She poured the batter into a pan. "That's a good question. He's off somewhere with Todd."

The bell on the front desk chimed.

Chantal whipped off her apron and trotted into the hallway.

I headed out the back door for fresh air. Now, to get a job before Chantal roped me into working here. I peered into the old kitchen building, trying to envision it as a luxury suite. Despite the bare wood floors and newly plastered walls, I imagined the wood stove in the center of the room, with the worktable to my left and the sink and counter against the right-hand wall. Cassie bent down to check something in the oven. My breath hitched. If I wasn't careful, I might go time-traveling without Todd's machine.

~

After dinner, I plopped onto the swing on the wraparound porch. With all the streetlights, few stars were visible, one of the only things I missed from my youth. Over the past few days, I'd thought more about my childhood than in the past ten years. This house and those journals were to blame. Maybe if I could read the rest of them, or ascertain how my family fared, I'd be able to stop thinking about it. Cassie had to have written more, so where were they?

An image of my father's journal flashed into my mind. I smirked at the memory of the day I'd stolen it from the closet. He'd written it to get Todd's attention, hoping Todd would come get him and take him back to 2010. It hadn't worked, and he'd been there thirty years when Cassie showed up by accident. That reminded me of Jenny, someone I'd never liked. She was truly to blame for the whole mess. If she hadn't used the time machine against Todd's wishes, my father never would have felt the need to follow her. And, if she hadn't reset the machine, Pa wouldn't have traveled back so far. Hmm. But then, I wouldn't have been born. I shivered, despite the seventy-degree weather.

I trudged inside, intending to raid the kitchen. After I shut the front door, shuffling noises from above drew me to the staircase. Could it be coming from the closets? Instead of heading to the kitchen, I crept upstairs. As I reached the halfway landing, a door creaked. It had to be one of the closets. I hurried the rest of the way and snuck around toward my right. When I rounded the last corner, the door to the two-story closet was open away from me. I thought about running past it and confronting the person, but Todd and Chantal were down the street at their house, and Jamal was still out for the evening. No way I would confront the person until I knew how big they were. I stood in the shadows and waited. A thump made my heart rate accelerate, but I stayed put.

When the door opened wider, I held my breath. A tall figure stepped out, closed the door, and padded toward the master bedroom. Was it a man or a woman? It was too dark to tell. I hurried back around the way I came and slowed down in front of my room. A man carrying a thick book opened the master-suite door.

"Wait!" I ran and caught his arm. I should have thought this through, but it was too late now. "What have you got here?"

He pulled away, but I grabbed the heavy book.

He glared at me. "Why do you care? Who are you anyway?"

"I could ask you the same question." I stared him down, hiding the book behind my back.

"Brian, come back to bed." The female voice came from inside the room.

Brian grimaced and closed the door behind him, leaving me the volume.

I hurried into my room and locked the door. Hoping it was a journal, I placed the book on the bed. Air whooshed out of my mouth as I laid my palm on Ma's family Bible, worn with age. I flipped the pages at the front and gazed at the family records, which contained dates from 1811 to 1950. It only took me a few seconds to locate Cassie and Nate's names. There were three children, the first was Melody, born July 3, 1873. Either she'd simply gotten too busy to write, or her journals had been lost through the years. My shoulders lowered as I placed the Bible on the desk. I'd return it to the closet tomorrow.

~

Chantal dropped a tray into the warmer on the sideboard as I entered the dining room.

"Chantal, you may want to lock those closets upstairs." I strode over, catching a whiff of bacon. "Last night, I caught one of the guests taking a family Bible out."

She tilted her head. "Brian?"

I nodded.

"I told him he could look through anything as long as he didn't take it out of the house."

I squinted. "So why was he sneaking around at night?"

She shrugged. "I need to finish bringing food in. Help yourself."

I glanced at the trays on the sideboard. Eggs, bacon, and pancakes seemed too heavy. Though it was similar to the hearty breakfasts Ma had served, I'd gotten used to toast or cereal. Instead, I headed to the drinks station on the other side of the room and fixed myself a cup of coffee, then sat at the head of the table so I could watch people walk in through the propped-open door to the small parlor.

I nodded as an older couple entered at the same time Chantal brought in more trays of food.

The wife surveyed the sideboard. "I love your breakfast scones."

I could take them or leave them, so I continued to sip my coffee while watching the small parlor and hoping Brian didn't go straight outside.

Brian and his wife arrived next, and while she went to the buffet, he charged directly to the table and sat next to me. "I promise I had permission to look in that closet last night." He stopped long enough for me to nod. "May I peek at that Bible?"

I stared at him. Ma would be able to size him up in a few seconds. Why hadn't I inherited that skill? She attributed it to the Holy Ghost, but I still didn't buy that.

"Well?" He peered at me. "Should I ask the owner?"

I lifted my chin. "It's my family's Bible."

He smiled and leaned back. "Hey, we might be related."

My jaw dropped.

"That's why I wanted to see the Bible. I think my grandmother's name is in it."

I didn't really want to meet any relatives, given that he would be much farther down the family tree, even though he was at least five years older. But what could I say?

His wife set down a full plate and sat next to him. She looked familiar.

The older couple settled at the other end of the table.

I sighed and stood. "I'll go get it. Meet me in the parlor."

"What about breakfast?" His wife waved her fork.

Brian pushed his chair back. "That can wait."

I plodded through the house but stopped at the stairs because he was right behind me. "Don't you trust me?"

He grinned. "Just excited. I've been tracking down this piece of information for a while."

"Then why were you skulking around late at night?"

He stepped back. "I wasn't skulking. We got in late, and it was the first chance I got."

I raised an eyebrow. "But didn't you check in yesterday afternoon?"

"I didn't know about the closet until I ran into that older lady." He jerked his head toward the dining room. "I'd been searching all the bookshelves."

I squinted. Why would one of the other guests tell him about the closet? "Take a seat in the parlor. I'll be right back." I trotted upstairs. What would I say about my name being in that book? Wait, he didn't know my name. Plus, Lydia Gardner was fairly common. I relaxed, grabbed the Bible, made sure the journals were in the top bureau drawer, and ran back down.

Brian stood and held out his hand when I entered.

"Not so fast." I perched on the edge of the sofa and placed the book on the coffee table, opening to the family tree. I patted the sofa next to me, and he took a seat. "What was your grandmother's name?"

"Betsey Gardner Duncan."

"Elizabeth?" I scanned the chart.

He pointed at the name. "No. Betsey."

There it was. She was my brother, Mark's, granddaughter, born to his youngest son, William, and his wife, Anna, in 1927. There was only one generation listed after Betsey. But even so, many nieces, nephews, and cousins were listed on these pages. My head swam.

"Are you all right?" Brian leaned in.

I blinked and cleared my throat. "Fine. Is that all you needed?" I reached for the Bible.

He held up his hand. "Do you mind if I photograph these pages? There are other names I want to note."

I dropped my hand into my lap and tried to sound nonchalant. "Why the interest?"

He pressed his lips together, then exhaled. "My gran died a few years ago, and a week before, she said something that made my dad think she'd gone off her rocker." He glanced at me. "It made me curious about her life and her family, so I started researching."

My chest tightened. "Oh? What have you found?"

He cocked his head. "Who are you?"

Thinking fast, I scanned the family tree. I couldn't tell him the truth, but I could say something close to it. I pointed to a line under Mark's great-grandson, a descendant of his oldest son. "If the last generations were listed, I would be here. "I'm even named after Mark's sister." I slid my finger to my name on the chart, the only one with no entries under it. Even Caleb had one child listed.

He leaned in, our shoulders touching. "What happened to her?"

I shrugged. "She never got married?"

He inched away. "Or she died young. It was unusual for a woman not to marry back then."

I never planned on getting married. Good thing I didn't say that aloud. How much did Brian know about my family? "So, maybe we can pool our info, huh? Cousin?"

"I haven't found all that much. Mostly, the connection

to this house." He slid away and peered at me. "I'm surprised you didn't ask me what Gran said that prompted my interest."

I smirked. "That was my next question."

He leaned toward me and chuckled. "She said that when she was little, her grandmother claimed to have met someone from the future. From 2020 to be exact. Wild, huh?"

I scoffed to hide my nerves. "And you think it's true?" Mark had married Emily, who never could keep a secret. She might tell her grandchild. But how could she have met someone from this year?

"No." He cleared his throat. "But I do think my grandmother and her grandmother believed it."

"What are you trying to find?"

"Any information I can." He leaned against the sofa. "Mostly mental health stuff."

I laughed. "I don't know much about my ancestors, but I can believe there were a few with loose screws."

He snorted and sat up straight. "Did you find anything else in the closet?"

I sucked in air. Why hadn't I been more prepared? Stupid.

"You did!" He pointed at me.

I blew out a breath. "I found some journals." Cassie's didn't mention time travel, nor did Nate's mother's, but my pa's did. It might substantiate Brian's theory of mental health issues. Shoot. Chantal had told him he could read anything here. "I think Chantal wants to keep everything in the house."

He nodded. "That was our agreement. I'll keep them in this room if you'll let me see them. May I photograph them?" He pulled his phone out of his back pocket.

"Yeah. I'll go get them." I stood and picked up the Bible. "Can you leave that?"

I blinked and laid it on the table. "Sorry, must have been a reflex."

Brian opened the Bible and snapped a picture of the family tree.

"Don't you want breakfast?"

"Too excited to eat. I normally don't eat much in the morning."

"No, that's me." His wife entered the parlor from the dining room.

I studied her for a second, then headed upstairs. Why did she look so familiar? Like I'd seen her somewhere else recently. But I'd only been here a few days and hadn't been out that much. Only Christmas Eve. I stopped on the landing, and my face flushed. Could she be the woman I'd seen arguing with Todd? She fit the general build, but I hadn't gotten a good look. I shook the thought out of my mind. That woman wouldn't come here. I continued into my room and retrieved the journals. Maybe Brian's wife didn't realize Todd owned this place. He didn't spend time with the guests.

When I returned, Brian was flipping through the Bible, and his wife had left.

I glanced around the room. "Was she bored?" Or keeping a low profile?

He reached for the books I carried. "She went outside to enjoy the beautiful day." He shook his head. "Vermont girl. She loves this weather. She doesn't go outside much at all in summer."

I handed him the journals and perched on the wingback chair. "I understand that. And I was raised here."

"Really?" He set them on the coffee table and sifted through them, allowing me to see the dates on the front covers. He opened the earliest and pointed to the name on the first page. "Frances Bridger."

She was Nate's mom, but if I told him, he might start asking more questions. "Do you know who she was?"

He flipped a page. "I think she was the mother of the man who built this house. Nate Bridger." Interesting. How much research had he done?

"Good to know." I picked up Pa's journal. It had been over ten years since I'd read it.

Brian skimmed Frances's journal. "I got the impression you grew up somewhere far away from here."

"No. I moved away after college." I leaned back in the chair and flipped to the first page. "I didn't grow up in this house. Just in the state. Foster homes mostly."

"Oh?" He glanced at me. "I'm sorry." He leaned against the sofa. "You don't have to babysit me."

"I'm not." I tapped Pa's journal. "I have one more to read, so I might as well do it now." At first, I eyed Brian over the book, waiting for an opportunity to ask him about his wife, but I became so engrossed in Pa's journal, I lost track of him. I couldn't let Brian see this book. It had too many blatant references to time-travel.

"Lydia?" Brian broke into my reverie.

I peered over the top of Pa's journal. He turned one of Cassie's journals to face me. I gasped.

He placed it on the coffee table and studied the pencil sketch of me as a fifteen-year-old. "You haven't seen this, have you?"

I shook my head, mouth still open. How had I missed

that?

He fingered the edge of the sheet. "I had to peel it from the previous page. She looked a lot like you. She's younger here, but dang, it could be you."

I laughed, trying not to sound panicked. Cassie hadn't started drawing until after I left. At least as far as I knew. I hadn't expected a picture of me in her journal. I slid from my chair and joined him on the sofa for a better look. What else had I missed? "Weird, isn't it? Any other sketches in there?"

"Yes." He showed me a picture of Nate.

I clamped my mouth shut to avoid uttering his name. "He's handsome. Maybe Cassie's husband?"

He flipped through a few more pages. "Yeah, I think so. Nate?"

I almost nodded, but forced myself to pick up the Bible and open it to the family tree. "Yep." I pointed to Nate and Cassie's names on the same line.

"It's nice to have an image in my head." Brian blinked. "Wait, how did you know this was Cassie's?"

My eyes opened wide, but I caught myself before he looked at me. "I read them last night and I remembered from the cover." Thankfully, Cassie's books had different covers from Frances's.

He leaned back and seemed to relax, but I feared he was suspicious of me. I should be careful around him. He would be gone in two days, though, so I needn't worry too much. That reminded me. I had no idea how long I'd be staying. Chantal wasn't charging me, but I couldn't accept her charity indefinitely. I needed to figure out what I would do next—and soon.

The front door chime jolted me into the present.

A distinguished-looking man rushed into the room, holding a sheaf of papers. "There you are!"

I startled and shifted to the end of the sofa. Did I know this man?

"Richard." Brian stood and extended his right hand.

I stifled a laugh. Duh. The gentleman had been addressing Brian, not me.

Brian shook Richard's hand. "Something interesting?"

"Perplexing is more like it." Richard sat on the edge of the wingback chair and thumbed through the papers, hands shaking. He looked to be in his fifties, with thick salt and pepper hair, horned rimmed glasses on a lined face, and a gray mustache. Were his hands trembling from excitement or age?

Brian sat on the edge of the sofa and leaned toward him, elbows on his knees. "So, tell me."

Richard glanced at me and then raised his eyebrows.

Brian grinned. "She's also on the family tree. I doubt she'd leave if we asked her."

"Darn right." Why'd I say that instead of my customary swear word? Cassie's sketch of Ma flashed into my mind, and I groaned.

Richard cleared his throat. "I asked the New Hope librarian to find some of the local newspapers from the 1850s through the 1930s. Your grandmother's wedding announcement was in one, but that was all I found pertaining to her."

"Anything unusual about it?" Brian asked.

Richard shook his head. "I found the owner of this place and ads for his cotton business."

"I already know that," Brian said. "Nathaniel Bridger."

He hadn't told me how he knew Nate's name. I should ask him.

"Yes." Richard pulled out a sheet of copy paper. "But look at this ad."

Brian rotated the paper 180 degrees.

Richard bobbed his head. "No, I gave it to you the right way. Look at the ads around it."

"Huh." He turned it back around. "November 12, 1873."

"What's so weird?" I stood and circled the coffee table to take a peek. "It's harvest time, so...." I furrowed my brow. This was a copy of the newsprint I'd found in the journal. I hadn't noticed the ad was upside down. Wait. I'd turned it around to read the date. How could I have missed that? "Could it have been a mistake?"

"I thought of that, so I searched subsequent papers." Richard waved his hand, still holding the rest of the printouts. "It was the only time they'd made that mistake."

"Still." Brian leaned back and allowed me to take the copy from him. "What does it mean?"

An upside-down flag, or stamp, had been traditionally used as a distress symbol. A slow burn started in the pit of my stomach, but I kept my mouth shut. Could it be a distress signal from Nate or Cassie? It took all my control to keep myself from bolting to the kitchen to ask Chantal where Todd was. He would argue with me, but I had a gut feeling this was a call for help.

~

While Richard and Brian discussed the novel they planned to write based on my family, I lifted Pa's journal and slid it into the inside pocket of my jacket. Then, I slipped out of the parlor and hurried through the kitchen toward the backyard. It was Saturday, so Todd might be in the carriage house. I paused on the porch and took a deep breath. Why was my pulse racing? Even if this was a distress signal, what could I do? I didn't have any responsibility to interfere, nor should I. The printout rattled in the breeze, and I stared at the upside-down ad. Todd might give me a rational explanation.

I marched out to the carriage house. Todd had two old cars here, but neither was connected to my family. He'd become interested in vintage autos soon after he'd bought this house. I strode through the open double doors and spotted legs sticking out from under the midsection of a sixty-seven Mustang. Todd was here, but he might not appreciate the interruption. I should go easy. "Sure is a beauty." I ran my hand over the glossy red finish on the hood.

Todd scooted out on his dolly. "Lydia, what are you doing here?"

I grinned and rolled my eyes. "Looking for you. What else?"

He stood and brushed himself off. "I could use a break, anyway."

"Well, you might not think that when you see this." I handed him the printout of the ad page.

He skimmed it. "So?" He walked over to a workbench and pulled a stool out for me. I followed him but stayed on my feet. He shrugged and sat, glancing at the ad.

I pursed my lips. "What do you make of it. Doesn't it seem a bit unusual?"

"Mistakes happen." Todd wiped his brow with a tissue from the table, even though it was only about sixty degrees in the garage.

I peered down my nose, muscles tensed. "What if it's a call for help? A message to the future."

He shook his head. "Cassie would put a note in the upstairs closet."

My shoulders lowered. "Right. That's how she communicated with you before."

Todd reached up and squeezed my hand. "Please relax. Don't worry about them."

I heaved a sigh and plopped onto the stool next to him. "I'll try. The missing journals are concerning."

He raised his eyebrows. "Why? It's been near a hundred and fifty years. Anything could have happened to them. Or Cassie got busy and stopped writing."

My chest constricted. "I don't think she'd do that. Clearly, she was keeping a log for us."

"Still." He blinked and swiveled away. "They could have gotten lost."

Case closed. It was what I hoped he'd say, but something still felt off. I meandered around the room in silence while Todd puttered at his workbench. What if Cassie had left a note in the closet and it had been lost? I whirled toward him. "Have you ever thought about rebuilding the time machine?"

He hopped to his feet and raised both hands. "No. I'm not going there again."

"I didn't ask you to." I closed the gap. "You've never thought about going back to check on them?"

"No!" Todd paced in front of the bench. "I'm sure they're all right."

I scoffed. "They're all dead."

He stopped pacing and shook his head. "You know what

I mean. Look for later articles. You'll see."

"I have a gut feeling about this. Something is wrong." I balled my hands into fists.

"Are you sure it's not you?" His voice lowered as he studied his feet.

I glared at him, hands on hips. "What are you saying?"

He touched my shoulder. "Well, you've been thinking about them. And you're at a crossroads. Maybe you just want to go back."

Did I? I wouldn't go without a good reason, but was I conjuring one? My stomach roiled. "No. I'm telling you, something is wrong." I leaned closer to him.

He stepped back. "Chill." He pushed the air down with his hands and breathed deeply. "Think about it real hard. Wait a while. You have time, you know. If I do reactivate the machine, you can go back to this date." He pointed to the ad. "Or before that."

I took a deep breath. "Wait. Reactivate? You mean you didn't destroy the machine?"

He rubbed the back of his neck and turned away. "I disabled it, but couldn't bring myself to destroy it. Stupid. It brought nothing but pain."

"Thanks a lot. If Pa hadn't gone back, I wouldn't have been born." I pursed my lips.

"I didn't mean it that way. I should have destroyed it after bringing you here."

I unclenched my hands. "If one of us decides to go back, how long will it take to prepare the machine?"

He rolled his eyes and then pointed his nose at me. "You mean if *you* decide to go." He ran a hand over his close-cropped hair. "Please do more research first. You'll probably find out they lived long, happy lives."

My muscles tightened even more. "What if I find out the opposite? Will you reactivate?"

He pressed his fingers into his chin. "I'm not sure. I'll need to pray about it first."

"Fine." I hoped to find good news, but feared I was more likely to find nothing.

Todd picked up a wrench off his workbench and lowered himself onto the dolly.

I slid between him and the car. "Would you keep the limits on the machine?"

"Yes." He glanced at the ceiling. "And remember, there was one constraint I didn't put on it, so you never know what will happen."

"What was that?" He'd never told me how the time machine worked.

"You won't be able to go back to any earlier than Nov of 1870. The last time we jumped."

"I don't want to." I retrieved the ad from his workbench. "I want to go to Nov 1873."

"Be careful." He closed his eyes and exhaled. "What am I saying? It's a bad idea. I'm not going to reactivate."

I took a deep breath and glowered at him. "Maybe I will."

He glared at me. "I won't tell you where the machine is."

"Then I'll find it." I stomped out. Just like the fifteen-year-old I was when I traveled here.

CHAPTER FIVE

I hurried toward my car, intent on going to the library and proving Todd wrong. Wait, I could start researching here. I veered to the house and entered the small parlor.

Brian rushed to me. "Where's that small journal you had?"

I shrugged. It was in the inside pocket of my jacket, but I wasn't sure I trusted Brian with it, and I didn't trust Richard.

"No one else could have taken it." Brian perched on the edge of the sofa and pushed some books around on the coffee table.

I sat on the wingback chair. "Why's Richard involved?"

"He's an expert on the time period. He and I are writing a novel based on my family." He motioned from him to me. "Our family."

If I played it right, maybe they'd do my research for me. "Hey, I'd like to help with your project. Cousin."

"That would be great!" Brian graced me with an open-mouthed smile. "You can start by showing me that other journal."

"It's not on the table?" I lifted a few journals, stalling. A flash of memory hit me. This wasn't the first time I'd hidden Pa's journal. Cassie must have found it under the mattress. Inwardly, I rolled my eyes. That wasn't the best place to hide it, but fourteen-year-old Lydia didn't know that.

"No." Brian peered at me. "Why are you hiding it?"

I tilted my head. "What makes you think that?"

He sighed and leaned back on the sofa. "If you won't let me see it, I'm not sure how much of my research I will share with you."

"Fine." I pushed to my feet, stalked into the foyer, and up the staircase. So much for my plan.

"Wait!" Brian called up the stairs.

I stopped on the mid-point landing.

He jogged to me and showed me his sheepish grin. "I'll trade."

"What?" I stared at him, hands on hips.

"I found a later journal of Cassie's in the large parlor."

I grimaced. Why hadn't I gone into that room? Since they hardly ever used it, the thought hadn't even occurred to me. Not smart, though, because I had no idea what successive generations used it for. "What are the dates?"

He laid a finger on his chin. "Eighteen seventy-four, I think."

I clutched his shirt sleeve. "Where is it?" It could have the information I sought.

"In my room." He extricated his arm from my grip and headed up.

I followed, patting the journal which was still in my pocket. I could demand the book he had, but would that cause trouble for Chantal? I'd better trade. Now would be a good time to pray that he wouldn't take Pa's journal seriously. That is, if I'd ever started praying, which I had not. Ma was probably turning in her grave.

He opened the door to the master suite and tried to slip in without company. I pushed it wider and waltzed into the room. "I've never been in this room. Had to see it!" It wasn't an outright lie. I hadn't been in the room in this century. My breath caught. The furniture was the same set Pa had made for Cassie, though the room was somewhat smaller. I opened the extra door into a modern bathroom.

Brian lifted the book off the top of the oak dresser. "Where's the other one?"

I fished it from my pocket and held it out. "I'm almost surprised you didn't have to pull yours out of your suitcase."

"I wasn't going to steal it." He nodded toward the book I held. "Trade?"

"You just weren't going to tell me about it." I pursed my lips and offered Pa's journal in my left hand, freeing my right one to grab his. "Okay, on a count of three."

"Here." He handed me Cassie's journal and took Pa's.

"Finally!" He flipped through Pa's short journal. "I'm not sure that was a fair trade." He grinned as he perched on the edge of the mattress. "Must be something juicy in here."

I smiled. "Only rantings of a lunatic." Sorry Pa. "I wanted to spare you, since he's your great-great-great-grandfather. I think."

He checked the inside cover. "Ed Gardner. If I'm remembering the family tree correctly, you're right." He began to read, then glanced at me. "Do I have to take this downstairs?"

I sighed and leaned against the dresser. "I guess not. Are you finished with the journals in the parlor?"

"Yes." He started reading again.

My anxieties wouldn't allow me to leave until I gauged his reaction.

"Wow!" He looked at me. "I see what you mean. And why his family might have talked about time travel. He seems to have really believed it."

"Yeah." I tilted my head and touched his shoulder. "I tried to spare you."

He grinned. "Well, I'm glad you didn't succeed. This is going to be fun."

"See you later." Whew. I needn't have worried. I hurried to my room with Cassie's journal.

The dates on the front were July 1874 - February 1875. The last one ended in 1873, so there was still at least one journal missing—unless Cassie skipped a year.

I opened to the first entry and sighed. She referred to something she'd written a week prior. Could Brian or Richard have the other journal? I'd find out later.

I sat in the rocker by the window to read.

When I noticed the light had shifted so it was harder to see the script, I checked the time on my phone. I'd missed lunch, and it was now two hours before dinner. I still had about a quarter of the journal left, and she hadn't mentioned anything that would give me a clue about a distress call in November 1873. Maybe the upside-down ad was a mistake.

Still, I enjoyed catching up with Cassie, Nate, my parents, and siblings. I switched on the light and continued reading. By the summer of 1874, Melody was one, and Cassie suspected another baby was on the way. The farm was doing well, and Pa had built the steam-powered cotton gin.

Ma and Pa were happily spending time with Melody and Mark's infant son, Mark Jr. Mark had married Emily in early 1873.

Lera and Simon had two kids as well. Simon Jr., born in summer 1871, and Andrew, born in early 1873. I enjoyed reading about them, but thank goodness I missed those years, with all that babysitting.

When I reached the next-to-last page, I gasped. Cassie wrote about Jenny, the time-traveler who could have helped Cassie go home, but wouldn't. I'd been suspicious of her the whole time she'd been there. I reread the entry.

Feb 7 1875

This afternoon, I caught a glimpse of a couple of travelers in the woods. One of them reminded me of Jenny. I hadn't thought about her since she left town the fall before last, shortly after she was released from jail. Aunt Mattie had graciously allowed her to live with them until she could find a means of support or a way home. When she'd vanished, we figured she'd gone home, so the woman I saw today couldn't be her. Weird how my mind plays tricks on me.

Cassie had told me she thought Jenny was the thief who had plagued New Hope, and I witnessed her causing my accident. Jenny must have been arrested the night I was injured and not released for three years. I flipped the page, but this was the last entry. Could Cassie have seen Jenny? If so, maybe she'd left the area and returned. But she'd vanished, and they thought she'd gone home. My jaw dropped. Was this Cassie's code for the fact that Jenny had gotten her hands on the time machine?

If Todd saw this, he'd never reactivate. But did that mean someone else would?

~

Starving, I hurried through the dining room to eat with Chantal, Todd, and Jamal in the kitchen. Brian and Allison had already helped themselves to the buffet and sat at the table. Allison sneered as I passed. What was her problem?

I took a big whiff as I entered the kitchen. "Dinner smells amazing."

Chantal laughed. She turned from the commercial stove and placed a bowl of okra on the butcher block table. "It's just pork loin." She squinted at me. "You're hungry."

I sat at my place. "Guilty."

"Go ahead and start. Jamal and Todd are running late." She exited toward the pantry.

I wolfed down the pork, mashed potatoes, and even some of the okra. Satisfied but not stuffed, I set my plate in the sink.

Chantal entered, head bent over her phone.

"Everything all right?" I touched her shoulder.

She startled. "Oh, yes."

I raised an eyebrow.

She swatted an imaginary fly. "Jamal and Todd are going to be later than they thought."

"Where are they?"

"They say they're stuck in traffic." She slumped into a chair. "I hope Jamal's not in any more trouble."

"You're worried about him." I sat next to her.

She snorted. "Always." She scooped a piece of pork

onto her plate. "Go on. I know you have better things to do."

"I can stay with you until they get here."

She pursed her lips. "I'm terrible company right now."

Allison's sneer popped into my head. If she was the woman Todd argued with, wouldn't he have said something? Maybe, maybe not. "Has Todd mentioned anything about knowing Allison?"

"No." Her brow furrowed. "I'm not sure he's even seen her. Why?"

"She looks familiar, is all." I didn't want to worry her any more than she already was. I glanced around the kitchen. "Any dessert in here?"

Chantal waved her fork. "In the dining room, if there's any left."

I snickered and strode toward the adjoining door, but stopped short at the sound of voices.

"This house seems more like a museum than a B&B," Richard said.

"My family preserved it as a tribute to Nathaniel Bridger," Brian said.

I leaned in closer, hoping to overhear something new about Nate, but Allison butted in.

"Please don't go into any more details..." She lowered her voice, so of course I listened closer. Ma always told me I had big ears. Unfortunately, not big enough. All I could hear were whispers.

"Later," Allison said.

"Yes," Brian said in a normal voice. "A walk out in the fresh air sounds good."

Brian sounded odd, plus it was an abrupt change to the conversation. What could they be discussing?

I took a deep breath and breezed into the dining room, straight to the sideboard. An older couple finished filling their plates. They must have been the reason for Brian changing the subject. I glanced at the trio seated at the table. "Hi, everyone. I'm just here for dessert." I zeroed in on the pie. "Ooh, chocolate pie."

"It was delicious." Brian pushed back from the table and ambled through the open doorway into the parlor.

I took his seat at the head of the table.

Richard and Allison left their dirty dishes and joined Brian.

Good. I could eat my dessert in peace and maybe hear more of their conversation. I tasted the pie and groaned in delight. Distracted by rich velvety smooth chocolate pudding in a graham cracker crust, I savored every bite of Chantal's heavenly chocolate pie and heard nothing from the adjoining room.

I stacked my dessert plate and all the others in the bin, intending to carry them to the kitchen later, and hurried into the parlor. The mysterious trio played cards as I passed through. Why hadn't they taken that walk? They were up to something, but what?

In search of more journals, I trotted upstairs toward the third-floor stairway. It was roped off, but I ducked under and climbed it anyway. At the top of what used to be an open entry to a playroom, they'd put up a make-shift door that wasn't locked.

Stacked boxes took up half the room. Ladders, paint cans, and building materials occupied part of the other. If they added a few walls, they could probably get at least one guest room out of it with some storage on the sides. The door on the back wall opened into the upper level of the closet, but it was empty. I slumped and crossed to the window seat in the center at the front of the house. Now what? I glanced out the window, but only the bright dots of the street lights lining one side of the street were visible.

I flopped onto the window seat, and it shifted. Wait. This seat opened. I hopped off, knelt in front of it, and lifted the lid. "Ha!" I clasped my hand over my mouth, hoping nobody had heard me, and reached in to take out three more books similar to Cassie's journals.

These were dated in the late 1880s and had large, scrawling handwriting. Inside the front covers, Melody Bridger appeared in the same scrawl. I flipped through them, but all they contained were animal sketches, random doodles, and laments over homework. No mention of her parents or siblings. Not even a mention of boys. Disappointed, I trudged back to the second floor with the journals. At least this told me Melody survived to her teens, and no mention of the family probably meant everything was normal. This, in addition to all the names on the family tree, gave me no reason to go back.

Why didn't I feel relieved? Had I wanted to go? Maybe to see my family once more. No, I couldn't risk tampering with time for a family visit. At my door, I stopped and squared my shoulders. I needed to concentrate on the present and near future.

CHAPTER SIX

Bang! I sat up as if I'd been spring-loaded. The curtains at the window were open, admitting only the soft glow of streetlights. I blinked sleep out of my eyes and retrieved my phone from the nightstand. Four a.m. Ugh. Who would be up at this hour? I crept to the door and opened it wide enough to peer out. Nobody stirred. Could the loud knock have been part of my dream? I checked the bathroom and looked out the window, but everything was quiet. With too much adrenaline to get back to sleep, I pulled out a pen and paper from the desk and sat in the wooden rolling chair. I'd never been a journal writer, but after reading so many of them in the last few days, I felt the urge to start one.

Sunday, Jan 5, 2020

I woke up from this weird dream. I'd been in this room, sleeping next to a woman I thought was Cassie, when lights shone in the window, and shouts came from outside. I panicked, and Cassie tried to calm me down. Someone pounded on the door. "We needed to leave now!" The voice was deep, unfamiliar. It was so vivid, it seemed real.

I set down the pen and rubbed my temples.

Did they mean I needed to leave this house or this timeline?

I pushed off the chair and slogged into the bathroom. After splashing cold water on my face, I dressed in jeans and a sweatshirt and padded downstairs. Chantal probably wouldn't be here to make breakfast for a couple of hours.

I crossed the room to the large stainless-steel refrigerator, opened it, and surveyed my choices. There were some leftovers from last night's dinner, but I didn't fancy eating pork loin for breakfast. I pulled out a plastic container of mashed potatoes. Potato pancakes would sit all right on my empty stomach. I grabbed a stick of butter and opened cabinets until I found a skillet.

"Stop or I'll... Lydia?"

I jumped, one hand on my heart and the other reaching for the cast-iron frying pan. "Don't scare me like that."

Jamal stood in the doorway. "Didn't intend to. Thought I heard an intruder."

I set the pan on the stove's front burner. "You couldn't have heard me from your room."

"No, I was in the hall. I woke up and couldn't get back to sleep." He wandered toward me. "Whatchya makin'?"

"Potato pancakes. Want some?"

"Sure." He glanced around the kitchen. "Need help?"

"Dig out some plates and utensils." I formed patties from the cold potatoes. "If you can find some spices, get those, too."

"Yes, ma'am." He rummaged around the kitchen. "Couldn't sleep either?"

"Woke up with a start. Don't know if I heard something or dreamed it."

"Me too!" He brought a jar of a spice blend to me. "But it was more like I felt something strange. Thought it could have been a mild earthquake."

"Huh." I sprinkled the spices on the patties. "Weird. About fifteen minutes ago?"

"Yeah." He stared at me, his brow furrowed.

"Do you know when Chantal usually gets here?"

"Oh, she sleeps in on Sunday." He grinned. "She'll be here at six-thirty, serve breakfast at eight, and then head to church at ten." He groaned. "She'll expect me to go too."

"Not surprised." I stifled a chuckle. "I hear ya. I went to church every Sunday until I was fifteen." I flipped the potato cakes. Of course, they fell apart, and I pushed them together.

"What happened when you were fifteen?" He set plates on the butcher-block table.

My pulse pounded. What could I tell him? "Uh, my parents died." Well, they did to me. "I ended up in foster care. Some of the foster parents took me to church. Others didn't."

"Oh." He opened a drawer. "Ah. Found forks."

I exhaled in relief at the change of subject. "Good, because the potato cakes are almost done. Hope they're edible."

"What do you want to drink?" he asked. "Coffee's ready. Chantal programs the pot every night."

"Is there any sweet tea?"

"Always." He opened the fridge.

I placed crispy, falling-apart potato cakes on our plates, and he set down two glasses of iced tea. I dug in right away.

He hesitated. "I'm so used to waiting for the blessing when I'm here."

I pointed my fork at him and swallowed. "Me, too. When did Chantal get religion?"

He cleared his throat. "She calls it a relationship." He leaned forward. "Chantal started going to church about a year before she met Todd. He snorted. "It was so simple. A friend invited her and she went. Hasn't missed many Sundays or ministry activities since."

I blew out a breath. Maybe someday I'd understand. I took another bite. Maybe I would never understand. Sorry, Ma.

Jamal wolfed down his food, then leaned against the chairback. "Too bad the chocolate pie's gone."

I scrunched my nose. "You can eat chocolate this early?"

He laughed. "You can't?" He sobered and leaned forward. "Chantal says you decided to stay for good."

"Hoping to find a new job in the area, but keeping my options open." I sipped my tea and squinted at him. "You?"

He glanced at the ceiling. "I'm kind of in a holding pattern."

The back door opened and closed with a bang. Both Jamal and I snapped our heads toward it.

"You two couldn't sleep either?" Chantal set a loaded canvas bag on the counter nearest the door. "Whew." She poured herself a cup of coffee. "We woke up at four. Thought I'd get a jump on breakfast prep."

My mouth went dry. "Four? That's when both of us woke up."

"Hmm." She lifted her cup in a salute and sat across

from me. "We didn't think you'd be able to hear or feel it."

"What?" Jamal joined us at the table.

Chantal touched her chest. "I thought it was an earthquake, but it was loud. Todd said it sounded like a low-hovering helicopter."

I glanced at the doorway. "Where's Todd?"

"Prowling around the garage when I left."

Why was Todd in his garage on Sunday before church? Was it related to the noise from this morning? In need of fresh air, I donned my hoodie and strode out the front door. Darkness hid all the houses on Todd's side of the street. I stopped at the edge of the porch and grasped the column. What had happened this morning? There had to be a rational explanation.

I pulled my phone out of my pocket, sat on the swing, and checked the local news. Nothing, but it was early, and helicopters might not make the news.

I sat, body frozen but mind swirling, until the sun peeked over the distant hills. Those journals, and all the talk about the past, had sent my imagination into overdrive. I wandered inside. In the dining room, Jamal and Chantal sat at the table, drinking coffee and chatting with a couple who appeared to be in their mid-fifties. She looked lean and had an open expression, while he slumped and rubbed the back of his balding head.

"Hi, Lydia." Chantal waved me closer. "This is Bob and Michelle. They checked in last evening."

I greeted them, fixed myself a cup of coffee, and sat where I could see the parlor door. It wasn't as good as the chair at the head, but Bob occupied that one. I didn't think Chantal would appreciate me asking him to move. My lips curled up at the thought, but I turned my face away so they couldn't see.

Jamal and Chantal chatted with the couple while they ate. I sipped coffee and listened. They lived in Atlanta and were just here for the weekend. Not nearly as interesting as Brian and Allison. Chantal checked the grandfather clock in the corner several times as Bob and Michelle finished their breakfast and left.

Chantal glanced at the clock again. "Curious. Bob and Michelle told me they woke up at four this morning."

I choked on my coffee. "That's too much of a coincidence."

Jamal scoffed, but Chantal closed her eyes and bowed her head. When she looked at me, she smiled. "Maybe God wanted all of us to pray for someone."

Now it was my turn to scoff.

Chantal clicked her tongue, but stayed quiet as we sipped coffee and waited for the other guests.

A few minutes before ten, the advertised end of breakfast on Sundays, Todd entered from the kitchen. He fixed himself a plate and brought it over, taking the recently vacated seat at the head of the table.

"Jamal, can you clean up?" Chantal asked. "Todd and I need to leave at ten to make it to church on time." She glanced at the clock. "Normally, the guests aren't this late."

"No problem." Jamal grinned. He'd probably rather clean up than go to church.

"I can help." *I'd* rather clean than go to church.

"I'll start you off." Chantal carried a tray to the kitchen.

Jamal lifted his plate and ambled after her.

Todd glanced at both doors and then leaned toward me.

"I wasn't sure I'd see you here."

I pulled back, surprised. "Why?"

"My machine has been moved."

My eyebrows shot up. "You think I did something with it? I didn't even know where it was."

His jaw tightened. "You didn't use it?"

"I might be able to get it working, but it would take me longer than a week."

He closed his eyes and sighed.

My breath hitched. Those suspicions I'd suppressed earlier surfaced. "The helicopter-earthquake this morning! Do you think someone used it?"

He pursed his lips. "It has Nov 11, 1873 in the date field. And it was warm when I found it downstairs in my garage."

I squinted. "I thought you said it had been taken."

He exhaled and shook his head. "I said, moved. It had been upstairs in my bonus room, but I found it in the garage."

I leaned forward, palms on the table. "But who?" A snatch of whispered conversation bombarded my mind. I sucked in air. "I think I know!" I told Todd about Allison, Brian, and Richard. "They could have found and reactivated the time machine, but how?"

He sat up and rubbed the back of his neck. "I only know one person, other than you, who's smart enough. It's not any of our guests." He snapped his fingers. "We've had break-ins in the neighborhood. My bonus room can be accessed from the stairs in the garage. It's at the other end of the house from our bedroom. They could have managed to get in without waking us up."

I huffed. "You really believe someone stole the time machine from your bonus room and left it in your garage?"

He groaned. "No. But when I found the pedestrian door jimmied..." He flashed me a sheepish grin.

"You thought I broke into your garage?"

"You were the only one who knew I still had the machine."

I slumped against the chairback. "Apparently, not."

CHAPTER SEVEN

Chantal entered the dining room from the kitchen, purse in hand. "Are you ready?"

Todd slid his chair back, lifting his plate. "Yep."

"Jamal will get that." Chantal grinned. "I'm looking forward to this trip."

"Trip?" My face flushed. She couldn't leave us here to man this place alone, especially with possible time-travelers.

Chantal chuckled. "Just for the afternoon. After church, we're driving out into the country for a picnic." She sidled up to Todd and closed her arm around his. "We'll be back in time to set out supper by six-thirty."

"Whew." I wiped my brow.

Chantal's lips parted into a wide smile. "Had you worried for a sec, didn't I?"

"Yes."

Jamal entered and stopped at the sideboard. "Still waiting for three of the guests? How long do you think we should keep breakfast out? They're already late."

"Go ahead and clean up." Chantal sighed as she followed Todd out.

I helped Jamal clear the dirty dishes and food trays from

the dining room. While he loaded the dishwasher, I replaced the tablecloth and the runner on the sideboard.

After depositing the linens in the laundry room, I wandered outside. Where were Brian, Richard, and Allison? Allison hadn't missed a meal yet. I trotted over to the small parking lot off the cul-de-sac. Three vehicles other than mine and Jamal's crowded the little lot. One for Bob and Michelle, one for Richard, and one for Brian and Allison. My jaw dropped, and my pulse quickened. I bounded up the steps to the porch, entered the B&B, and trotted upstairs. First, I knocked on the master suite door. Then I pounded. No answer. I put my ear to the door. Silence. I raced down the hallway to the first room on the opposite landing. No answer and no noise there either. Where were they?

Or when?

~

The view from my rocking chair on the front porch would have been idyllic for a lazy Sunday afternoon. The sun lowered toward dusk, and activity on the street waned. A silver blur turned onto the street. I jumped up. When the Prius pulled into Todd's driveway, I bolted off the porch and raced to them.

Todd climbed out of the car and held his hands up as if I was about to arrest him. "Whoa." He grinned. "Didn't think you'd be that excited to see me."

"We have to do something. They're gone." I wrung my hands together as I'd been doing all afternoon.

Chantal rounded the back of the car and squinted. "Who?"

"Brian, Allison, and Richard." I pointed toward the

small parking lot. "They're gone, but their cars are still here."

Chantal frowned. "Hmm."

Todd coughed. "Um. I'm sure there's an explanation."

"Of course." Chantal pecked Todd on the cheek. "I have to set supper out." She strode down the street toward the B&B.

"I'll be there in a few," Todd called after her. He turned to me. "Calm down—"

"Don't tell me that." I leaned toward him. My pent-up anxiety flowed through my quavering voice. "Those people could be messing up the timeline."

"Nothing's changed." He backed away.

I stepped toward him. "You don't know that. I think one of us needs to go after them."

He sighed. "We don't know for certain that they're trapped."

"Todd, I think we do. They're nowhere to be found, but their cars are here."

"So is my time machine."

I took a breath. "Have you changed it? When Cassie used it, it disappeared on her. Didn't it pop back here?"

He lowered his head. "Yes. But they could have ridden it back."

"You just want to believe that."

"If you go back, you don't have to go right away. Take your time."

I raised a hand to my hip. "We have to go. If nothing else, to retrieve them."

Todd closed his eyes. "I don't want to strand anyone but. . ."

"What?" I shot him a glare.

He huffed. "They stole the machine."

I raised my arm to the side. "I can't believe you."

He lifted his index finger. "If they time-traveled."

"You know they did. Should have known it this morning." I stalked toward the B&B.

"What are you going to do?" Todd trotted over and stopped me with a hand on my arm.

I glared at him. "Go up and check out their rooms. There's bound to be proof."

He scoffed. "Chantal won't let you. Guest privacy."

I pulled my arm out of his grip. "I'm the cleaning person."

He scooted in front of me. "Wait, just until checkout tomorrow morning. You'll feel silly if they show up from a day-long hike."

"They're not the type."

"Wait, please." He strode toward his front stoop.

"Only until check out tomorrow." I grumbled and stomped toward the B&B, glancing at the woods behind it. If only they'd come tramping in from a hike, I could concentrate on my future instead of the past. The knot in my stomach tightened. I had a long night ahead of me.

~

Monday morning, I sat in the dining room, pushing food around on my plate and willing Brian, Allison, and Richard to walk into the room.

Chantal entered from the kitchen. "Still no sign of them?"

I grimaced and turned my head from side to side.

The grandfather clock in the corner of the room struck

ten. Check out time. Chantal stared at the clock and huffed out a breath. "At least Bob and Michelle already left." She stared at the open parlor door.

"Well?" I rubbed my hands on my thighs.

"Ten more minutes." Chantal picked up her coffee mug and took a sip.

Jamal pushed his chair away. "They could be hurt."

"All three of them?" Chantal glanced at her brother.

Jamal stood. "Well, something's not right. We need to check out those rooms."

I nodded, looking at Chantal out of the corner of my eye.

"I'll do it if you don't want to," Jamal said.

I pushed my chair back. "I'll take Brian's and you can open Richard's."

"If anyone goes in those rooms, it'll be me." Chantal set down her cup and placed her hands on the table. She pushed herself up, marched out the door, and through the small parlor toward the foyer.

Jamal and I scrambled after her.

When she reached the top of the stairs, Chantal turned right, walked to Richard's room, and knocked. "Richard?"

I held my breath.

After about thirty seconds, she knocked again and then tried the door. When it wouldn't open, she pulled a key out of her apron pocket and unlocked it. She opened the door a crack and peered in, then opened it wider.

Jamal and I rushed into the room. I stopped short and gaped at the unmade bed and the open suitcase.

Jamal peeked into the bathroom. "Nobody in here."

"And he hasn't even started to pack." I motioned to the

clothes in piles on the bed and chair.

"You search here. I'll check on Brian and Allison." Chantal waved her key and left.

I opened the wardrobe. It was empty except for the Bible on the shelf. I picked it up and flipped through the pages. On a hunch, I flipped to the family-tree page. It didn't look quite as full. I should have studied it more closely before. Or photographed it. I checked for all my family. We were still there, but a few other names might be missing. Brian's grandmother was still listed, but she was the only other person I remembered specifically. Gooseflesh crept up my arms. Something wasn't right. I snapped my fingers. Brian had taken pictures. But even if his phone was still here, it was probably password-protected.

Jamal eyed the Bible. "Why would Richard have that? It's Brian's family, right?"

I slipped the Bible under my arm. "Well, they were both working on the book."

Jamal and I hurried down the hallway to the open door on the opposite wall. Chantal stood in the room, which appeared in a similar condition to Richard's.

Jamal peered into the bathroom, shook his head, and turned toward us. "Wherever they went, they must have expected to be back by now."

Chantal slumped against the door frame. "I need to call the police and file a missing person's report."

I took a deep breath. "It's not your fault."

She shook her head, a tear escaping. "I know, but...What if they were hurt on our property? We should have looked for them sooner."

Jamal gave her a short hug. "You were honoring their

privacy. Besides, you wouldn't have been able to report them missing until today anyway."

"I'd better get it over with." She plodded downstairs.

I spotted two phones and a wallet on the dresser.

Jamal jerked his head. "We should go downstairs."

I grimaced but followed him and stopped on the stairway as Chantal finished her call.

"Yes. I will, and thank you." She set down the receiver and glanced up at me. "They're allowing me to clean the rooms, but they want me to photograph them first. Someone will be out to pick up their things eventually."

I made eye contact. "Do you think you should call Todd?"

She pulled her head back. "Why?"

"Oh, uh." How could I forget she didn't know about the time machine? "I need to call him about that job opportunity. Do you want me to tell him about this?"

"No. I'll tell him tonight." She headed upstairs. "I have guests in the master coming in this afternoon. I guess I'll store their stuff in the attic, for now."

"Let me help." I wanted a peek at those phones. Maybe I'd find something to indicate their motives. Now, there was no doubt in my mind they'd used Todd's machine.

~

As soon as Todd pulled into his driveway, I hopped up from the porch swing and raced toward him, arriving as he opened his car door. "Todd, I know for certain they used the machine and didn't return."

He climbed out and stared at me, then averted his gaze and shut the car door. "Look. I shouldn't have told you.

Anyone could have moved it without using it."

"Brian, Allison, and Richard were researching my family's history. They were supposed to check out today, but they didn't show."

He stepped past me, but I shifted to block him. "Wait. Saturday evening, I interrupted the three of them having an intense whispered conversation. They stopped when they noticed me. Then Sunday morning..."

"You really don't want to go back." He closed his eyes, took a deep breath, and opened them again, making eye contact with me.

I bit my lip. "No, but I think I have to."

He walked around me.

I followed.

He shook his head. "No. I can't let that happen again."

"But it's already happening." I fished the Bible from the canvas bag draped over my shoulder. "The family tree in here is different."

He turned around to look at me, his eyes wide. "How do you know?"

I pulled Richard's phone out. We'd found both Brian's and Richard's, but this one hadn't been protected. I showed him the photo with two names that were now missing from the Bible.

"Dang." He rubbed the side of his neck. "How did they find it?"

"How could they reactivate it?" I doubted Brian, a lawyer, or Professor Richard could do it.

Todd pursed his lips.

I leaned in. "What do you know? Could Brian's wife have done it?"

He groaned. "I didn't realize it was her until Chantal described Allison yesterday."

I squinted at him.

He glanced away. "The only person, other than you, who I thought could reactivate the machine is a woman who works in the lab next door to mine, but her name is Jessica Gentry. I hadn't seen her here." He exhaled. "Jessica's been trying to get me to share my research." He rubbed his temple. "I heard a rumor that she's stolen other people's work. She could have activated the machine."

An image of the woman at the soda fountain flashed into my mind. "She's the one you argued with on Christmas Eve."

He nodded and lowered his head.

I stomped the ground. "You knew this yesterday and didn't tell me?"

"Nothing you could do." He locked eyes with mine. "I hoped they'd show up."

I took a deep breath, trying to slow my heartbeat. "We have to go and stop them from whatever they're doing." I peered at him. "Would they be able to retrieve the machine?"

"Only if they have a remote." He rubbed the back of his neck. "Both of mine are here. I'll show you." He led me into the garage.

Jenny had carried something that resembled a TV remote, though at the time, I'd had no idea what it was.

"So, they *are* stuck." I placed my hand on my hip and nodded at the remotes he pulled out of his workbench drawer. "Do they both work?" They were black and slender, but one was a bit shorter than the other.

"Yes." With a sigh, he handed me the shorter one. "Let me show you how to use it before you leave."

We walked over to the time machine in the corner.

"You're not coming with me?" My grip on the remote was so tight, my knuckles whitened. I'd only ridden this once, ten years ago, and I'd been in so much pain I was barely conscious.

"I can't." What he meant was he wouldn't. "I'm not going to take off the restrictions either. You won't be able to go to an earlier date than they did, and you won't be able to return until at least a minute after you left."

I nodded. "Got it."

He held up his index finger. "Also, you can't bring them all back at once. It's limited to three people."

"Anything else?" I stepped onto the machine.

"Wait!" Todd pulled me off. "Get ready first. Eat something. Find something more suitable to wear. Give Chantal an excuse, just in case..." He angled his head away.

"If I have the remote, I'll be fine, right?"

He lifted his hands and gazed at me. "It's risky. I still don't fully understand it. That's why I disabled the machine. I should have destroyed it." He bobbed his head toward my outfit. "Get ready before you go."

I took a deep breath and scanned the jeans and t-shirt I wore. He was right. But I didn't have anything that would blend in. Though waiting wouldn't make any difference, my gut wanted to leave immediately. Before I chickened out.

CHAPTER EIGHT

Todd ushered me onto the platform and handed me the remote control. If I needed to step off to locate the travelers, the machine would pop back. The remote would allow me to call it after I rounded them up. I secured it in the pocket of my riding pants and grasped both handrails.

"I would have moved this to the yard behind Nate's house, but I thought someone might notice." Todd strode to the garage door, giving me a wide berth.

I shrugged. "From a distance, you would have looked like you were moving a treadmill."

"But one of the guests could see it up close." He glanced out the garage windows.

"They wouldn't know what it was, though."

"Well, I don't want to take any chances." He tapped his foot to a swift beat. "Ready?"

"Yeah. How do I look?" I wore a vintage white blouse over riding pants, with my hair pulled back in a low chignon.

"You'll blend in long enough to get them home. If the machine is accurate, they should still be in the vicinity."

With any luck, they'd be relieved to see me.

Todd had convinced me to wait until Saturday, when he

could stand guard by the machine. He'd told Chantal that we were working on a project. He hadn't needed to elaborate because Chantal had enough to worry about with three missing guests and Jamal still here, hiding from thugs. The whole operation was programmed to take five minutes 2020 time. That is, if the machine worked correctly.

I took a deep breath and let it out on a count of ten. "Here goes." After checking for the fifth time that the date and time were correct—two minutes after the trio would have landed—I pushed the activate button.

The machine shook so hard, I maintained a death grip on the railings. He should add a seat, straps, or something to this thing. My vision blurred as a mist rolled into the room. No idea why that happened, but I didn't understand time travel. If I hadn't experienced it in the other direction, I'd never have believed it was possible. A wind picked up and nearly blew me off the platform. I doubled over and almost vomited from the motion.

When the machine stopped vibrating, the mist cleared. My breath came in gasps as if I'd run a 5k in record time. I straightened and raised both hands to my brow to shield my eyes from the sun. Why hadn't I worn a hat? I scanned the horizon for the trio. Two people stood near the tree line, but I couldn't see the third, and they were too far away to identify. I stayed on the machine to keep it from popping back to Todd, and waved my arm over my head. They started toward me. My stomach settled as Brian and Richard came closer. Maybe this would be easier than I thought.

Hoof beats and the rumble of rolling wheels invaded the quiet. I whipped around to see a carriage carrying a man and a woman. Who could they be? None of my family ever used this road. I waved for the men to hurry. I'd have to leave with Brian and Richard and come back for Allison later.

"Yoo hoo!" The carriage stopped, and the woman stood and waved. It was Mrs. Kelley. Bile rose in my throat. If I let her come any closer, she'd recognize me. Then she'd tell Ma's friend, Mrs. Hodges, and the whole town would believe I'd come back from the dead. Ma and Pa would never get any rest after that. I waved Brian and Richard off and activated the machine. Mist swirled in, and the platform shook harder this time. I could only hope Mrs. Kelley would think she'd seen a spirit.

I held on tight as darkness overcame me, and my body vibrated so much I feared my teeth would fall out. When the platform stopped shaking and the mist evaporated, I heaved. My breakfast landed on Todd's sneakers.

Todd pulled me off the platform. "What happened?"

I collapsed onto him. "I'm sorry about your shoes."

He closed his arm around my back. "Don't worry about that." He led me to a bench along the garage wall and sat next to me. "Breathe."

I gulped in air. "The pastor and his wife saw me. I panicked and hit the return button."

"Hmm. How long were you there?"

"Long enough for Richard and Brian to get halfway to the machine from the trees. So, not more than a minute. Two, tops." I tilted my head toward him. "Why?"

He blinked. "Sorry. The scientist in me. Your reaction to the travel is more extreme than normal. Probably because your body didn't have time to adjust."

I rolled my eyes. "Now, what are we going to do?"

He slapped his thighs. "That's up to you, but if you go

back, I suggest you wait at least until tomorrow."

"Will you be able to monitor then?"

"Yes. Meet me here after lunch." He stood and glanced back. "If you still want to go."

I shuddered. "I have to."

~

After lunch on Sunday, I excused myself, telling Chantal I planned to go for a hike to clear my head. I felt rested enough for another attempt after spending the remainder of Saturday in my room, poring over the journals. No hints of time travelers, but then I didn't have a journal for the time my trio had landed. As Chantal cleaned the kitchen, I donned the riding pants, blouse, and an old wide-brimmed hat, and snuck out the front. I strode to Todd's house and entered his garage from the side door.

He waited next to the time machine. "I've set it for the next morning. You ready?"

I took a deep breath and stepped onto the platform. "After being stuck for a whole day, they should be ready to return." I tamped down the queasy feeling in my gut. "How do I find them?"

He shook his head. "No way to know where they've gone. I've been praying they didn't wander too far. You'll probably have to make your presence known to Cassie at least."

I nodded and bit my lip. "I hope she's happy to see me." My breath hitched. "Will she recognize me?" I had aged ten years, but it would only have been three for them.

Todd peered at me. "You don't look that much different." He checked the display panel on the machine and handed me the remote. "Be careful. I'll be here when you get back in five minutes. Send two of them back, then call the machine, and come back with the last one."

I leaned toward him. "What if I can't find them, or they won't come?"

He searched my eyes. "Come back alone. If you don't return in five minutes..."

I clutched his shoulder. "Will you come find me?"

"If I can." A sweat broke out on his brow.

I nodded and let go. "You know this thing isn't perfect. Check the closet in the B&B first." It was the place where Cassie had left messages for Todd before.

He exhaled. "Will do."

Hopefully, nobody would be around this time. I pocketed the remote, clicked the activate button, and hung onto the rails with an iron grip. The mist swirled in as the machine shook, and a low tone increased in volume and pitch. When the shaking finally subsided, I opened my eyes. Must have closed them by instinct.

I stepped off the platform onto a field and stood for a moment as my heart rate slowed to normal and my stomach recuperated. It hadn't been as bad as yesterday, but maybe I should have waited more than a day. The machine disappeared, and I patted the remote in my pocket. Todd had told me that with this controller, the machine will come to wherever I am when I call it.

A glance to my right revealed Nate's house at the end of the lane with a dirt circular driveway in front of it. From the height of the sun, it was morning, probably around eight—the right time. I strode toward the house, hoping it was the next day and not later. Couldn't think about that now. Cassie would most likely be in the kitchen or out in the cowshed.

Keeping a lookout for Brian, Allison, and Richard, I hurried to the kitchen door and peeked in. Nobody was there, but the wood stove was in use. The aroma of baking bread wafted from it. Cassie had to be close. I could check the cowshed, but instead, I tidied up the worktable, which was sticky with bread dough. I also washed the teacups that had been left on the table. So many memories came crashing in on me, I felt grateful to have this time alone to readjust to life here. I hoped it wouldn't take long to check on my family and retrieve the time-traveling trio.

"My kitchen isn't a rest area for travelers."

I clasped my hand on my heart, my pulse racing, as I whirled to face her.

Cassie stood in the doorway, one hand on her hip. She looked radiant, even through her scowl.

I raised my hands and smiled. "Cassie. You look wonderful."

"Who are—" Her eyes widened, and she gasped. "Lydia?"

I nodded.

She ran over and gave me a fierce hug. "I wondered yesterday if you'd come. After the Kelleys' stories about flashing lights in the field." She pulled away and held me at arm's length. "You're grown."

"Yes. I'm twenty-five. It's 2020, my time." More or less. I wasn't sure whose time was whose anymore. "Did the Kelleys see anyone?"

"Is that why you're here?" She pulled a chair out and motioned for me to sit.

"A couple of reasons." I swallowed. The upside-down

ad was still on my mind. "Have you seen any travelers?"

"No. Just evidence." She sat opposite me. "A loaf of bread went missing. I thought it was some kids, but there haven't been any untended lately. Caleb's the only one of ours big enough, and he's past that."

"He's eleven, now, right?" I leaned in, palms on the worktable.

She nodded. "Eleven going on thirty. He's so smart. And wise. And he's made great progress in reading. I know he'll be a scientist or inventor someday."

A smile formed on my lips as I blinked back tears. Maybe I missed my family more than I realized.

"What about you?" Cassie clasped my hands across the table. "Tell me everything."

"I'd love to, but I really need your help." I pulled my hands away. "I think three people traveled here using Todd's machine, but they didn't have the remote, so they couldn't get back."

"Oh." She placed a hand on her cheek. "I know what that's like."

"Yeah. Anything you can tell me would help."

She let her hand fall to the table. "The only thing that was missing was the bread."

"When?"

"This morning." She motioned to the stove. "That's why that one is in there, and the mess on…did you clean this up?"

I smirked. "Old habits."

"Thank you." She stood abruptly. "The theft put me off my schedule. Come with me, and I'll tell you the rest."

I followed her across the walkway to the back door. "What day is it?"

"November 12, 1873. Why?" She led me through the mudroom and dining room to the small parlor.

"So, they've been here a little less than a day." I smiled at the wooden cradle with little fingers wriggling over the side.

"She's awake. I'm surprised she's not screaming." Cassie lifted her baby and turned her to face me. "This is—"

"Melody." I hurried toward her. "I read the family tree in the Bible."

Cassie smiled. "Don't tell me anything else."

Melody's face turned red, and she grunted.

I laughed. Even though I hadn't spent much time around babies, I knew what came next.

Cassie grimaced. "Don't laugh unless you want to change her."

I pressed my lips together. "No, thanks." She headed to the sofa, and I stayed put, but I peeked over the back. She laid Melody on top of the blanket draped over the cushion, took off the cloth diaper secured with safety pins, and wiped her off with a rag she'd taken out of a pail of water. Then she pulled a clean diaper out of a different pail and put it on Melody.

"I'm impressed at your efficiency."

"Four months of practice." Cassie picked up her daughter, put her on her shoulder, and paced across the floor. "Now. To answer your question. It was about an hour ago the bread went missing. I only saw one set of footprints in the mud near the walkway." She jostled the baby, who scrunched her little face. "I didn't see or hear anything else."

"I'm going to walk around." I walked to the foyer.

"Oh, Lydia." Cassie stopped me with a hand on my arm.

"Jenny is out of jail. She's staying with your ma."

Why was I not surprised? "Figures. Ma always has to meddle."

"Your mother loves people. She's one of the few who care about Jenny." Cassie meandered away, Melody cradled against her shoulder. "She dragged me with her to visit Jenny in jail, baked goods and a Bible in hand."

I snickered. "How did Jenny handle that?"

Cassie grinned. "She gobbled the bread and cookies and tolerated the Bible reading. I got more out of it than she did."

"Thanks for the reminder about Jenny."

The grandfather clock struck the hour. Cassie jerked her head toward it. "I have work to do, and you should start searching. Don't let Jenny get her hands on the time machine if you go to your ma's." She took a breath. "And, you really should go there. She'd be so hurt if she found out you were here and didn't visit her."

"You sound just like her." I stuck my tongue out.

She chuckled. "Not a bad thing at all."

I blew out a breath. She was right. I had to visit. I wanted to see Pa, too. First, I prowled around Nate's house and grounds but didn't find any clues.

~

I walked the wooded path toward my parents' house. How many times had I traversed this dirt trail? Countless times, especially in the seven months Cassie was with us. Although it had been ten years, my body seemed to know where the roots waited to trip me and branches stuck out to scratch me. Muscle memory. Funny, they'd be in the same places after all this time. Wait. I'd only been gone from this time for three years. Ugh. Time travel had my mind spinning.

When I entered the clearing, I spied Pa's work shed and beelined to it. Since harvest was over, he'd probably be there. I wanted him with me when I met Ma. I'd always had a close relationship with Pa. Now we had even more in common. We were both time-travelers.

The rough but rhythmic buzz of a saw cutting through wood emanated from the shed. Grinning, I opened the door wide.

"Grandpa." Caleb kept his head down. "I can explain."

My breath caught, and I froze in the doorway. Caleb looked almost full-grown. He'd only been eight when I left.

He lifted his head, his reddish-brown hair flopping into his blue eyes. "You're not Grandpa."

I straightened to my full height and entered. "I'm looking for your grandpa." No need to announce my identity if he didn't recognize me. "Do you know where he is?"

"Right behind you," Pa said. "What do you want here?"

I spun and stopped just short of hugging him.

His eyes widened in recognition, and he smiled big. "Uh, let's go outside to discuss business." He glanced over my shoulder at Caleb. "Put that saw down, and stack those planks like I told you."

Caleb grunted but obeyed.

Pa and I walked outside. He pulled the door closed and escorted me several yards behind the shed. He crushed me in a bear hug, then pulled away and held my face in his hands. "Lydia." A tear rolled down his weathered cheek. "I knew you'd come back someday. How long?" He looked me up and down.

"I'm twenty-five, Pa." I studied our feet and fidgeted.

"Did it take you that long to get Todd to let you use his machine, or did you have to make your own?"

I heaved a loud sigh. "I'm not here for a visit."

He turned and paced away from me. "I was afraid of that."

"It's not that I didn't want to." Not totally a lie, though I hadn't thought about it much. "Um. It seemed bad form to risk changing history just for homesickness."

"I know." He faced me and placed his hands on my shoulders. "It's so good to see you."

"You, too." I wiped a tear off my face.

He slapped a hand on his thigh. "Your ma will be over the moon!"

"Uh." I pulled away. "I'm not sure I want to see her yet."

He raised his eyebrows. "Why?"

I squared my shoulders. "I have something important to do here. Three people used Todd's machine and didn't have the remote with them. They must have gotten stuck here."

He pulled at his collar. "Geez! That's all we need."

"Right." I nodded, searching his face.

His deep brown eyes intensified as the skin surrounding them crinkled. "I'll help you find them, but you have to see your mother."

I shifted my weight. "I don't want anyone else to see me. Caleb didn't seem to recognize me."

"Oh, I won't bring you to the house." He pulled a toothpick out of his shirt pocket and pointed it toward the yard. "Jenny's there. I'll bring Mattie to you."

"Where?"

"Go back onto the path. Sit on that old stump, and we'll be there as soon as we can."

I tapped my foot. "I need to find those people ASAP."

"Your mother might be able to help." He tucked the toothpick in the corner of his mouth, then hurried toward the house. When had he picked up that habit?

I ambled to the stump and sat, willing Pa to return post-haste. The few leaves on the trees rustled in the wind, small animals skittered between the trees, and birds chirped. This far south, there were always birds around. When I lived in Seattle, I hadn't realized I'd missed these sounds.

Why had I let my mind drift when I needed to concentrate on finding the time machine thieves? When Ma and Pa came into view, I stood.

Pa led Ma to me, both of them breathing hard.

As they approached, Ma squinted, then her eyes lit up. She trotted over and hugged me harder than Pa had.

"Ma." I tried not to choke.

She pulled back but kept her hands on my upper arms while she looked me over. Her eyes twinkled, and a corner of her mouth crooked upward. "Took your time coming, didn't you?"

"I'm sorry—"

"I'm glad." She tucked a strand of hair behind my ear. "I get to see you grown. You look beautiful."

Startled, I pulled back. "Really?"

"Of course." She let go of my arm and settled onto the stump. "Have I ever lied?"

"Uh, stretched the truth. Especially to make people feel better."

"Pish." She flicked her wrist and then peered at me. "So, tell me everything. What have you done in nine years?"

"Ten. And that's not important. I—"

"Yes, it is important. I'm your ma. I want to hear everything." She clasped her hands in her lap.

Pa laid a hand on her shoulder. "She has some urgent business. I told you."

"Short version then." Ma waved toward Nate's. "And then you can get on with it."

I wouldn't be able to leave until I told her, so I filled her in on Todd getting me an ID, growing up in foster homes, and earning my way through Georgia Tech. Pa was impressed with that. I told her about the software job in Seattle, and Pa said he'd explain later. I ended by informing her of my current predicament. Thankfully, she listened and didn't ask many questions, making my story faster than I'd expected.

Ma clapped her hands on her thighs, a gleam in her eyes. "Now, tell us about these three people you're searching for."

"Two men and a woman. One of the men is in his fifties, and the couple are probably mid-thirties." I provided a general description. "No idea what they're wearing."

"We'll keep a lookout for them." Ma stood and clasped my hands in both of hers. She closed her eyes and moved her mouth as if she was speaking, but didn't make a sound. When she opened them, she peered at me, a serious expression on her face. "If you need a place to stay, I'm sure Nate and Cassie will put you up." She pulled me close and embraced me tightly, as if she didn't want to let go. "Please visit us again before you leave," she whispered in my ear.

I rested my head on her shoulder. The urgency to get on with my mission warred with the need to be comforted by my mother.

When she broke away, Pa pulled me to him and hugged

me even harder, then let go but kept his gaze on me. "We'll head back to the house. If we see anything, I'll leave a message in the shop. We'll keep Jenny away from Nate's."

"Wait." I touched his arm. "Maybe Jenny knows something about them. Could she have put an upside-down ad for Nate's business in today's paper?"

Ma tilted her head. "Now, why would she do that?"

I rubbed my temple. "As a distress call. To get someone to come back for her."

Ma's brow furrowed. "She hasn't mentioned anything about going to the future. She's happy to be out of jail and seems content here. Even started husband hunting." She laughed, then held up a finger. "But all that could be a cover. I never could read Jenny, like I can everyone else."

Pa nodded. "Best to keep Jenny away from the travelers and the time machine."

I squinted. "That's what Cassie said, but why? Jenny used the time machine. Maybe I should talk to her." Not that I wanted to. I'd never liked her.

Pa shifted from foot to foot. "It's for her own good. She went back and forth on that thing too many times." He circled his finger at his temple. "It made her a bit off kilter."

I lifted an eyebrow. "You mean crazy?"

He held up a hand. "I didn't say that."

Ma grunted. "Didn't have to."

Pa laid a hand on my shoulder. "It's best if Jenny doesn't recognize you and doesn't know about the time travelers. We'll do our best to see to that." He gave me one last squeeze. "So glad to see you."

Ma accepted Pa's proffered elbow. "I'll be praying for your success. Looking forward to seeing you before you leave."

"Me, too." I tried to smile, but with the tears rolling down my face, I'm not sure I pulled it off. What had gotten into me? I'm not a crier.

CHAPTER NINE

My vision blurred as Pa escorted Ma down the path. Was I crying about being home? Well, not home but back where I started. I wiped my eyes with my sleeves, squared my shoulders, and strode down the trail toward Nate's house. Brian, Allison, and Richard could be there, prowling around trying to find the time machine. At least that's what I would have done. Too bad I didn't know my quarry that well.

Squirrels skittered in the brush, and an owl called from a tree along the path. Nothing out of the ordinary. When I emerged into the clearing, I circled the property to the dirt road in front. The grass at the side of the house had been trampled, but anyone could have done that. I veered toward the field where the machine had deposited me. They could be hiding in the woods in that direction. If I called out, would they trust me? Having no idea what their motive was for coming here put me at a disadvantage. If they were just trying to ascertain whether they could time-travel and then got stuck, they'd want my help. What if they had some other reason in mind? I winced at the mess they could make of the timeline. Even coming to retrieve them was risky.

I wandered toward the kitchen. Maybe Cassie would

have some ideas.

"Stop right there, fella." A male voice I didn't recognize startled me, and something sharp poked me in the shoulder blade.

My breath hitched, and I raised my hands.

"What are you doing here?"

"Visiting Cassie." I peeked over my shoulder.

"Uh, I'm sorry." He lowered the knife, shifted from foot to foot, and lifted his wide-brimmed hat, revealing mussed sandy-brown hair. "The way you were dressed."

"It's okay, Lucas." Cassie stepped from the kitchen door. "This is my... cousin, Lydia." She turned to me. "Lydia, this is Lucas Sullivan. He works for us."

"Hello." My face flushed as I stared at the tall, lean cowboy with piercing blue eyes. Her sketch hadn't done him justice.

Lucas fidgeted with his hat, his face reddening. Was he embarrassed by his action or my stare?

I blinked and walked toward Cassie. "Didn't know you needed a bodyguard."

She chuckled. "That's a bonus. He helps Nate with the farm work. Since your...I mean, Ed has been spending more time working on the steam-powered mill."

I bounced on my toes and clapped. "I'm glad. He always wanted to do that."

Lucas tilted his head and squinted, then returned his expression to neutral. "Nice to meet you, ma'am." He cleared his throat. "Well, I'll get back to work." He replaced his hat and sauntered away.

Cassie pressed her lips together, suppressing a smile. "I think he finds you attractive."

I snorted. "He thought I was a guy."

"From behind. He was looking at your oversized breeches, I'm sure."

"Well, I didn't have anything else from this period. The dress I was wearing when—" I glanced around, uncomfortable speaking about time-travel. "It was ruined. It wouldn't fit now, anyway."

Cassie ushered me to the back door. "Let me find you something else to wear while you're here." In the small parlor, she checked on Melody asleep in her cradle and walked upstairs. "I should have thought of that earlier."

"It's okay." I trudged behind her. "I hoped I could get away with this."

"Well, if you want to go into town, you probably shouldn't." She continued toward the master bedroom and pointed to the room I occupied in 2020 as she walked by. "I'll make up the bed for you in here, in case you need to stay."

"Thanks." This morning, I'd awoken in that room, a hundred and fifty years later. I couldn't help but shudder at the weirdness.

Cassie opened her wardrobe. "Nate will be happy to see you."

"I'd like that, too. But this can't be a social call." I fingered a navy-blue skirt and jacket. "Can I wear that one?"

She smiled. "Still like to blend in, don't you?"

"Just like you." I snickered, but then pointed to a jade green gown. "Maybe not. That's gorgeous."

She grinned and held it up. "Guess who advised me to get it."

"Lera."

"Of course."

"How's she doing?"

"Well. She and Simon stayed with us for nearly a year while they rebuilt." She turned away and rehung the jade dress. "They built a smaller house, not too much larger than this one. Caleb has two baby brothers. Two and a half and eleven months."

I blinked. "Wow. They're close in age."

She handed me the navy-blue outfit. "Yeah. She has her hands full, but she has a part-time nanny. Caleb and Simon help. Plus, there's Mrs. Jones."

"Is she still living at Ma and Pa's?" I laid the navy skirt on the oak sleigh bed and took off my breeches.

"Yes. Your pa and Nate built another house for Mark and Emily. They got married last January." She handed me a full slip.

"Not surprised about that." I put on the slip and started to don the jacket over my blouse.

"Wait, you'll need a different blouse, and one of these." She smiled and dangled a corset in her hand.

I groaned. "Really? My bra works fine."

She smirked. "Yes, but you don't look right in it."

I exhaled and allowed her to help me into the blasted corset. I'd started wearing them shortly before I left. One more reason to stay in the future. "These don't bother you?"

She laughed. "I've gotten used to them. And I don't wear the crinolines."

"I can see that." I glanced at her full skirt. "No bustle either?"

"Nope, and even if that becomes the fashion soon, I don't intend to." She pointed to the laces on the front of my corset. "But bras haven't been invented yet, so I have to wear these. Honestly, they're more comfortable than some bras, and I think they're more flattering."

"Well, that's the last thing I'm worried about." I pulled the laces tight, tied them, and put the chemise and blouse on over.

"Not even for Lucas?" She crooked up one side of her mouth. "I saw that longing gaze you gave him."

My face heated. "No way. I'm not interested in anybody." I coughed. "From this time."

She studied me for a second. "Recent breakup?"

I jerked my head back. "How'd you know?"

She smiled, a gleam in her eye, and twirled her finger in front of my face. "Your expression right now. The 'I hate men' look."

I pursed my lips. "I don't hate them. Just don't want to get involved right now."

"Okay, I get it." She looked me up and down, then dove under the bed and pulled out a pair of boots.

I let out an exasperated sigh. "My boots don't work either?"

"Nope." She handed me the granny boots mine had been patterned after.

I sighed, but pulled on her shoes. "I'm not going to be here long enough for anyone to scrutinize my costume."

She placed one hand on her hip. "That's just it. It can't look like a costume."

Rolling my eyes, I finished buckling the shoes and stood. "Good enough?"

She smiled. "You'll do."

"Wait!" I fished the remote out from my riding trousers.

"I need a pocket."

"Oh yeah. You need to keep that on you." Cassie pulled a set of pockets sewn onto a ribbon out of her dresser and tied them around my waist under my skirt.

I slid them around to land on my hips. Too bad I couldn't wear my bike shorts with the pockets. The remote would be snug. With these, it wouldn't show, but it would dangle. I slipped the remote through the slit in the over-skirt and inside the pocket, patting it against my thigh.

She led me out of her room, carrying my shirt, riding pants, and boots. "I'll put your clothes in your room."

"Thanks." Where should I search first? I stopped at the top of the staircase. "Have you heard or seen anything else amiss?" I called back.

She exited my room and closed the door, motioning for me to lead down the stairs. "No, but I'll keep a lookout. If you want, you could take one of our horses to town."

It had been seven years since I'd been on a horse, and that had been one ride at a dude ranch. I'd been rusty then. And I now wore a skirt. I blew out my cheeks as I exhaled. " Okay. I hope horseback riding comes back to me."

"It will." She stopped in the foyer and peered at me. "Mr. Ed?"

"Sure." I grinned at the name Pa had given Nate's gentle white horse. Todd had found a rerun of that show on YouTube.

"Wait." She held up her hand. "You never learned to ride side-saddle, did you?"

"I did, but I was never good at it."

"You'll need my riding habit." She smiled as she ushered me upstairs to her room. "I've never been able to ride side-saddle, so Lera and I designed pants that resemble a dress."

Cassie exchanged the skirt I wore for a color-matching set of flowing trousers with long panels in front and back.

I turned this way and that in front of her mirror, marveling at the craftsmanship. "Amazing. It looks like the skirt I had on. Even matches the jacket."

She lifted her chin. "Most people hardly notice. You can only tell when you see me from the wrong side of the horse."

I raised an eyebrow. "And Ma's okay with it?"

Her face lit up. "She's not nearly as stuffy as you'd think." She led me down the hallway. "Emily had Lera make one for her, too. And, I've seen a few young ladies in town wearing them.

I laughed. "You've made your mark on fashion."

"Only in this town." She checked on Melody as we passed through the parlor. "Still sleeping."

When we entered the stable, the horses shuffled in their stalls and whinnied softly.

Cassie's brow furrowed as she approached Mr. Ed. "What's up, fella?" She stroked the side of his face, and he quieted. "I think someone's been in here."

"I wondered if something was off." I walked down the aisle between the stalls, counting. "How many horses do you have now?"

"Eight. Plus, Lucas's." She bridled Mr. Ed and led him out of his stall.

"There are seven here." I grabbed a saddle from the tack room and lugged it toward her.

"Nate and Lucas may each have one out." Cassie took the saddle from me and hefted it over Mr. Ed.

I grinned. "You've gotten a lot more comfortable with the horses." Cassie had been terrified when she'd arrived.

"Mr. Ed is my horse now." She patted his withers. "Isn't that right, sir?" She finished buckling the saddle, then handed the reins to me.

"I'm impressed." I led Mr. Ed out of the barn and stopped next to a stump.

"Wait!" Cassie yelled. "Lucas's horse is here. If he had one out, it would be Codger."

"They stole two of your horses. I need to hurry." I started to mount.

"No. You shouldn't go alone." She ran toward the barn.

"You can't go!" I called. "What about Melody?"

Cassie stopped next to the barn door and cranked on a handle. A loud siren blasted.

My hands flew to my ears. That was new.

"Give them five minutes, maybe ten. Depending on how far they are away." Cassie walked toward me. "I can't believe I didn't think of it sooner."

"I'm capable of searching by myself." I stayed put, though, unsure how well I could still ride. The last thing I needed was to get hurt falling off a horse.

Less than two minutes later, Lucas ran toward the barn. "What's wrong, Mrs. Bridger?"

"Do you or Nate have a horse out of the barn?"

"No."

"There are two missing." Cassie waved toward the barn. "Is Codger there?"

"Yes." Cassie nodded. "I think they've been stolen."

Lucas rubbed his clean-shaven chin. "I believe you're right. Must have been recent. I'll saddle Codger and go looking."

"Where's Nate?" Cassie asked.

"He's mending a fence over in Brentwood." He trotted into the barn.

I grinned. "Is Pa, I mean Ed, naming the fields now?" Hopefully, Lucas hadn't heard me.

"Actually..." Cassie ran after Lucas.

When they returned, Cassie led a large brown horse with a black mane and a white diamond shape above his eyes, and Lucas carried a western saddle. He nodded at me. "Miss Lydia."

"Lydia, Lucas has agreed to ride into town with you to find your friends as well as the horses."

I cleared my throat. "Thank you."

While Lucas saddled Codger, I pulled Cassie aside. "How much did you tell him?"

"Just that you were traveling and got separated from three friends. Also, you're Nate's cousin from his mother's side."

"Got it." I hoped to keep the story straight.

Lucas finished buckling the saddle and led Codger to us. "I'll also keep an eye out for Lucy and Ethel."

"Don't tell me." I held up my hand. "Lucy is red and Ethel is gold?" The first time I saw some of those old reruns, I screeched. It hit me why Pa loved to name the animals so much. It was his little joke from the future.

Cassie smirked. "Ethel is more tan than gold, but you got the idea."

I shook my head. "Ed again?"

She flashed a grin and lifted her hands, palms up, in a playful shrug. "I can't let him have all the fun."

I hooted so loud, Lucas jumped.

"Ma'am. Are you all right?"

I snorted and wiped a tear from my eye. "It's so good to see you, Cassie." I hugged her and then stepped onto the stump. "I'm fine, Lucas. Shall we?"

Without the aid of a stump, Lucas mounted, making it look easy.

I hooked my left foot in the stirrup and jumped up, lifting my right leg over Mr. Ed, but the front panel of my trousers got in the way and I didn't make it. Cassie ran over, gave my bottom a shove, and I managed to fall into the seat. I had to pull wool fabric out from under me. At least I could ride astride. Once I settled, I grabbed the reins and lifted my chin. "Now, shall we?"

Lucas peered at Cassie. "I could go to town and tell the sheriff. Then Miss Lydia wouldn't have to—"

"Please wait to get the law involved." Cassie pushed her palms out in front of her. "Since they're Lydia's friends. And we don't know for sure if they stole the horses."

"Yes, ma'am." Lucas tipped his hat and nudged Codger to a trot. I had hoped we'd walk for a while, but I managed to get Mr. Ed going. We kept a quick pace. At that speed, we couldn't talk much, which was a good thing.

At the edge of town, Lucas slowed to a walk, and I followed. He rode next to me as we entered Main Street. "What do these folks look like?"

"Two men and a woman. One man is probably early fifties, tall, and a bit overweight. The woman and the other man are early thirties. He's tall and lean, and she is taller and broader than me, with straight dirty-blonde hair. They'll probably all be wearing trousers."

He raised an eyebrow. "They shouldn't be too hard to spot." He glanced from side to side as we rode to the opposite end of town. I recognized most of the people, but nobody seemed to notice me. I had the advantage. Most of the town thought I died right after the fire.

Lucas waved and shouted greetings to most folks. How long had he lived here, and where did he come from? I would ask, but I didn't want to know any more about him than was necessary.

"Lucas!" Mrs. Hodges waved from in front of the mercantile. "Who's your friend?"

Lucas rode over and stopped. "This is—"

"Ellen!" I pulled Mr. Ed next to him. I couldn't use my real name. Why hadn't we thought about that?

Lucas turned to me and narrowed his eyes. "I thought your name was Lydia."

I took a calming breath. "Cassie knows me by Lydia, but that's my middle name. My first name is Ellen. I can't believe I didn't correct her when she introduced you."

He scratched behind his ear and faced Ma's friend. "Mrs. Hodges. This is Ellen. Nate's cousin."

Mrs. Hodges furrowed her brow.

I flinched. "From his mother's side." Everyone knew his father's relatives.

Lucas nodded. "She's visiting for a short spell."

"How nice." Mrs. Hodges clapped her hands together. "Cassie will have to bring you to our quilting group."

"Thank you." I forced a smile, hoping I wouldn't be here that long.

Lucas asked Mrs. Hodges if she'd seen our quarry and described them. I fidgeted with the reins, my cheeks red. The town gossip was the last person I wanted to tell about the trio.

"Oh, yes!" Mrs. Hodges pointed to the other end of the street. "They rode through town about a quarter hour ago. I remember them because the older man and the woman rode one horse, and the younger man couldn't handle his."

"Thank you, Mrs. Hodges." Lucas tipped his hat.

Mrs. Hodges, of all people, had seen Brian, Allison, and Richard. But if anyone noticed or remembered something odd, it would be her or Ma.

CHAPTER TEN

At the opposite end of town, Lucas increased Codger's speed to a gallop.

I spurred on Mr. Ed, and he responded, catching up to Codger and almost bumping me off in the process. I grabbed the pommel and squeezed my legs to stay mounted. Mr. Ed sped up, and my bottom bounced against the saddle. *Relax into the rhythm.* Pa's instruction from my childhood popped into my mind. My body refused to obey, and I struggled to maintain control. About the time I despaired of being able to stay seated, Lucas slowed. Thank goodness. I pulled back on Mr. Ed's reins and loosened my grip on the pommel. My focus widened from Mr. Ed's withers to the area around me.

A buggy with a single driver turned toward Lera's house.

"Hi, there," Lucas called.

The woman pivoted to meet his gaze. Jenny!

I lowered my head. What was she doing out here? She was supposed to be at Ma's.

Lucas raised his hand. "Hey! Have you seen two men and a woman riding two horses?"

Wincing, I pulled up and kept my eyes trained on him.

"No, Lucas." She smiled too brightly and pushed a blonde ringlet off her face. "Who do you have with you?"

Lucas hesitated. "Oh, this is—" *Please don't use my real name.* "Ellen. Nate's Cousin."

Now, I had to turn in her direction. Otherwise, I risked drawing her suspicion.

She peered at me. "I didn't know Nate had other cousins."

I cleared my throat, lowered my voice, and thickened my southern accent. "From his mother's side. I'm passin' through. Headin' to South Georgia from North Carolina."

"How nice." The scowl on her face belied her words. "Sorry, I couldn't help."

"Sorry to bother you, Miss Jenny." Lucas tipped his hat and continued down the main road.

I heaved a sigh of relief and followed Lucas while Jenny drove her buggy toward Lera's. Would Lera find out I was here? Nobody had mentioned if she even knew I was still alive. I wouldn't put it past her, though. She had acted like she didn't know about the time travelers, but she wasn't stupid. In fact, Lera had more street smarts than most of us.

After running the horses for another couple of miles, I slowed Mr. Ed and called to Lucas. "I don't think we're going to find them out here."

"I'm of the same mind." He wiped his brow with his sleeve. "We need to rest the horses soon, anyway."

"Let's walk back."

He nodded toward the turnoff. "Do you want to check out Ms. Lera's?"

"No." I closed my eyes and exhaled. "Do you?"

He frowned. "I'd be obliged to avoid Miss Jenny. Thank

you."

I laughed, but then sobered. He wasn't supposed to know I knew her. "Why?"

He shook his head. "I shouldn't be talking bad about anyone."

"It's all right. I won't be here long, and I won't tell anyone what you said." Why did I want to know? I wouldn't ask him any more questions, but this one was already out.

"She got out of jail about a month ago. Ms. Mattie was the only person who would take her in. She's trying to get away from Ms. Mattie by snaring a husband." He grimaced. "She's not going to catch me."

"How do you know she's husband hunting?" Why couldn't I keep my mouth shut?

He shrugged. "She talks all pretty to all the menfolk and doesn't give the women the time of day."

I pressed my lips together, willing myself to stay quiet.

Lucas stared off into the distance and rubbed his chin. Then he unleashed a steely gaze at me. "Who are you, really?"

I sucked in air. "Nate's cousin."

"You've been here more recently than you're lettin' on. You're trying to keep people from recognizing you."

I blinked and used my most innocent facial expression. "Why would you think that?"

"You changed your voice back there." He motioned behind us. "What happened that your friends abandoned you?"

"They came here without me. And they're not my friends."

"Ah." He squinted. "They're here to cause mischief for

you?"

"Yes. And for Nate." Bringing his employer into it might put Lucas back on track. "Can we keep looking?"

He heaved a sigh and mumbled, "Something strange goin' on. I'd feel better getting the law involved." He closed his eyes for a moment, then fixed his gaze on me. "Okay, Miss Ellen. I'll continue, for now."

I scanned the area for other turn-offs and tried to remember anyone else who lived out this way.

He pointed down a narrow path. "Maybe they went out toward the Oldhams' place."

I shrugged. "Worth a try. Who are the Oldhams?" For once, I didn't have to pretend not to know someone. They must have moved in after I left.

"They're a big family. They have a lot of land by the creek, but not much to show for it."

I nodded. He meant they were poor, either for lack of work or bad luck with crops.

"There's a lot of shacks in the woods or clearings for campsites. Do you think they're hiding?"

"I have no idea what they're doing." All I could do was hope that when I found them, they would come back with me before they changed the timeline. If they hadn't already.

Lucas led the way onto a trail so narrow, we had to ride single-file and slow the horses to a walk. He held branches for me, and I grabbed each one as he continued ahead.

After at least half an hour, we entered a small clearing. A little shack stood on the bank of the creek. Smoke floated from the chimney, a sign someone was cooking. Two children ran out of the home, one chasing the other. Three older children trudged over the bank of the creek. A skinny kid in overalls and no shirt held a string of fish.

Lucas jumped off his horse and strode toward the oldest boy, who shooed his younger brother inside.

"Howdy." Lucas nodded toward the boy carrying the fish. "Nice catch."

"Yes, sir." He looked to be about Caleb's age. Dirt smudged over his face, blending with his auburn hair.

"Have you seen two men and a woman with two horses?"

The boy turned his head slowly back and forth, his lips in a straight line.

"Much obliged." Lucas strode toward Codger. "We'll keep going."

"Mister," the kid called. "You don't need to go any farther up that road. There's only one way in here, and if they came this way, I would've seen 'em."

Lucas squared his shoulders. "Weren't you down at the creek?"

The kid lifted his chin. "Yep. And we come up when we heard ya."

"So, you've been within earshot all morning?"

"Yes, sir."

"Well then." Lucas tipped his hat and mounted his horse. "Thank you for saving us some time."

"Welcome, sir." The boy smiled, showing crooked teeth.

Lucas reached into his saddlebag, pulled out an apple, and tossed it to him.

The boy caught it. "Thank you!"

Back on the trail, I waited until we were out of earshot. "So, they're that poor? Aren't there apple trees around here?"

"Not on this property." Lucas held a branch for me until I grabbed it. "It wasn't just the apple. What he truly responded to was the praise. I doubt he gets much of that."

"How would you know?" I dropped the branch and continued behind him. "Do you know his parents?"

"I'm not blaming the parents. They're focused on feeding all their kids. And I know because I grew up in a similar circumstance."

"Oh." I concentrated on the trail until we came out onto the main path. Why had Lucas come here? It wasn't my business, and I didn't need to get to know anyone new. Still, the way he handled that boy impressed me.

At the main road, Lucas stopped. "Where should we go now?"

The sun was high in the sky, and my stomach started to growl. "I guess back to Nate's. Maybe they've heard something."

We trotted toward town. When we approached the turnoff to Lera and Simon's, a buggy careened around the corner from that direction.

"That's Miss Jenny," Lucas said.

Something must have happened at Lera's. Should we go there or follow Jenny? Maybe she was chasing our trio. "Let's keep her in our sights."

We picked up speed, but I didn't see anyone in front of her, even when she slowed down at the edge of town.

We passed her when she pulled her cart in front of the livery. I faced forward, keeping her in my peripheral vision, but Lucas tipped his hat toward her.

She climbed from the buggy and yelled at the man who worked there.

I wanted to head back to Lera's, but it would look strange if we turned around in the middle of Main Street. Lucas greeted everyone we passed as we rode through town. I stayed several paces behind to avoid more introductions.

At the other end of town, we picked up speed and trotted the four miles to Nate's. Now, I understood how Cassie felt when she first came here. Horseback riding was tough when you weren't used to it. I would be sore tomorrow. How had I taken cars and paved roads for granted? I'd have to tell Cassie that. She'd get a kick out of it.

When we reached Nate's, we tied the reins to a hitching post next to a filled water trough. Cassie must have expected us because she'd dumped a pile of oats next to the trough.

Nate stepped onto the walkway from the kitchen. "Lydia!" He opened his arms wide, and I ran into them.

Lucas cleared his throat. "She asked to go by Ellen."

Nate released me and grinned at Lucas. "That's for anyone not family." He sobered. "I take it you didn't find my horses."

Lucas frowned. "No, sir."

I touched Nate on the shoulder. "Any more signs of intruders?"

Nate shook his head.

"They took bread and two horses. That's enough." Cassie stood in the kitchen doorway.

Lucas held his hat in his hands. "I'll head home."

"Don't you want some dinner?" Cassie shooed us into the house. "Go in. I'll be right there."

We entered the dining room to a table laden with food and the heavenly aroma of fried chicken.

"What else could she possibly bring in?" I asked.

Cassie entered carrying Melody.

Lucas and I chuckled.

Nate sat at the head of the table, and Cassie took the seat opposite, leaving Lucas and me across from each other. Cassie seated Melody on her lap.

I helped myself to the fried chicken from a platter in front of me. Nate cleared his throat, and I dropped the drumstick on my plate. He folded his hands and bowed his head. I placed my hands in my lap and glanced around at my companions. All three of them closed their eyes, bowed their heads, and squished their faces in concentration. Maybe faith worked in this time period, but I couldn't find much use for it in mine. Come to think of it, I didn't find any use for it when I lived here either.

"Amen." Nate offered me a dish of scalloped potatoes.

I smiled and accepted it. Other than the blessing, I enjoyed dinner. I'd almost forgotten they had their big meal in the middle of the day instead of the evening. After the work was done, they'd have supper. Many times, within an hour of going to bed. It made sense that it was the lighter meal.

We chatted about the farm, steering clear of time-travel or my past. I glanced at Lucas every now and then, but he let Cassie and Nate lead the conversation. If he was attracted to me, like Cassie thought, he didn't show it.

To keep myself from saying something I didn't want Lucas to hear, I spent most of the dinner either chewing or making faces at Melody.

After my last bite, I dropped my napkin on the table. "That baby is so stinking cute." I knelt next to her, smiled, and shook my head, babbling in baby talk.

Cassie chuckled. "You've changed some, Lydia."

I leaned back. "She's the first baby I've seen in, like, years."

"Do you want to hold her?"

I lifted my hands, palms out. "Uh, I'd better not."

"Miss Ellen." Lucas dropped his napkin on the table and pushed his chair back. "Did you want to ride back out?"

My gaze stayed on Melody. "Oh, all right." I held out my arms to accept the baby. She studied me for a second, smiled, then nestled her head on my shoulder.

Lucas stood. "Miss Ellen?"

I startled. "Right. Lucas." Was that a blush on his face?

Cassie snickered. She must have figured out I'd forgotten I'd told him to call me Ellen. It was my middle name, but nobody ever called me that.

"Yes, Lucas. Give me a minute?" I paced with Melody, jostling her up and down even though she wasn't fussy.

"I'll be out back." Lucas hurried outside.

Nate smirked. "I'll go out and talk business. That'll make him more comfortable."

Cassie chuckled as Nate left.

"I'd better go." I surrendered Melody and flexed my fingers at her. "Bye-bye."

~

I stepped off the back walkway and strode toward Nate, Mr. Ed, and Codger.

Nate patted Mr. Ed's flank as he swiveled his head toward me. "I've been thinking. The people you're trying to find. Maybe they wouldn't stick to the main roads."

"The shortcut through the woods!" I clamped my mouth

shut. I shouldn't know about it.

"Yeah, they could have seen it." Lucas sauntered to us. "I'll show you."

"Sounds like a plan." I widened my eyes at Nate and jerked my head toward Lucas.

Nate grinned and shrugged.

Lucas seemed sharp when it came to dealing with people. Why did he pretend he hadn't caught my blunder? Was he letting us keep our privacy, or was he uninterested? And what did I care, either way?

Nate hoisted me onto Mr. Ed. I shifted in the saddle and arranged the wool panels of my ensemble. This was better than riding sidesaddle, but a pair of jeans would be much more comfortable. I leaned toward Nate. "Are you coming with us?"

He shook his head. "I'll continue searching around here."

"Thanks for not getting the law involved."

He cleared his throat and glanced at Lucas, who was several yards behind me. "The last thing we need is to draw attention to time-travelers. Had a devil of a time explaining your disappearance. Folks are finally starting to act less suspicious of us."

I grimaced. "Sorry for this. I'll get them out of here as soon as possible."

Nate tapped my arm and stepped back. "Keep her safe, Lucas."

Lucas tipped his hat and rode out behind the house toward the woods on the other side. The shortcut to the main road on the opposite end of town would lead us near the turnoff to Lera's. How could I suggest going there without tipping him off that I knew them? I kept my mouth shut, for now.

We kept a steady walking pace, riding either side of a winding trail wide enough for only one wagon. Daylight filtered through the mature maples, pines, and sweet gum trees that towered over us. Shrubs and smaller trees lined the rutted dirt road. My shoulders tensed as the road seemed to narrow.

Lucas slowed his pace. "Should we venture off the path?"

I blew out a breath. "It's like looking for a needle in a haystack." Would we ever find them? Why hadn't they stayed close to Nate's? They wouldn't have needed transportation. Could someone else have stolen the horses? I glanced around the area and shrugged.

He nodded. "We make a good team, though."

I shot him a questioning glance.

He grinned. "You know what the people look like, and I know what the horses look like."

I chuckled and pointed forward. "Let's see where this leads."

"Oh, I know where it leads. The other side of town. Near the road to Highland's place."

I jumped at the opportunity. "Let's go there. Ask if they've seen anyone, and then head back to Nate's."

"Good plan." He clicked his heels against Codger's flanks and trotted ahead of me. Mr. Ed and I followed slightly slower. Whatever happened this evening, a nice long soak in the clawfoot tub would be a necessity. I groaned, reminding myself I needed to get in better shape. I was only twenty-five.

When we exited the woods onto the main road, a wagon rolled along ahead of us.

Lucas pulled up and greeted the driver by name, asking if he'd seen the people and horses we were hunting. After the man shook his head, Lucas tipped his hat, and we continued toward Lera's. I looked forward to seeing her, but didn't want her to recognize me. Lucas would introduce me as Ellen, though, so that would help.

When we turned off the main road, Mr. Ed trotted over to the side of the path, avoiding the wagon ruts. Lucas rode on the opposite side, scanning the woods.

In 2020, most of these trees were gone, and a subdivision with large houses surrounding a golf course occupied this area. Progress. I blew out a breath, allowing my lips to flutter and make noise.

"Chin up," Lucas said. "We'll find them."

He couldn't have known what I was really sad about, but he did recognize my mood. I forced a smile. "I'm beginning to wonder. Maybe I'll have to go home without them."

"I hope that's not the case. Wouldn't want Nate to lose Lucy and Ethel."

I squinted at him for a moment. "Oh, the horses."

"Good mares. Solid. Worth a pretty penny." Lucas led me to a hitching post at Simon and Lera's house. Or at least, I assumed it was their house. Though the road leading to it was still flanked by the large oaks, the house looked nothing like the original. It was about half the size and built to resemble a simple farmhouse rather than the stately mansion from my youth. I liked this better.

Lucas jumped down from Codger and rushed over to help me dismount. Normally, I would have waved him off, but I was a bit out of practice and getting sore. He must have noticed that, too.

He led the way to the front door and flipped the knocker. We waited for a while. He reached for it again, and the door opened. Instead of a maid or butler, Lera appeared.

"Mr. Sullivan." She opened it wider and stepped back. "Come in." Her voice sounded slightly more cultured than before, but otherwise the same. She'd gained a little weight and looked healthier than the last time I'd seen her.

Lucas took off his hat as we entered.

She led us into a cozy parlor. "Won't you stay for tea?"

"No, thanks." I used my lower tone with the thick southern accent.

"Beg pardon, Ma'am. We just had dinner. And we're in a hurry." Lucas pointed his hat at me. "Miss Ellen, here, is Nate's cousin. She traveled here with some friends, and they got separated. Have you seen two men and a woman you don't recognize around here?"

"Nice to meet you, Ellen." She peered at me as she gave a slight curtsy.

I lowered my head to avoid being recognized.

Lera cleared her throat. "Simon may have seen your friends. He saw a young man he didn't recognize near the hen house earlier and chased him off the property. Please have a seat. I'll fetch him."

She left the room, and we took seats in adjacent parlor chairs.

Lucas rubbed his hands on his thighs. "That has to be them."

I sat on the edge of my chair, willing my legs to be still. We had to be close.

When Lera brought Simon in, Lucas and I stood, but he waved us down and sat on the sofa. Lera settled next to him. He looked more than three years older than he had when I'd left, but he'd been in his early forties and suffered smoke inhalation the night I'd been injured.

Simon peered at me. "Good afternoon, Miss?"

I swallowed hard. Why hadn't I thought of a last name? "Ellen Granger."

Simon gave a short nod. "Good to meet you. I hope it wasn't your friends I saw."

"Why?"

"Because they're thieves." His eyes burned bright. "They stole one of my hens."

"I'm sorry. If your thieves are my friends, they're desperate." What else could I say that might diffuse the situation? "Can you describe the man you saw?"

"Early thirties. Tall, medium build. Short, dark hair." In other words, Brian.

"Did you see any horses with them?" Lucas asked.

"No, but I heard horses approaching. That's why I went out to investigate."

I leaned forward. "Do you mind if we wander around your property?"

"Go ahead." He shifted to the edge of the sofa. "Do you want assistance?"

Lucas and I locked gazes. He blinked and gave a short head shake.

I looked at Simon. "I think we can handle it. They might hide from you."

Simon furrowed his brow. "I think they would. I shouted after the man I saw, and I'm pretty sure he heard me."

Lera touched her husband's shoulder. "You mean, dear, that you threatened him."

Simon cleared his throat. "I said the first words that came to mind."

I stifled a chuckle.

At the sound of a baby's cry, Lucas and I stood. "We should let you get back to your day," I said. "Thank you so much for your help." Good thing I'd kept my low tone and accent throughout the conversation.

"You're welcome." Lera hurried to the staircase. "That'll be baby Andrew."

"Two little boys." Simon grunted as he pushed to his feet. "Keeps us busy."

"I'll bet," Lucas said. He and I hurried outside to our horses, and he helped me onto Mr. Ed. Before he mounted, Lucas turned in a circle, scanning the horizon.

"Trying to divine which way to start?"

"Looking for smoke. I figure they're trying to cook that chicken."

"Good point." I craned my neck as far as possible, but the air was clear.

"Let's head that way." He pointed in the opposite direction from where we'd come. "There's a clearing beyond the tree line. We might see smoke or smell it on the way."

I followed him. The sooner I found them and convinced them to come with me, the better. I patted the remote in my pocket. It was my only way back to the time period I belonged in, even if I wasn't born in it.

CHAPTER ELEVEN

The sun hung low on the horizon when we clopped into a clearing and found the remnants of a fire.

I pulled Mr. Ed's reins to stop. "Well, somebody's been here."

Lucas dismounted Codger and helped me down. He let go of my waist and backed up as soon as my foot touched the ground. "I'm sorry, Miss Ellen. I picked the wrong direction. If we'd come this way first, we would have found them."

"It's okay. We went with the best idea at the time." I poked around the fire pit, searching for anything that might suggest which direction they'd gone. My mind and gaze kept wandering to Lucas. He'd assisted me in dismounting several times today, and each time he'd acted more uncomfortable. I focused on my task. Why had I expended mental energy on Lucas?

"Here!" Lucas stood near the edge of the clearing and held up a scrap of fabric. "It was hanging on this branch. Looks like it got snagged."

I ran over to inspect the red flannel fabric. "Could it

have been here a while?"

"I don't think so. We had lots of wind last night. That would have knocked it off." He peered off into the thickly wooded area adjacent to the tree where he'd found the fabric. "If we search that area, we'll have to go on foot."

I motioned toward the horses. "Should we secure them, first?"

He glanced at the sky. "I think it'll have to wait. Nate said to be back before dark."

"But we'll lose them!" How could he give up now? "Are you afraid of Nate?"

"No, ma'am. But I respect him, and I don't want to cause him worry." He strode toward the horses. "We'll have to run to make it back if we leave now."

I set my jaw and ran to Mr. Ed, but instead of mounting him, I walked him to the tree where the red cloth had been.

"Where are you going?" Lucas trotted over on his horse.

"To find my friends!"

He jumped down and stood in front of me, arms out with an inch gap between us. "No, you're not."

"You can't tell me what to do." I gritted my teeth and tried to veer around him, but he shifted in that direction. We kept up that routine for at least a minute. I folded my arms over my chest. "This is not getting us anywhere."

"Exactly." He peered into my eyes. "I'm not going back without you, and I'm not continuing the search tonight. We need to leave."

I closed my eyes, held my breath, and counted to ten. My hands hung at my side, balled into fists. When I opened my eyes, Lucas wore a silly grin. I took another deep breath and made a break for it, trying to run past him into the woods.

He stopped me, holding both upper arms. "I didn't want to lay hands on you, but you gave me no choice."

"Let me go!" I struggled to escape his grasp, but he was too strong.

"No." He stared down at me, his blue eyes sad but gentle. "Your safety is more important than finding your friends or the horses." He lowered his tone. "Please don't make me carry you home."

"You don't know where I live." Stupid. I didn't want him wondering about my past. Why couldn't I keep my mouth shut? I pulled out of his grasp.

"You know what I mean. Nate and Cassie's, at least for now."

The sun was nearly on the horizon. I hated to lose, but practicality got the best of me. Getting lost in the woods at night with no lantern wouldn't help anybody. "Oh, all right."

He lifted me onto Mr. Ed, then mounted Codger and escorted me to Nate's.

When we clopped into the back yard, there was just enough daylight to open the barn door and light one of the nearby lanterns.

I dismounted onto the stump. "Please don't tell Nate about our, uh..."

"Me having to force you to come back?" He waited for me to hop down and offered a brush. "I won't if you won't."

I accepted the brush. "Thanks. Of course I won't tell."

"Good." Lucas stroked Codger. "I wouldn't want Nate thinking I'd been violent toward his cousin."

I snorted. "Not even close." I'd never experienced violence, except a couple of times when Austin squeezed my wrist so tight, it hurt. Thank goodness that was over. Lucas had stayed in control during our argument, much more than Austin. When the time was right, I'd look for someone like Lucas.

I brushed out Mr. Ed and cleaned his hooves as if I'd done it yesterday. More muscle memory. Wild.

~

After closing the barn door, Lucas tipped his hat and strode toward the woods.

I climbed the two steps to the walkway between the kitchen and the house and started into the kitchen.

The back door opened, and Nate stood in the entrance. "About time you got here. Did Lucas go home already?"

My face flushed. "He walked into the woods behind the cowshed."

"He has a cabin in a clearing back there." Nate stepped inside, allowing me to enter.

"Isn't that your land?" I followed him into the mudroom and hung my wrap on a wall hook next to the door.

"Yes. I helped him build it, and I take out the rent from his pay." He led me through the pantry and into the dining room. "She's back."

"Thank goodness." Cassie sat in her chair at the other end of the table, Melody on her lap, feeding her something gooey from a spoon. "Do you want supper?" She shifted Melody.

"Thank you. I'll get it." I surveyed the casual meal laid out on the sideboard and picked up the only clean plate.

She shoveled the mushy orange stuff into Melody's mouth, but more came out than what went in.

"Is she getting anything?" I plopped potatoes and ham

on my plate and sat at the table.

Cassie chuckled. "I wonder that myself. She isn't losing weight, though."

"She's chunky." Nate knelt next to his baby girl and tousled her fine hair. "She just prefers to wear sweet potatoes."

"You've grown soft there, Nate." Pa stood in the doorway. They never did knock.

"Look who's talking." Nate stood and strolled toward Pa. "I've seen you with your children."

"And your grandchildren. Talk about soft." Cassie smirked.

"Well, that's to be expected." Ma passed Pa and hurried to me. "You must have recently gotten back. Did you find them?"

I shook my head. "Only where they'd been. They stole a chicken from Simon and cooked it." I almost laughed as an image of the three of them plucking a chicken popped into my mind. They must have been desperate.

Ma sat next to me, and Nate resumed his seat at the head of the table.

"That means they're more outdoorsy than most city people." Pa pulled out the chair across the table and sat. "That might make them harder to locate."

"I would think they'd want you to find them," Cassie said. "Especially if they know they're stuck here."

I leaned back in my chair and sighed, my supper untouched. "That's what I thought."

"Mmm." Ma closed her eyes and lifted her head toward the ceiling.

Nate tapped Ma's shoulder. "What, Aunt Mattie?"

She raised her index finger, opened her eyes, and focused on me. "I think they have an agenda. They're trying to change something."

Pa groaned. "Mattie, I know you have insight, but I so hope you're wrong this time."

"Me too," Ma said.

Nate pressed both palms on the table. "So, my plan for drawing them to Lydia probably won't work."

I pushed food around on my plate. "What is it? It wouldn't hurt to try." My stomach empty, I forced myself to eat the lukewarm potatoes while Nate detailed his plan. When he finished, I swallowed hard. "I don't want to parade around town, being introduced as Nate's second cousin or not."

"Well, if they know you're here, they might seek you out," Pa said, a hopeful tone to his voice.

"I think they already know I'm looking for them." Brian and Richard saw me arrive, but they also saw me leave. I pushed a forkful of ham into my mouth and chewed.

Nate turned to me. "I can spare Lucas if you want to keep searching for them."

"You might find them," Pa said.

I slumped in my chair. "I don't know what to do."

"You haven't prayed yet, have you?" Ma asked, her voice low.

"Please don't start that." I focused straight ahead, but could see her in my peripheral vision.

She lifted her hands and stayed quiet. She'd changed in three years. Or maybe she'd backed off because I was so much older than I would have been if I'd stayed here. Time-travel could warp your mind.

"Well, I'll be praying." Cassie peered at Ma. "And we need to keep an eye on Jenny."

"Oh." Ma's hands flew to her mouth. "Why hadn't I thought of that? The last thing we need is for her to find out the time machine is within reach."

I patted my pocket. "Thankfully, Brian and his crew don't have the remote."

Nate narrowed his eyes to slits. "Could you go back and get a fake remote?"

I squinted. "Why?"

"You could hide the real one, and if you get within earshot, tell them you have the remote. Then if they try to steal it, they'll get the wrong one. It might get them out of hiding." Nate smirked. "Or we could leave them a note when they come back for more bread."

Pa stroked his chin, deep in thought.

Though all of us faced him, he didn't make eye contact. Where had he gone in his mind? He'd tell us when he was ready, but until then, every muscle in my body tensed.

After an eternity of about two minutes, Pa glanced around the room as a slow smile spread on his lips. "What?"

"Out with it, Uncle Ed," Nate said. I smiled at the fact that he still called Pa uncle after working together all these years.

"Well, she might not have to return for another remote." Pa paused. "Remember when Jenny was going to the future and back a lot?"

We all nodded.

"She buried a bunch of tools and other gadgets under the carriage house. I pulled a remote out and hid it." He held up his hands. "Now, it could work, so I will at the very least cut some of the wires or take out the battery."

I blew out a breath as my shoulders unclenched. "After three years, it's doubtful the battery would work, anyway."

Cassie raised her index finger. "Still, better to be cautious."

CHAPTER TWELVE

The next morning, Pa showed up as we were finishing breakfast. He whispered something to Nate, and they both headed out the back door. I glanced at Cassie, but she continued eating while nursing Melody.

"Maybe I should go see what they're doing." I laid down my fork and stood.

Cassie swallowed. "If Uncle Ed wanted you there, he would have asked you."

I plopped into the chair and tried not to glare at her. "Do you think they're searching for that remote?"

She nodded, pulled Melody to her shoulder, and patted her back. "Lucas will probably be here soon. You should finish your breakfast."

"Not hungry." I took a sip of tea. "Do you ever make coffee?"

She grinned. "When I can get it already ground. Or have the extra time to roast and grind it."

"Oh. Right."

She raised her eyebrows. "Easy to take a lot for granted, isn't it?"

I nodded. Simple pleasures like watching puppy videos on my phone popped into my mind. "Do you ever wish you'd gone back?"

She startled, glanced at Melody, smiled, and shook her head. "No. My place is here. I do, however, try not to think too much about cars, air travel, and having any fruit or vegetable you want all year."

I shook my head. "I don't understand how you do it. I can't stay here."

"I know that." She covered my forearm with her free hand. "You were born for the twenty-first century. You deserve to be able to reach your goals as a scientist."

My face flushed. I didn't have the heart to tell her what I'd been doing for a living. Programming video games I didn't enjoy playing would not impress Cassie. Instead of disappointing her, I finished breakfast and considered where to search for Brian, Allison, and Richard. What could they possibly want to do here?

My eyes flew open wide as it occurred to me. Could they know more than I do about the present? "Cassie, are you writing in a journal right now?"

"Not at this second." She flashed a cheesy grin.

"You know what I mean."

"Yes. I started a new one in July." She tilted her head. "Why?"

"I found several of your journals, but the last one ended in June, and the next one started in 1874."

"That's about right. You're missing the one I'm writing in now." She shrugged. "If someone found it and hid it, I can't help you."

I leaned in. "What did you write recently?"

Melody let out a loud belch. Cassie and I both chuckled, then Cassie peered at her daughter. "My writing isn't that bad."

"She has great timing, doesn't she?" I sipped my tea. "Well?"

"Normal stuff." She held up her finger. "I wrote about the harvest and Nate's trip to Atlanta. I still hate that."

"I remember." I suppressed a smile.

"Let's see. I wrote about Jenny being released, and Aunt Mattie taking her in when Simon wouldn't."

"Hmm." Jenny's name kept popping up. Had I discounted her because I didn't want her to have anything to do with this? "Exactly when did she get out?"

"Three weeks ago." She settled Melody on her lap. "Why?"

"Do you know if she's left Ma's house at all before yesterday?"

"Of course. She's been to town a few times." She jostled Melody on her knee.

I rubbed my chin with my thumb. "Did you take out an ad for yesterday's paper?"

"No. We placed one a couple of weeks ago."

"Do you have this week's paper?"

She squinted. "Ed brought in a copy last evening, but in all the excitement, I didn't read it." She motioned toward the small parlor.

I jumped out of my chair and tore into the parlor. The newsprint lay on one of the end tables. My hands shook as I unfolded it and turned to the ads at the back. The upside-down ad stood out in the center column. I dashed back to Cassie and plopped it in front of her.

She took a deep breath as she studied the paper. "What are you thinking?"

"Jenny placed this upside-down ad."

"Why?"

"A distress call." That had been my first impression.

She stared at me, her eyes narrowed.

"It's a distress symbol. An upside-down flag or stamp." I studied her face, but she didn't change her expression. "When I saw the ad, I thought you were trying to get a message to me. Then I saw your later journals."

She sat back. "Wow. I'm glad I've been keeping journals. I promised your mother I would. To let you know what happened to us."

I cocked my head. "Why didn't she?"

"We knew her house didn't survive that long, but we hoped ours did. I guess this house is still standing?"

"Yep, passed down through the generations until about eight years ago when Todd bought it. His wife is now running it as a B&B."

Her face lit up. "And my journals were still there?" She nearly bounced off her chair.

"Except the one you're writing in now." I didn't tell her I hadn't found any later than the 1880s. I hoped to find those after I returned.

"That's too cool!" Cassie opened her mouth, then snapped it shut. "I'm not going to ask anything else. I shouldn't know that much." She leaned back and sighed. "But thanks for telling me."

"No problem." I stood and picked up my plate. "You already know more about the future than you should anyway. I won't tell you more." I carried my plate out the door.

Cassie called, "Don't go trying to find your pa."

I rolled my eyes as I crossed the wooden walkway and entered the kitchen. While I set my plate in the sink, I glanced out the window toward the carriage house. Nate and Pa came out and headed this way.

I hurried out of the kitchen.

"Lydia." Pa held up a small black object.

Behind him, Lucas strode from the direction of his cabin. I shook my head. "Wait, Pa."

"We found—" He stopped mid-sentence when Nate nudged him. Pa pocketed the remote before Lucas approached.

"Did you find Ethel and Lucy?" Lucas's shoulders drooped. Was he disappointed? No. I had to be reading something into that.

"No," Pa said.

Lucas nodded and studied his feet. Was he trying to hide his expression?

"We found only one saddle missing." Nate waved toward the barn. "They must not have had time to saddle both horses."

Lucas snapped his gaze to Nate. "I hope they put the saddle on Lucy. She hates bareback riders."

"I suppose they figured that out pretty quick, if they didn't." Pa pulled his toothpick out of his mouth and then went back to chewing on it again.

Nate pulled Lucas aside, and Pa slipped the remote to me.

"Has it been deactivated?" I asked.

He nodded and held up a battery. "Hand me yours and I'll hide it."

"I'll do it." I patted the real one. How could I part with it?

He pursed his lips and peered at me with one of the scolding looks that made him Pa. I slumped and handed him the real remote. "Where will you hide it?" I whispered.

"Somewhere Jenny'll never suspect." Pa slipped the remote into the pocket of his overalls.

My gut soured as my lifeline disappeared into Pa's pocket. No matter how much I trusted Pa, I needed that controller. "Wait." My hands trembled as I held out the non-functional remote. "You keep the fake one. See if Jenny tries to steal it." I gave him my best pleading expression. "Please."

He pursed his lips, then heaved a sigh. "It would give us an indication if she's involved." He pulled the remote out of his overall pocket and handed it over. "Please tell us before you leave."

"I will. I promise." I smiled, and my hand stilled as the real remote landed in it. It was the first time I'd ever had a security object.

~

After searching in vain all morning, Lucas and I stopped Codger and Mr. Ed at the posts near the kitchen door of Nate's house. He dismounted, tied the reins for both horses, and strode over to me with his hands up, ready to help me down. Normally, I'd already have dismounted, but we'd searched all morning and found no trace of the trio. I sat there, wallowing in self-pity. Not one of my best moments, but Lucas didn't seem to notice.

I allowed him to help me down, and when his hands touched my waist, my skin tingled through the shirtwaist. As soon as my feet hit the ground, he cleared his throat and backed up. The same thing happened when he helped me down yesterday.

"Sorry, we didn't find them." Lucas glanced away. "I hope they're taking good care of Nate's horses."

I stifled a giggle. He seemed to care more for animals than people. But that was unfair. He'd never met Brian, Allison, and Richard. To him, they were just thieves. Come to think of it, if they'd stolen Mr. Ed, I might care more for the horse.

Lucas held the door as I walked into the mudroom. He followed, helped me out of my wrap, and hung it on a hook.

"Right on time." Nate clasped hands with Lucas and ushered us into the dining room, where the table was laden with food, ready for the midday meal. The aroma of onions permeated the room.

"You needn't have waited for us." I sat in the chair Lucas pulled out for me.

"We were already starting." Cassie shifted Melody's bib. "You really were just on time."

Nate smirked. "Lucas's stomach is on a clock, I swear."

"What can I say? Always look forward to Miss Cassie's cooking." Lucas slid into the chair opposite mine.

I squinted and wrinkled my nose. He wasn't here for supper or breakfast, but I didn't have time to ask why. All three of them closed their eyes and bowed their heads as Nate blessed the food. Only Melody and I had our eyes open. I would have made faces at her, but she might've started giggling.

"Any luck this morning?" Nate took a big bite of venison.

I hadn't had any in ten years, and I hadn't missed it, so I answered instead of eating. "No. Didn't even see any evidence."

"Hmm." Nate continued chewing. Everyone was silent, but Cassie coughed a little, like she was trying to choke something back.

Nate swallowed and looked from Lucas to me and back. Did they have some news they didn't want to tell me in front of Lucas? I nodded and took a bite of green beans.

"If you don't need me this afternoon, we can go back out." Lucas watched Nate.

Nate turned his attention from Cassie to me. "Lydia, can you spare him for about half an hour? I have a quick chore I need help with."

"Sure." I glanced at Cassie, who nodded. Did Cassie have something to tell me, or did Nate really have a chore? I wished she'd tell me now, though I didn't want to explain everything to Lucas, or let him think we were all stark raving mad.

I ate what little I could and listened to them talk about the farm and Mattie and Ed's family. Lucas hardly said anything and nothing about his own family. Not that I cared, though. When Jenny's name came up, I perked up my ears.

"I hope she finds a husband soon." Lucas shook his head.

"Why, Lucas?" Cassie said at the same time Nate said, "You don't want her sights set on you."

Lucas gave an exaggerated nod toward Nate. "Exactly."

"How do you know she's looking for a husband?" I feared she was looking for a time machine.

"Anything to get out of Aunt Mattie's." Nate waved his

fork. "If she could, I think she'd try to support herself."

"Why can't she?" I peered at Nate.

"You should know that." Cassie touched my arm. "She doesn't have the right skills."

I sucked in air. "How would I know that?"

"Oh, yeah." Cassie lowered her head. "You wouldn't know she can't sew, or do any farming, or gardening."

"And we already have a teacher," Lucas said.

Nate pushed back from the table. "Lucas, can you come to the barn for a few?"

"Sure thing, boss." Lucas stood and lifted his plate.

Cassie reached her hand out, palm down. "Leave those. I'll get them."

"I'll help." I cleared the table as she put Melody in her cradle.

Cassie brought in the last dish and closed the door.

I stood at the worktable where I'd covered most of the leftovers. "Are you going to tell me your news now?"

She set the dish on the counter and leaned against it. "Aunt Mattie has been keeping an eye on Jenny. She went out yesterday."

I held my hand up to interrupt her. "We saw her going to and coming from Lera's."

"She's also been acting strange this morning. She tried covering her anger, then went out for a couple of hours. She's been subdued since."

I rested my hip on the table. "Hmm. No idea what that means."

"Well, this morning, Aunt Mattie had one of Mrs. Jones's boys follow her, and he said she met three strangers in a clearing about a mile from Simon's place. They talked for a while, and then she got mad and rode home fast."

"Were the strangers two men and a woman?"

She shook her head. "That's where we're confused. He claimed it was three men."

"Hmm." I paced the room. Allison had shoulder-length blonde hair, which she kept in a ponytail. If she had it tucked in a hat, and he saw them from a distance, could he mistake her for a man? "Has this boy ever seen a woman wear pants?"

"Oh! Probably not." She snapped her fingers. "That's got to be it."

"Maybe Jenny's made contact and found out they don't have the means to return." I picked up a rag and wiped the worktable.

"You don't have to do that." Cassie picked up the cloth-wrapped leftovers and headed to the cold storage in the cellar.

I dropped the rag on the table and followed her, grabbing the rest of the packages. "This way, we can do it in one trip." Wait. Melody was in the dining room. "How do you do all this yourself? With a baby?"

She chuckled. "The same way your ma and every other mom does it."

I shook my head, glad I would never have to. If I ever had a baby, it would be in a hospital. At home, I'd have baby monitors and use disposable diapers.

~

I slowed Mr. Ed to a walk and slumped in the saddle. We'd been riding all afternoon and seemed to be going in circles. My back ached, and my thigh muscles screamed in protest.

Lucas glanced over his shoulder and slowed Codger until he rode next to me. "About to give up for the day?"

"Yeah." We turned around and headed toward Nate's. A flash of red streaked from behind a copse of trees and disappeared around the next bend. I spurred Mr. Ed, and he responded with a gallop. When we rounded the curve, two horses and three riders came into view. "Stop!" I cupped my hand to the side of my mouth. "I have control of the machine. I can get you home!"

The single rider slowed, but the others urged him on, and they disappeared into the forest.

Lucas caught up to me and held out his hand. Then he slowed Codger and waited until I caught up. "I think they heard you. You tried."

"I know." I heaved a sigh. "What are they up to?"

He shrugged and glanced at the darkening sky. Normally, we'd have a couple of hours of daylight left. "A storm's coming. We should hurry. Shortcut or road?"

The last time I'd heard that question, we'd been in the wagon and taken the road. Then we'd gotten stuck in the mud and walked the rest of the way in a downpour. I snapped my head toward him. "Shortcut."

He nodded, and we trotted down it. Thankful Lucas kept quiet, I mulled over everything that had happened the past few days. Brian must have connected with Jenny. Had the ad been enough to lure them here? How was Jenny keeping them away from me? They had to know she didn't have the means to get the time machine back. Should I return and leave them here and hope they didn't mess anything up? Or should I stay and try to get them to come back with me? I blew out a breath.

"Miss Ellen? Are you okay?" Lucas slowed to a walk.

"You heard that?" I searched his face.

"Heard what?" He squinted. "You weren't keeping up."

"Oh. Just thinking too much." I clicked my heels against Mr. Ed's flanks, urging him to go faster. He shot past Codger and kept going. I narrowly missed a branch hanging close to my face, dodged around it, and ran right into another one. "Ow!" I clapped my hand to my face, nearly tumbling off Mr. Ed.

Before I could fall, Lucas held the reins and leaned toward me, using his body to keep me mounted. "Careful."

"Thanks." I sat up as Mr. Ed slowed to a walk.

"We should walk for a while." Lucas sat up straight and glanced at the lighter clouds ahead. "I wanted to talk to you anyway."

Alarm bells went off in my head, but I shooed them away. He probably just wanted to get to know me better. After all, we'd spent a lot of time together the last two days, yet we were still practically strangers.

"Who are these people you're looking for? Really?" He kept his focus on the path.

Why hadn't I come up with a cover story? "Uh, they're adversaries."

He scoffed. "I gathered that. What did you mean you have control of the machine?"

My breath hitched. That had been dumb. How had I not realized my blunder and tried to mitigate it? "I said that?"

He nodded, eying me. "Yes. So?"

My mind raced. "Uh, it's a code word. I wanted to let them know that I could make it right. All the thefts. They could come home."

He furrowed his brow. "Uh huh."

I grimaced. Did he believe me? Probably not. I stayed silent until we got close to Nate's. "Thank you for all your help the past two days, Lucas."

"It wasn't much." He continued to lead through the trees, holding branches for me when needed, but he wouldn't look at me.

"Not your fault." I smiled and tried to make eye contact. Why did I care how he felt about me?

A gentle rain started to fall as we left the woods. We picked up speed and trotted to the barn. Lucas hopped off Codger and ran to open the door. I waited a second and then realized he didn't plan to help me down. I lifted my leg over, trying not to let any underclothes show, not that Lucas was watching. He lowered his head as he led Codger into the barn. I jumped down, pulled Mr. Ed in, and accepted a brush from Lucas.

We unsaddled, brushed down the horses, and scraped their hooves in silence.

When I finished with Mr. Ed, Lucas had already put his horse in his stall. He took Mr. Ed's reins. "Good night, Miss Ellen."

"Good night, Lucas." I turned on my heel and marched to the kitchen. The aroma of baking bread called to me.

Cassie set a loaf pan on the worktable as I entered. "What is his problem, anyway?" I mumbled.

She smiled. "Lucas?"

I shook my head. "It doesn't matter."

"No luck?"

"We saw them. I even called out to them, and I'm pretty

sure they heard me. They just kept going." I slumped in one of the chairs near the table. How could I convince them to return with me when they wouldn't even talk to me?

Cassie touched my shoulder. "We're all praying."

Like that would do much good.

~

I paced my room, debating going to church with Nate and Cassie this morning. On the one hand, I would see my family. On the other, I'd have to keep up the ruse of being Nate's cousin Ellen. What if someone recognized me? I'd put Ma and Pa in an awkward position.

"Lydia," Cassie called through the door. "We need to leave soon."

I took a deep breath and exhaled. The image of Brian, Allison, or Richard lurking around the churchyard trying to talk to Jenny propelled me outside. I patted the remote in my pocket and hurried downstairs, through the house, to the carriage waiting out back. Nate held the reins, and Cassie sat beside him with Melody on her lap. I hopped onto the back seat, surprised Lucas wasn't with them. He must not go to church. Did that make him more or less attractive? I blinked and shook my head. I wouldn't start mooning over Lucas.

On the hour-long ride to church, I mulled over the past few days. Everything had gone wrong. I should have retrieved the errant trio and been back to 2020 by now. Why did they keep running from me?

Yesterday, Lucas accompanied me on my search. We'd spotted them near Lera's, and they'd run in the opposite direction, again. I started to chase them, but Lucas stopped me. Instead, we kept a steady pace and noted their location.

Frustrated, I asked why he didn't want to get the horses back. But the squint in his eyes revealed he had a reason for his caution. One he wouldn't disclose to me. Other than common courtesies, he hadn't spoken to me since my gaffe when I mentioned the time machine on Friday afternoon. Obviously, he didn't believe my explanation. Was he angry?

We reached the edge of town, and I sat up straight. I should have kept a watch for Brian or Richard during the ride. Mrs. Hodges' house was dark, as were the mercantile, the livery, and all the other shops. At the other end of the street, a few people milled. "Where is everyone?"

Cassie glanced over her shoulder. "It's Sunday. They're either on their way to church or still in bed."

How could I have forgotten? Nothing was open on Sunday.

Nate drove the wagon off Main Street down a grassy path next to the church. I clutched the seat tighter as we bounced over uneven terrain. It didn't seem to faze Cassie. When we pulled up to the hitching posts, Nate hopped off and secured the wagon.

I lowered my bonnet and kept my head down as I climbed out. Cassie handed Melody to me, and Nate helped her down. The baby was asleep, which astounded me after all the jostling on the ride. I nestled Melody on my shoulder and scanned the crowd as we walked toward the entrance. Mrs. Hodges and the rest of the quilters chatted on the other side of the lawn. Emily's family walked past us, but nobody paid me any attention. Good.

"Aunt Mattie!" Cassie said too loudly. She linked my arm with hers and ushered me over to Ma, then took Melody out of my arms. "This is Nate's cousin, Ellen."

"Good to make your acquaintance, Ellen." Ma's eyes sparkled.

"Likewise," I said, unable to keep a grin from escaping.

Ma patted my shoulder, and Pa kissed my hand. Jenny stood behind them, her arms crossed over her chest.

Ma glanced at her, then leaned in and whispered, "She's probably waiting for Lucas, trying not to look too obvious."

I stifled a chuckle. "He already knows she's after him."

Ma smiled, her eyes still twinkling. "Maybe she'll get the message, sooner or later."

I wanted to ask how long Ma would let Jenny stay with them, but I already knew the answer. Until she could support herself or find a husband. It would probably be a while. My eyes opened wide at a third possibility. Until she traveled into the future. Why were Ma and Cassie adamant about keeping Jenny away from the time machine?

CHAPTER THIRTEEN

While Ma played the piano prelude, I fidgeted on the unpadded wooden pew and glanced around the plain, mid-sized sanctuary. Jenny sat on the other side of Pa and didn't appear to recognize me—good. Nate and Cassie sat to my right on our pew. Mark and his wife, Emily, accompanied Emily's family across the aisle. The congregation included most of the same people as when I'd lived here before. I hoped they didn't recognize me.

Just before the service started, Lucas slipped in the door and sat on the end of the back pew. So, he did attend church, just not with Nate and Cassie. He worked for them and ate dinner with them every midday, but other than that, kept to himself. Nate and Cassie hadn't talked much about him when he wasn't around. Again, I wondered what his story was, but tried to kick it out of my mind. I needed to concentrate on my task.

The pastor motioned for the congregation to stand, and Ma played the first hymn. I stood, but instead of singing, I let my mind wander.

It was good to see Ma and Pa. They seemed to be doing

well, enjoying life. Cassie and Nate, and Mark and Emily, too. Even without me. I swallowed hard. Good for them.

After Pastor Kelley began to preach, a rustling in the pew across the aisle and behind us caught my attention. I glanced back to see Lera pull a little boy close and shush him with a finger to her mouth. She looked good, too. Happy. Simon faced forward, seemingly concentrating on the sermon. Even Caleb looked content, though he fidgeted a bit. He'd grown a lot in three years and was taller than me. He'd probably pass Lera before long.

After the final hymn, I wanted to run down the aisle to see if my time-travelers were outside waiting for Jenny, but I was sandwiched between Cassie and Pa as we filed out of the pew and down the center aisle. Jenny followed us, instead of racing out. That surprised me. It probably meant she wasn't expecting anyone. Still, I kept my eyes peeled as we exited the church.

Cassie introduced me to Pastor Kelley. Hoping he wouldn't remember me, I lowered my head and curtsied. It wouldn't do to draw attention to myself with a modern handshake. As soon as I could extricate myself, I scanned the crowd in front of the church. Since it took nearly an hour for most people to get to town, they used the after-church time to catch up on the news. Pa called it gossip. Today, I didn't mind. It gave me a chance to check out my surroundings.

"Morning, Miss Ellen." Lucas startled me.

I pressed my hand to my chest. "Morning."

He flashed a sheepish grin. "Sorry. Didn't mean to scare you. See anyone you know?"

I shook my head. "Not sure they'd let me see them," I

whispered.

He nodded. "I can't help search today." He shifted from foot to foot. "But, if it's all right with Nate, I'll go out with you tomorrow."

"Thank you." He must have a family obligation or some other commitment. "I had hoped I'd find them by now, but it looks like I'll still be here tomorrow."

"Yes, ma'am. See you then." He threw me a hasty salute and hurried off. I stayed where I was, hoping against hope I'd see Brian. Since I knew him the best, he might listen to me.

I locked eyes with Jenny for a split second. I'm not sure who looked away first, but she also watched the crowd. I pretended to listen to Cassie and Lera's conversation. Instead of gawking, I focused on my peripheral vision, keeping Jenny in sight. When she dashed off, I followed at a distance, and Pa joined me.

Jenny met a man. Or was it Allison? They were too far away to be certain. After about a ten-second conversation, Jenny whirled around and headed toward us.

"Did you see that?" Pa whispered, still focused on Jenny.

"Yes. What do you make of it?"

"I didn't know she had a remote." He pulled me toward Cassie, Ma, and Lera.

My eyes flew open wide. "She handed him something?"

He nodded. "We've been watching her. No idea where she would have hidden it. It doesn't still work, does it?"

I shook my head, more to clear it than to answer. "I have no idea." I glanced back to where she'd been. The man had disappeared into the woods. "What do you think I should do?"

"Pray." He closed his eyes.

I rolled mine. He could pray. I needed to take action. I broke ranks and marched toward the woods.

Lucas trotted out from behind the church on Codger and called out to Jenny. I pivoted to see her right behind me, but Lucas claimed her attention. He stopped next to her and kept her talking while I hurried toward the woods, not caring if Nate and Cassie left me. Finding Brian was the only thing on my mind.

At the tree line, I stopped and listened. Only the sounds of nature filled the air, so I followed the narrow path. Voices drew me to the edge of a clearing. I hid behind a tree and peered at two men and a woman.

"Why can't we use it now?" Richard sounded agitated, like he was past ready to leave.

"She can't get away right now. She has something to check out," Brian said.

"Are you sure this Jenny is who she says she is?" Richard asked.

Allison reached for the remote, but Brian held it away from her.

"I just want to make sure it brings the time machine." She held out her hand. "I'll send it right back."

"With me on it." Richard waved his arm to the side. "I can check out of the hotel. Explain your absence."

No, he couldn't, because if they summoned the time machine, they couldn't return to any earlier than when I left, which was almost a week after their checkout time.

Allison grabbed the remote and pushed some buttons. I held my breath. She shook it and banged it on her palm a couple of times, and I exhaled.

"Why would she give us this if it doesn't work?" Allison slammed the remote into Brian's outstretched palm.

Brian shrugged. "Maybe she doesn't realize."

She flashed him a glare and slapped his arm. "She'd have to know. She'd have already used it."

That remote might have worked for the original time machine. But my remote might be the only one that would work now because it was the last one that came through the portal, or whatever it was. That had to be it!

I sighed in relief and walked toward them.

Allison glanced around. "Do you hear something?"

I raised my hand in greeting. "Hey guys."

"It's Lydia." Allison grabbed Richard by the collar. "Run."

"Why would she come here?" Brian trotted after them.

I stood, mouth agape. Why did they run from me? It hit me like a crash of lightning. They'd contacted Jenny first. Either she told them not to trust anyone from their time, or she knew who I was and why I was here. Why would she play games like this, though?

~

"Are you sure this is a good idea?" I asked Nate as we rolled into the patchy grass beside my old home.

Nate glanced over his shoulder. "We always have Sunday dinner with Aunt Mattie. If we don't today, Jenny might get suspicious." He stopped the wagon and hopped down.

"But what if she recognizes me?" Part of me feared she already had, but if not, I didn't want to give her more of a chance.

"She thinks you're dead." Cassie glanced at me, her mouth in a straight line.

I slumped. "That's a pleasant thought."

She reached back and touched my shoulder. "I'm sorry to be so blunt."

I lifted my chin. "Truth can be that way. It's okay. How do I avoid Jenny?"

Cassie blew out a breath. "We'll introduce you as Nate's cousin, Ellen. Stay at our end of the table."

Nate held his arms up to take Melody from Cassie. Was it to aid Cassie in getting down, or an excuse to hold the baby? He nestled her onto his shoulder and cooed at her. I don't think I'd ever seen a prouder expression on his face than when he gazed at his little girl.

I took a deep breath and hopped down from the cart. I planned to eat, listen, and lay low.

Pa walked out of the house and caught my eye. He wore a similar expression to Nate's. Too bad I didn't deserve his pride. I'd avoid telling him what I did for a living. When I returned to my time, I'd find a job that not only paid the bills but served a function other than entertainment.

"Good to see you, Ellen." Pa ushered me inside and introduced me to Jenny.

Before I could say anything, Ma instructed Jenny to help her bring in the food. Ma and Pa made a good team. Maybe someday I'd find someone to team up with for the long haul.

When Ma declared that everything was ready, I headed for the chair Cassie pointed to across the table from her and next to Nate, who sat on one end. Jenny sat on the same side of the table as me, next to Pa at the other end, with Lera and Simon between us. We'd both have to lean around Lera and Simon at the same time to be able to see each other. I winked at Cassie to let her know she was a genius, and she nodded back, smiling.

Cassie's lap was empty. I glanced at the other end of the table at Melody on Ma's lap. One of Lera's boys sat in a high chair, and the other sat on Lera's lap and slapped the table next to me. It was fine. I could handle that for an hour to avoid sitting near Jenny.

The conversation revolved around the farm and the upcoming winter months. Ma had all sorts of plans to keep Jenny busy. I enjoyed the roast chicken and stewed tomatoes, probably canned from Ma's garden. The dinner brought back happy memories, and I almost forgot I didn't belong here anymore.

"So, how long is Ellen staying?" Jenny asked.

I almost choked, but coughed to cover it.

Nate shrugged. "Just a couple of days."

"Miss Mattie said that two days ago." Jenny's voice sounded shrill.

Ma wiped Melody's face. "I must've been mistaken. It really doesn't concern us how long she stays, now does it?" She lifted her chin and peered across the table.

I would have loved to witness Jenny's expression because she stayed mute for the rest of the meal. Was she on to me, or was she afraid I'd distract Lucas? Jenny had always been hard to read. I suspected it was because she had lots of contingency plans on her mind. If she couldn't get to the future, Lucas would be a way to get away from Ma. Or, more likely, he would be a stop-gap while she manipulated someone into taking her to the twenty-first century. She must be disappointed that Allison didn't bring a remote when they time-traveled.

Maybe I should confront her. No. I needed to convince Brian, Allison, and Richard to return with me. But how?

~

As soon as Ma put her fork down, I jumped up and volunteered to help clear the table. Lera placed a hand on my arm and shook her head.

"We have pumpkin pie for dessert," Ma said. "Let's have it on the porch, shall we?"

Lera let go of my arm. "Yes. We should enjoy the mild weather while we can."

Ma brought Melody to Cassie and enlisted Jenny and Lera to help her clear. "We'll have the pie and coffee out soon. Why don't the rest of you go outside and enjoy the afternoon?"

Simon stood, gave Lera a peck on the cheek, and offered his arm to me. "May I escort you, Miss Ellen?"

I put away my disdain from when he and Lera were courting, and crooked my arm around his elbow. He didn't seem to recognize me. Considering his interaction with Lera and attentiveness to his sons, he'd mellowed quite a bit in three years.

Nate, Cassie, Pa, and Caleb joined us on the porch. I almost asked if Mark always ate Sunday dinner with his in-laws, but clamped my mouth shut just in time. They hadn't explained his and Emily's absence, so that was a guess. But Mark had been sitting with her family in church. It hadn't surprised me. My brother had always deferred to Emily.

"Looks like we're in for a cold winter." Pa stared at the steel blue sky.

"How can you tell, Grandpa?" Caleb sat on the bench next to Pa and gazed in the same direction. I smiled, remembering how close they'd always been.

"I'm amazing." Pa winked. "And we'll see if I'm right."

"How long do you usually stay on Sunday afternoons?" I whispered to Cassie, who occupied the wooden rocker next to mine.

"We chat for a bit after dessert." She studied me, then smiled. "I might develop a wicked headache. Depending on how Jenny's acting."

I chuckled. "Or I could."

She glanced over at Nate, who leaned on the porch railing next to Pa and Caleb, and chatted with Simon. "Please don't do it too soon, though. Let Nate have his pie." She chuckled. "He doesn't get many good sweets these days."

"It looked to me like you'd mastered the wood stove."

"Yes, but I can't bake goodies and do anything else." She bounced Melody on her knee. "And, I have more to keep me occupied these days."

"Are you still tutoring Caleb?"

She shook her head. "Ed does that now. He's backed off the farm work the past few years. That's why we hired Lucas."

"What about Mark?" I suspected Mark wasn't doing his share, or was working more for Emily's family.

"He was working before Ed stepped back, and Nate's planted more cotton."

I mulled over all she'd said, letting myself get caught up in life with my family. When Lera, Ma, and Jenny brought out trays of pie and coffee, I shook myself out of my reverie. I needed my wits about me, and I didn't want to get sucked back into this life. I wanted, needed, to go back to the twenty-first century. Part of me thought I should just go and not worry about the three who'd gotten themselves stuck here.

I glanced up at Jenny, who handed me a slice of pumpkin pie on a china dessert plate. She narrowed her eyes in a menacing glare. I blinked and accepted the plate. Her face resumed a neutral expression. Maybe I imagined it.

At any rate, she had some kind of plan involving the trio. I couldn't let her carry it out. Dang.

CHAPTER FOURTEEN

Nate set his fork on his empty dessert plate. "Mighty fine pie, Aunt Mattie."

"Thank you." Ma grinned, then turned toward Cassie and frowned.

Cassie closed her eyes and pinched the bridge of her nose.

Ma took Nate's plate. "You'd better get your wife home. One of her headaches is coming on."

Nate squinted. Cassie must not have clued him in on her plans.

Ma shooed us toward the carriage. "You'd better go, too, Ellen. In case Cassie needs help."

I flashed Ma a smile. She knew exactly why Cassie had a headache. Maybe she also wanted to keep my exposure to Jenny to a minimum.

Instead of taking care of Melody that afternoon, I prowled around the outbuildings searching for clues. Brian, Allison, and Richard landed near here, but had stayed on the other side of town since then. I kicked the dirt floor of the tack room. This was probably the most important mission of my life, and I had no idea what to do next.

As I left the barn, rustling from the woods caught my attention. Since there wasn't any breeze, it could be Lucas coming from his home. That shouldn't have compelled me to investigate, but it did. I plodded toward the woods, glancing around.

A large hand covered my mouth, and the other arm went around me. I gagged at the smell of perspiration and struggled against his hold as he dragged me farther into the woods. Who was this? What did he want? My heart pounded, and sweat rolled down my back as he forced me deeper into the thicket. I couldn't let him get me any farther away. I dug in my heels, but he bent his knees and grabbed my waist as if to lift my feet off the ground. Adrenalin surged. I pushed away, whirled around, and kneed him in the groin.

He doubled over and staggered back. "You didn't have to hurt me," Richard hollered.

"You didn't have to kidnap me!" I leaned over, hands on hips, catching my breath. "What was that for?"

He glowered at me. "What are you doing here?"

"Answer my question first. Why did you accost me?"

"I thought you might scream, and I wanted to talk to you away from the house." He kept his voice low and held out his hands, palms down. "Why did you come to this time?"

I looked behind him for Brian or Allison, but we were alone. "I could ask you the same thing."

"So, I guess you know about the time machine." He leaned in and peered at me. "Do you have control of it?"

"I can get it." I narrowed my eyes. "Where are Brian and Allison? And what were you three thinking?"

He glanced behind him. "Allison wanted to see if Todd's time machine worked. Brian wanted to meet his ancestors."

"And you?"

"I didn't believe them and ended up coming along by accident." He grimaced. "Can you take me back?"

My shoulders relaxed for the first time in three days, and a smile spread across my face. "That's why I came." I stepped toward him. "Get Brian and Allison and meet me behind the barn in two hours." That should give me enough time to say goodbye.

He frowned and studied his feet. "Uh, *I* can meet you back here."

My breath hitched. "Why not Brian and Allison?"

"They don't want to go back yet." He shifted from foot to foot and gazed past me.

My shoulders tensed as my fingers curled into fists. "What are they up to?"

He blinked. "They won't tell me."

"But?" I gave him the side-eye.

He let out a breath. "They changed their minds after they talked with that blonde woman."

"Jenny?"

"I don't know her name."

"Blonde ringlets?"

Richard nodded. "Yes. Sharp features, too."

That was Jenny all right. "When did they talk to her?"

"The first day we were here. And earlier today." He leaned against a tree.

"That first day? Did she get angry and race off after she talked to you?" If so, I'd seen her driving fast in her carriage. Wait. They were here a whole day before I arrived, at least to stay longer than a minute. "Where did they meet?"

"In town. Outside the newspaper office."

I leaned toward him. "Did they mention the upside-down ad?"

"The blonde talked to Allison. I didn't hear what they said."

I stamped my foot and swore. "What about today?"

He shook his head. "Didn't hear that either."

"You need hearing aids." I rolled my eyes, then glanced around. "Where are they now?"

He shrugged. "They told me to meet the blonde here."

Tall trees surrounded us, with no real landmark. "Here?"

Richard blinked. "No. Behind the barn." He ushered me back the way we came. "I'm supposed to stall her until they come. I don't know why we're meeting her. The remote she gave Allison doesn't work." He clasped a hand over his mouth as we emerged into the clearing behind the barn.

"Don't worry. I already know. Mine is the only one that'll work." I started to pat it in my pocket, but then thought better of it. Maybe carrying it on me wasn't such a good idea. Jenny had to know I had a working remote. Was that why she wanted to meet here? To steal it? Jenny would probably be here soon. Should I hide to watch what she would do, wait in the house, or confront her?

"I think she's coming." Richard pointed over my shoulder.

"Don't let her know I'm here." I dashed behind a large oak tree. A speck of a person on horseback rode toward me, so I hoped she hadn't seen me. I stayed behind the tree with my back to it, waiting to hear their conversation.

"Don't remember seeing you around here." Lucas's voice startled me.

I peered around the tree at Lucas perched on Codger about ten yards from us.

"I'm just passing through." Richard sidled toward me.

Lucas tipped his hat and kept it in his right hand. "Miss Ellen? Is this one of the fellows?"

"Yes." I stepped out from behind the tree. "Now we have to find the other two."

"And Lucy and Ethel." Lucas dismounted and strode to me, not taking his eyes off Richard.

Richard scanned the horizon, a deep furrow in his brow, as if willing the others to show up.

Lucas strode to Richard. "Where are the horses?"

"What horses?" Richard's voice cracked, making him sound like a teenager rather than a fifty-year-old man.

"The ones you and your friends took from my boss." Lucas pointed toward the barn but kept his steely gaze on Richard. I was surprised he didn't use the word, stole.

"Oh, uh." Richard shifted his weight and lowered his head. He must have felt out of his element with someone like Lucas glaring at him. Lucas was not quite as tall as Richard, but still appeared to look down on him. Maybe because Lucas was in the right, and Richard knew it.

"Well?" Lucas stood his ground.

Richard hesitated. "Uh. I'm waiting for them. They should be meeting me soon."

"I thought they told you to stall Jenny." I bit my lip as soon as her name escaped me.

"Jenny?" Lucas wheeled around to face me. "How would they know her? She's been in jail three years."

"What?" Richard jumped, and his eyes widened. "What for?"

"Theft. I wouldn't get mixed up with her." Lucas stopped short. "Unless that's how you know her. Is she part of your gang or something?"

Richard's eyes narrowed, and his lip quivered.

I suppressed a grin at the image of gears grinding in Richard's brain.

Lucas scratched his temple. "No. You didn't know she was a thief, did you? Did you know your friends were?"

"No." Richard squared his shoulders. "I think they just borrowed the horses. We found ourselves in a tight spot."

"You know, you could have asked for help." Lucas placed his hat on his head. "Folks around here are neighborly, even to strangers."

"Thanks for the information." Richard shifted his weight. "We're not used to that where we come from."

"Where is that?" Lucas asked.

I glanced at Richard's gray slacks and white shirt. They didn't scream twenty-first century, but I would bet they weren't from this time. And if Lucas noticed Richard's feet, he would be suspicious. Nobody here had shoes like those black leather loafers.

Richard took a deep breath. Was he buying time? "Atlanta."

"Probably so." Lucas turned to me. "Well, if you're all right, Miss Ellen, I'll take my leave."

I smiled. "I'm fine, Lucas. Good night."

"Night." He pulled Codger behind him and walked onto the path.

"That his cabin back there?" Richard asked.

"Yes. Have you seen it?" I was almost curious enough to follow him.

"Yeah. It's not very big. Not surprised he lives alone. He does, doesn't he?"

I shrugged. "As far as I know." Who would he live with? Why did I care?

~

About an hour later, we still stood next to the tree line and gazed around the large clearing from the path to Ma's, to the road out front of Nate's house, and the fields and trees across the yard. Richard didn't appear to know which direction Jenny would be coming from. He jingled something in his pocket.

I raised my eyebrows. "Did you bring change from the twenty-first century?"

He pulled his empty hand out of his pocket. "It was an accident. I didn't believe it would work."

I rolled my eyes. "Does that explain your shoes, too?"

He winced. "I was hoping no one would notice. One of the reasons we've been laying low."

"What are Brian and Allison wearing? I haven't gotten a close enough look."

He shifted his weight. "They're more in period, though Allison is wearing riding breeches."

I nodded. Similar to what I wore when I traveled.

He looked me up and down as if he noticed my dress for the first time. I wore the navy suit Cassie had lent me that first day.

"Where did you get that?" He moved closer and felt the fabric. "It's from this time period, isn't it?"

"Yes. Cassie lent it to me."

He squinted. "How?"

"They're kind people, and they don't ask many questions. They're passing me off as their cousin, Ellen." I didn't want him to know I originally came from this time.

"Hmm." He nodded and seemed to accept my explanation, but he glanced at me out of the corner of his eye. Was he skeptical?

I cleared my throat. "What if Brian and Allison don't come? What will you do?"

He slumped. "Appeal to your good graces to take me back, I suppose."

"I can take you whenever you want to go." I peered at him.

At first, he appeared to cave, but then he stood tall and lifted his chin. "I'll wait a bit longer, thank you." Did Richard have an agenda? He side-eyed me. "You don't have to wait with me."

I felt torn. I wanted to listen to their conversation, but I didn't want Jenny to see me yet. What would Ma do? That was easy. She'd pray. I shook my head and walked away from Richard. An image popped into my mind, and I blurted it out. "Maybe Brian and Allison are meeting with Jenny someplace else."

He scoffed, jiggled the coins in his pocket, and paced back and forth. Maybe I was getting to him. If I could get him to go back now, we'd have one less person who shouldn't be here, and the rest of us could go together.

He planted his feet. "They're coming."

Had he seen someone? No. He stood, back rigid, head high. He'd resolved to stay for now. Drat.

I feigned nonchalance as I strolled toward Nate's house. "Suit yourself." The sun dipped low on the horizon, a red-gold haze surrounding it. It was probably about an hour before twilight. I wouldn't put it past Jenny to wait until then so she could lurk in the shadows better. But wouldn't she have told them a time?

When I reached the other side of the barn, I glanced back. Good. Richard wasn't watching me. I sidled over to stand behind it, my back to the barn wall, watched the house, and kept my ears open for Jenny, Brian, or Allison.

At twilight, rustling sounded behind the barn. I peered around to see Jenny ride a brown pony across the yard and stop in front of Richard.

"Where are they?" Her voice sounded shrill.

"They'll be here." Richard's tone quavered.

"They're late. Tell them to bring the remote back here tomorrow at this time." Jenny spurred the pony and pranced off toward the path to Ma's.

"Lydia!" Cassie called from the kitchen window.

Eyes wide, I put my finger to my mouth.

Jenny disappeared down the path.

I let out my held breath. If Jenny had heard, she didn't want Cassie to know.

Cassie disappeared inside the kitchen, so I peered around the corner of the barn. Richard was nowhere in sight.

I strode toward the house and around the kitchen to the walkway.

Cassie opened the kitchen door and beckoned me in. "I'm so sorry! Were they out there?"

"Jenny and Richard were. They left, though."

She wrung a dishtowel with both hands, no doubt a habit she picked up from Lera. "I shouldn't have used your real name."

"It's all right." It wasn't, but I didn't want Cassie to feel guilty. It really wasn't her fault. "I should have told you what was going on. I've been out there waiting for her to show up most of the afternoon." I sighed and surveyed the clean kitchen. "Anything I can do to help?"

"No. Supper's on the table." She led me across the walkway to the back door of the house. I hung my wrap in the mudroom, and we entered the dining room. Nate had Melody on his lap. Runny rice cereal covered them both.

Cassie and I laughed.

"I'm afraid she knows I'm an amateur." Nate smiled. When Cassie moved to take Melody, he stuck his elbow out. "No. I'm determined to get the hang of this." He continued to smile, coo, and attempt to shovel rice into his daughter's mouth. She spit out more than went in.

"I knew you'd be a good Pa," I said.

Even though this mission wasn't going well, I felt grateful I'd gotten to see my family again, especially meeting Melody and witnessing Nate and Cassie as parents. I smiled and relaxed despite my circumstances.

~

The sun slid closer to the horizon as I paced the walkway behind Nate's house. Because Jenny planned to meet up with the trio behind Nate's barn this evening, Nate had declared today a normal Monday morning. He and Lucas left for the fields. I ventured down the path to Ma and Pa's, and they said Jenny had left early, skipping laundry day.

To repay Cassie for her kindness, I helped with her laundry, but it wasn't anywhere near as much as my Ma and I used to do when I was fourteen. Cassie only had hers,

Nate's, and the baby's. Washing Melody's tiny clothes was fun.

It was now close to twilight, and I'd been on edge since dinner.

Cassie, Nate, Ma, and Pa had assured me they were praying. I didn't see how it had done any good, but they seemed less worried than I was. What if Jenny or the trio changed the timeline? I stood at the end of the walkway and faced the barn. Someone had to stop them. Who better than me?

With any luck, I'd take them to 2020 in the next hour. I still had the real remote, so when Allison, Brian, and Richard turned up, I'd retrieve the time machine. I tapped my heel and clutched the railing, staring toward the barn. Where were they?

"Ms. Cassie said you might be leaving soon," Lucas said from behind me.

I jumped and whirled toward him, my hand on my chest.

"Sorry. I didn't mean to sneak up on you." He doffed his hat and held it over his heart. "I wanted to tell you it was a pleasure to meet you."

I nodded once. "Likewise. Thanks for all your help."

"'Twasn't anything. Nate was paying me." He looked at his feet and then at me, his lips in a straight line. "Do you need any help with your, uh, friends?"

I smirked. "You didn't like Richard much, did you?"

He shook his head, then flashed a shy smile. "Not much. No."

"Thanks. I'll be fine. You can go on home." My cheeks flushed. He'd softened a little since yesterday.

"Well, my cabin isn't too far back. Holler if you need

help."

I nodded again and willed him to go before I asked a foolish question or told him I'd miss him. How could I have gotten to that point in four days?

He replaced his hat and loped across the yard toward the trees.

I sighed. Jenny better not get her claws into him. Concentrate, Lydia. I wandered across the yard, where I would be closer when Jenny arrived. If she arrived.

Lucas disappeared into the woods, and my curiosity got the better of me. I hurried over to the tree line, stopped behind the largest tree, and peered around at the barn, corral, cowshed, carriage house, and the tranquil grassy area between me and Nate's house. Good, no people. I followed the trail, staying far enough behind that Lucas wouldn't see me.

"Stop!" Lucas yelled.

I ran toward his voice. Lucas dashed in the opposite direction and vanished down the path on the other side of the clearing, leaving me alone in front of a small cabin. It resembled one of the tiny homes that had been popular a few years back. The front door was ajar. No one else in view, I pushed open the door and stood on the threshold. One glance showed me the whole place. It had a loft bed over a desk and chair on the left side and on the right, a fireplace with a spit and a kettle hanging over it. In the corner near the fireplace, one comfortable-looking chair sat next to a small table holding a Bible.

I backed out, right into a muscular chest and did a one-eighty. "I'm sorry."

Lucas stepped back, his mouth open and his brow

furrowed. "What are you doing here?" There was an edge to his voice.

"I heard you yell. I came to…help?" I pointed to the door. "It was open."

He placed a hand on either side of the door frame and stared at me. His jaw tightened as his lips pressed together.

My feet stayed planted on the inside of the threshold. "Was someone here? Did you catch them?"

"Yes and no." He rubbed the back of his neck and turned away from me.

"Why would they be in your house?"

He swiveled and leaned in, his steely gaze boring into my soul. "That's a good question. Why would they?"

I stepped back. "How would I know?"

He poked his finger out, just short of touching me in the chest. "They're your friends."

"How do you know it was them?" I pointed back at him. "Did you see them?"

His eyes narrowed. "I saw enough. Besides, haven't had any trouble 'til you came."

I huffed and stamped my foot. "I don't control them. If I did, we'd all be gone."

He walked around me into the cabin. "I wish you were gone." He mumbled so softly, I barely heard him.

"Is anything missing?" I walked outside and held my breath.

He scoffed and glanced around the room, then groaned. "Just my supper."

My shoulders slumped. "I'm sorry. I'm sure Cassie will feed you."

He locked gazes with me. One hand gripped the open

door. "She already feeds me dinner every day. I can fend for myself at supper, thank you."

"Fine. Fend for yourself." I turned and stalked down the path to Nate's house. Proud man. When I reached the barn, only a sliver of the sun shone over the horizon. I hadn't missed the meeting, though. Richard, Brian, and Allison didn't have plans to leave tonight. Not if they were stealing food. Ugh.

~

I pushed the scrambled eggs around on my plate while Nate and Cassie chatted. Why hadn't Allison and the guys shown up yesterday? I'd thought they were ready to go home. My stomach flip-flopped. I was more than ready. I sipped my tea.

"Do you need Lucas to help you search for your friends today, Lydia?" Cassie's voice broke into consciousness.

I heaved a sigh and set down my cup. "I don't know what to do."

Cassie and Nate exchanged a glance, a raised eyebrow, and a couple of head bobs in my direction. A nonverbal conversation. How cute.

Cassie shifted Melody on her lap and leaned toward me. "We've been praying. So have your ma and pa. We think you should stay here and wait for them to come to you."

"We'll all keep our eyes and ears open," Nate said. "Your ma and pa especially."

"I know they've already been watching Jenny." I picked up my fork, but laid it on my plate. Weird, I'd never lost my appetite like this before. "But she disappears on them. And I don't expect any of you to follow her around." I looked at

Nate. "Lucas has already spent way more time than he should on this. I know you need him around the farm."

"Well, it happened at a good time of year. Not nearly as busy now."

"Why don't you stay until Thanksgiving?" Cassie said. "We'll say that we talked you into staying for the holiday since we haven't seen you in so long. That's a week from Thursday."

My stomach roiled. Were they trying to suck me back in, and get me to stay for good? "And then what?"

She took a deep breath. "You could go back without them." She took another quick breath. "I doubt they'll let you, though."

I tensed my shoulders. "I'm worried that Jenny has a trick up her sleeve. She wants the remote and has to know I have it, even if she doesn't know who I am."

"Where is it now?" Nate asked.

I patted my pocket, but it wasn't there. "In my room. In the pocket I forgot to put on this morning."

Nate glanced at Cassie. "You might want to give it to Ed."

I narrowed my eyes at him. "Is there something you're not telling me?"

Nate looked down at his empty plate.

Cassie cleared her throat. "Aunt Mattie overheard Jenny talking to Allison. She knows who you are. And she knows you want to keep her from gaining access to the time machine."

I blew out a breath. "Tell me something I hadn't already figured out."

Nate stuck up his hands. "That's all we know."

"Wait." I spoke my thoughts as they came to me. "If I could get Brian alone, I think I could convince him. He's a descendant of Mark. He has something to lose if the timeline gets messed up."

"You really think that'll happen?" Cassie peered at me. "Because your Pa doesn't."

"He doesn't know that for sure." I studied her face and then Nate's. Either they were in denial, or they truly believed Pa. "What's he basing his theory on?"

Cassie leaned toward me. "God exists outside time. He's allowed us to travel in it, but ultimately, we can't mess up anything He's done. We've accepted that by faith."

I snorted. "I wish I had that kind of faith."

Cassie reached over and covered my hand with hers. "You can. All you have to do is ask. You know that."

I took a deep breath and let it out. "I've heard it all my life, but I just don't buy it." I pushed my chair back and stalked to the parlor door. "But thank you for taking me in." I whirled around. "I'll consider staying until Thanksgiving. If you really think it helps, please pray that I can get those three back to 2020 where they belong before they do any damage." I about-faced and stopped short of Lucas, who stood just inside the dining room door, his mouth agape.

Lucas strode into the room. "I knew something weird was going on."

"Ha, ha." Cassie stood, hoisting Melody on her hip. "We're joking."

"Didn't sound like a joke to me." Lucas stared at Nate, then Cassie, then me.

I wore a neutral expression, but I'm sure he could read Nate's and Cassie's guilty faces. I stepped toward him and tried to smile. "You don't really believe in a time machine, do you?"

He scratched behind his ear. "I didn't, but a few things are starting to make sense now."

Nate groaned and lay his head in his hands. I couldn't believe he'd cave that quickly.

Lucas seemed too innocent to learn about time travel, and I wanted him to stay that way. I tilted my head. "How could a time machine make sense?"

Lucas waved his arm as he spoke. "Things like you and your friends appearing pretty much out of nowhere. No method of transport here. What you called to them about having the only way back. Them having to steal to eat, and you relying on Cassie and Nate."

I raised my hand. "That's enough."

"Plus. I know the Bridgers, and they wouldn't take you in and lie for you if you weren't close family."

I groaned and turned away.

"Do you want help getting your friends to return with you or not, Miss Lydia?" Lucas asked.

I closed my eyes and slumped against the door frame, but kept my back to him.

"You are Mattie's youngest, aren't you?" His voice was just loud enough for me to hear.

"Yes." I trudged upstairs to my room, thoughts and feelings colliding in my mind. How could he see right through me? Why were Cassie, Nate, Ma, and Pa so serene about this whole thing? About everything?

I closed the door behind me and flopped onto the bed, bone tired despite having woken up less than an hour before.

My eyes fluttered open as a siren sounded. I blinked and

pushed myself up. Had I traveled to the future? Wait. That was Cassie's alarm. She must need Nate for something. The sun shone brightly through my window, so I must have slept for a few hours.

Before I could haul myself off the bed, a fist pounded on my door. "Lydia!" Cassie's unnaturally high-pitched voice quavered. "I need your help."

I catapulted myself off the bed and to the door. When I opened it, Cassie, eyes red and tear-filled, fell into my arms. "Someone's taken Melody!"

CHAPTER FIFTEEN

"What!" I patted Cassie's back. "Could Nate have her?"

She pulled away and shook her head. "No. He and Lucas are working in the fields. I left her in her playpen in the parlor and went to the kitchen to check on a loaf of bread in the oven." She blew her nose on her apron and sobbed. "I was gone for a minute!"

I hugged her again. "It's not your fault." My knees wobbled as I ushered her to the door. "What do you need me to do?" How was my voice so steady when my heart felt like it was beating out of my chest?

"Find Jenny! She did this!" She followed me out the door and downstairs, mumbling about how she'd pummel Jenny. If it weren't for Melody being missing, I would have smiled at the irony of Cassie wishing someone harm. Mama bear was a real thing.

I glanced around the small parlor. "Anything else missing?"

"Why would I care?" She threw up her hands.

"It may give us a clue. I don't know. Did she have a toy or a blanket in there?"

"A blanket and pillow."

I inspected the playpen. "Well, whoever took her, took the blanket too." I pushed my hair out of my face and plodded through the dining room to the mudroom. "That makes me think they'll take care of her." I swallowed hard, willing myself to believe my own words.

"How are you able to stay so calm?" She stood, hands on hips, and glared at me.

"One of us has to!" I glared back, then softened my expression. "Stay here in case someone comes back. I'm going to run to Ma's. Then I'll go get Nate and Lucas. Ma will probably start Mark and some of the Joneses searching. We'll find her."

I raced off down the path, not stopping to saddle a horse. I could run a mile faster than I could get a horse ready and ride. Why would Jenny do this? There were other ways for her to trick me into giving her the remote. It didn't make sense. Part of me hoped that when I got to Ma's, Melody would be happily bouncing on Ma's knee, some kind of miscommunication with Cassie.

When I reached the house, I stopped and caught my breath. It had been a week since I'd run any distance. "Ma," I called as I walked into the kitchen.

"Uh, Miss Ellen." Ma shook her head, her eyes wide. Behind her, Jenny wiped off a plate.

"It's okay, Ma. I'm pretty sure she knows already." I stomped toward Jenny. "Where is she?"

Jenny jerked her head back and squinted at me as if she had no idea what I was talking about.

"Who?" Ma faced me, one hand on her hip.

"Melody. She's missing."

Ma's face blanched, and her mouth formed a perfect O.

Jenny's eyes widened. "I have no idea what happened."

"Right." I jabbed my finger at her apron. "It has something to do with you."

"Why do you say that?" Ma's trembling hand touched my shoulder.

I let my arms flail. "Who else would have kidnapped Melody?"

Jenny snorted. "How do you know she was kidnapped? She could have wandered off."

I planted my fist on my hip. "She's four months old and was in her playpen."

"Oh." Jenny bit her lower lip.

Ma took a deep breath and squared her shoulders. "Don't let's keep jawing about it. Go out to the barn and tell your pa and Mark. I'll get the Joneses looking. Then I'll head over to Cassie's."

"Right." I trotted outside. Did Jenny really not know what had happened, or was she that good an actor? It didn't matter now, though. We had to get everyone out searching for the baby.

"Pa!" I entered the dim barn. "Mark!"

Mark walked toward me carrying a wrench. "What's going on?"

"Get your pa. Somebody took Melody. We're all out looking."

Mark gasped and ran off to the shop at the other end of the barn.

Pa hurried to me, wiping his grease-stained hands on a towel. "When?"

"Maybe about ten minutes ago?" I blinked. "Cassie said

she was only out of the room for a minute, but Melody's missing."

"We'll find her." Pa gave my shoulder a soft squeeze. "Go get Nate. Where was the last place you saw your friends?"

"Near the path to Lucas' cabin." I squinted and tilted my head. "You think they would do this?"

"Desperate people do desperate things." Pa raced to the first stall and brought out Ginger. "Did you run here?"

I nodded.

"Do you want to ride Mary Anne?" He turned to Mark. "Saddle up Mary Anne, for your sister."

Mark furrowed his brow and then studied me. He hadn't spoken to me before now, and we were never close. "Lydia?"

"Don't have time to explain," I said.

"Later," Pa said at the same time.

Mark pulled Mary Anne out of her stall and saddled her, mumbling to himself the whole time.

They got the horses ready in record time, and Pa and I mounted. When we left the barn, Mark was getting Elvis out of his stall.

Pa and I raced toward Nate's, or tried to. Mary Anne wasn't used to novice riders, and I had trouble getting her up to speed. "Move!" I kicked her hard. She accelerated fast and nearly jolted me off. I clung to the saddle horn and willed myself to stay on as she galloped down the path.

When we arrived at Nate's, Cassie stepped off the walkway. "Nate and Lucas must not have heard the siren."

Pa nodded and signaled for me to head toward the cotton fields. He rode down the path toward Lucas's cabin.

About halfway to the field, I gulped. My remote was

still in the pocket I'd neglected to add to my costume this morning. Could the kidnapping be a diversion to get everyone out of the house in order to get that remote? A war raged inside. Go back for the remote, or find Nate and Lucas?

Mary Anne made my decision for me and galloped toward the cotton fields. I yelled Nate's name as I rode across acres of flat, near-barren land. How could he hide in this open space? He had to be somewhere else. A dark blot on the horizon morphed into the shape of a horse and rider, then another farther behind. Nate waved one arm over his head as we approached each other.

Thank goodness I found him. I slowed Mary Anne, and we stopped opposite each other.

"Nate, you have to come quick." I huffed, trying to catch my breath.

"Is it Cassie?" He leaned forward, wide eyes locked with mine.

"Somebody's taken Melody."

His face blanched, and he spurred the gray horse and galloped toward the house.

Lucas rode Codger to me. When I told him about Melody, he frowned and lowered his head. Then he scrunched his nose and mouth together and narrowed his eyes.

I swallowed hard. "What are you thinking?"

"Come with me." He turned his horse at approximately a ninety-degree angle from the direction Nate had headed.

"Where are we going?"

I lagged as he galloped away.

"Please let me catch up," I whispered under my breath.

Who was I talking to?

We rode through spent fields, past a creek, and into a thickly wooded area. Lucas slowed when we hit the woods and didn't let any branches hit me so hard that they knocked me over. I got scratched a few times, though.

Finally, he slowed to a walk, and a clearing came into view. I reined in Mary Anne and stayed behind a large oak next to Lucas. He dismounted and tied Codger up to a smaller tree, then he came over and helped me down.

"I had a hunch they might be staying here." Lucas pointed to a ramshackle cabin, larger than his but almost falling apart. "I stumbled on it last summer. On Sunday, I remembered it, but haven't had a chance to check it out, yet."

"So?" I peered at him. "What now?"

He tied Mary Anne to the same tree as Codger and pulled me over to crouch next to him behind the oak. "Let's watch for a bit." But he didn't. He closed his eyes and lowered his head, moving his lips slightly. Praying.

Well, he could pray while I kept watch. Too bad there wasn't anything to see. Not even smoke coming from the chimney. However, the brush had been cleared from around the front of the cabin, and the threshold looked cleaner than the windowsills. Someone had been there. I took a few steps into the clearing to investigate, but Lucas stopped me with a hand on my arm.

"Nobody's here now," I whispered. "But somebody has been."

"I can see that, but they could be hiding." He motioned for me to stay back, and he started toward the cabin. Then he stopped, glanced around the forest floor, picked up a rock, and headed back out there.

"Don't you have a better weapon than that?" I whispered as I followed.

He faced me and raised his hand. "Stay back there."

I planted my foot and shook my head.

"If I don't return, you need to go get Nate."

"Fine." It made sense, so I crossed my arms over my chest and leaned against a tree. What gave him the right to act so superior? My face flushed, and I flared my nostrils.

He smirked.

I squeezed my hands into fists, but stayed put. Men!

Lucas crept to the cabin and peered into the window. I couldn't help being impressed at how stealthy he was.

He locked gazes with me, put his finger to his lip, and rushed the door.

CHAPTER SIXTEEN

After a bang and a scream, Lucas ran out of the cabin carrying a red-faced, bawling Melody. I sprinted to them, and he handed her to me. "Take her home to Miss Cassie." He raced back toward the cabin.

"Poor baby." I bounced her up and down as I approached my horse. "Big man scared you, didn't he?" She hadn't been crying until Lucas went in. Had she been asleep by herself and he scared her, or had someone been with her and escaped? I stepped my left foot into the stirrup, but needed a hand to hoist myself up. Melody wiggled so much I couldn't hold her in one arm. I'd have to wait for Lucas.

Melody screamed in my ear, so I rubbed her back, bounced her up and down, and whispered, "Shh." With all this wailing, how would I think well enough to figure out what was going on? Keeping a lookout, I paced in front of the horses. I wouldn't let my guard down and lose her again, but she made it easy for someone to track us.

"I know, I'm not Mommy, am I?" I patted her. She burped and hiccupped, and her wail subsided to a whimper.

Lucas came into view from the opposite side of the clearing. He shook his head as he strode toward us.

I leaned forward. "Was anyone with her?"

He jerked his head toward the cabin. "The older gent. He ran as soon as I hit the door."

"It was Richard. I'm surprised you couldn't catch him." I clamped my mouth shut.

"Well, I brought the baby to you first." He eyed her. "Is she all right?"

I took her off my shoulder and searched her tear-streaked face. "I think so." I glanced up at the horses. "How far is it to Nate's?"

"A couple of miles." He tilted his head. "Why didn't you head back?"

I nodded toward my horse, my hands full with Melody. "Couldn't mount."

He smirked. "Oh, right. If I help you up, do you think you can carry her on Mary Anne?"

I gulped. "I'll try. I'm kind of rusty at riding."

"No..." Sarcasm dripped from his voice.

"All right." I secured my grip on her and used my free hand to swat him on the arm.

He pulled back, chuckling. "I'd take her if she'd let me." He held his hands out to her, but she buried her face in my shoulder.

"You scared her, maybe more than they did when they took her."

"Yeah." He flashed me a sheepish grin. "The door slam. I wanted to scare Richard. That part worked."

I smiled. "Help me up?"

Lucas lifted me, still holding Melody, onto my horse and had to help me arrange the fabric on my riding costume.

Blushing, he rode beside me, keeping hold of Mary

Anne's reins as I held Melody with one arm and the pommel with the other hand. Thankfully, the baby had calmed down and only whimpered a little. When we left the woods, we were still about a mile off. I kept watch as we got nearer, not sure what to expect. Cassie would be there, and probably Ma, but the men would all be off searching. Thank God for Lucas's hunch. I blinked and shook my head. No, I should thank Lucas.

He flashed a lopsided grin, then turned away as if he could read my mind.

"What was that about?" I sounded more annoyed than I'd intended.

"What?" He wore an innocent expression.

"That smile." I resumed my forward gaze, and his smile reappeared in my peripheral vision.

"I don't know. Maybe I'm just happy we found her." He lowered his voice. "And to be riding next to you."

I flushed. "I can't wait to get her to her mother."

"That, too." He faced forward.

I tightened my hold and kept the same slow pace so I could safely deliver her to Cassie. When we arrived at the house, the kitchen door opened.

Cassie walked out. "I'm supposed to send you two into town—" She stopped and stared at me with her mouth wide open. Then she let out a yelp and a sob and rushed over, arms extended to Melody. "Thank you! Thank you!" She took Melody in her arms and hugged her, pivoting back and forth.

"What's the commotion?" Ma stepped onto the walkway, then raised her hands in the air. "Oh! Thank you, Jesus!"

Lucas dismounted and reached up to help me down. "I'll

take the horses to the barn."

"Mary Anne belongs in Pa's barn." I leaned toward him.

"I'm aware. But she'll be fine in our extra stall. At least for a while." Lucas clasped my waist and lowered me to the ground

A shiver ran through me, and I stepped away from him. Always before, he'd been the first to back up.

Lucas cleared his throat and led the horses away.

As Cassie entered the kitchen with Melody, Ma hugged me tight. "Thank you, Lydia. God used you and Lucas today."

My first impulse was to scoff, but Ma didn't deserve that. She truly believed, and I shouldn't make light of it. "I'm glad I could help."

She held me at arm's length and studied my face. It probably resembled hers. Happy tears streamed down my cheeks.

"Come in." She motioned toward the kitchen.

I hesitated. Cassie was probably nursing Melody. "Shouldn't we give her privacy?"

"Na." Ma ushered me inside. "She'll want to hear how you found her."

I sat at the worktable and explained Lucas's hunch, finding the old shack, and Richard running away.

Ma poured tea into my cup. "Why would they take her and then not try to use her to get the remote?"

I shrugged. "I wondered the same thing." My eyes shot open wide. The remote was still upstairs in my room. It had better be.

"Lydia," Lucas said from the doorway.

I jumped. How had he put the horses in the barn so

quickly? He must have left them in the corral.

He touched a finger to his mouth and motioned for me to go with him.

I followed him because, even after only knowing him for a few days, I trusted him.

We walked directly to the barn, then he guided me to the corner near the tack room. He stood behind me and looked over my shoulder as I peered out the small window. Jenny and Brian stood about a foot apart, red-faced and talking in low tones, their hands waving. Too bad I couldn't make out what they said. And where was Allison? Did anyone other than Richard know we had Melody?

We watched for several minutes until Jenny stalked off toward Ma's house, and Brian headed in the direction of the old cabin. I pivoted toward Lucas. "What do you make of that?"

He shook his head. "That's why I wanted you to see. I hoped you'd be able to figure it out."

"I've got no idea what's going on between them." I rubbed my temple. "What do we do next?"

"I'll keep praying. In the meantime, I'll find Nate and Ed. At least we have good news for them." He smiled as he escorted me out of the barn.

After Lucas rode off, I plopped onto the walkway steps near the kitchen. I took several deep breaths and let them out on a count of eight. Now, maybe I could process this morning's events. What were Allison, Jenny, and Brian trying to accomplish? Kidnapping Melody made no sense. Wait! I scrambled to stand and raced to my room. I grabbed the pocket I'd forgotten to don this morning and pulled out the remote. Whew. I plopped onto the mattress and caught my breath as I checked it over. It was the real one. Either they didn't bother to search for the remote, or they didn't find it.

Breathing easier, I slid the set of pockets under my riding skirt and replaced the remote. I kept my hand on the lump in my pocket as I strode to the kitchen, where Ma prepared dinner and Cassie sat at the worktable, cuddling her baby.

"I knew we'd find her." Ma pointed at Melody as she carried a pie to the worktable. "I had a peace about it after praying."

"I have faith, too, Aunt Mattie." Cassie patted Melody's back. "But I also know that God doesn't always answer our prayers the way we want."

"Correct." Aunt Mattie cut the pie, then shrugged. "I just sensed she was all right."

"I'm grateful to Lucas for thinking so quick." Cassie kissed Melody on the top of the head. "I can't imagine what it would have been like if she'd been gone any longer."

I clamped my mouth shut to avoid mentioning I'd expect her hair to turn gray. Belittling her for an honest fear reaction wasn't the way I wanted her to remember me. "I've been thinking." I stirred the stew. "Maybe I should go home today and take the remote with me."

"I thought you were going to wait until after Thanksgiving." Cassie's voice squeaked.

"Well, if I go now, they won't have a reason to do any more harm." I cleared my throat. Maybe I wanted to go home before I got sucked into life here. Before I got attached to my family. I don't think I was attached before, except for Pa.

"Please stay." Ma closed the gap between us and laid

her hand on my shoulder. "Just until next week. I've been praying. And I believe that's the right time."

"Another one of your feelings?" I gave her the side-eye, unable to keep the acid out of my tone.

"Yes." Ma let go of my shoulder and carried one of the dishes out of the kitchen.

"You know she's often right, don't you?" Cassie said in a low tone.

I sighed. "No, but I'll take your word for it."

Cassie shifted Melody to her other shoulder. "Then it's settled. You'll stay until next Friday at least."

"Next Friday at most." I left the ladle in the pot and faced her. "I just hope I don't have to leave anyone from the twenty-first century behind."

Her mouth fell open, and she shook her head.

"Except you," I added quickly.

"What about Jenny?" She rose off her chair for a split second, then settled back into it. "You can't take her."

I squinted. "I guess I don't think of you or her as from my century anymore, but why not take her?"

Cassie pressed her lips together. "It's better that she stays here."

I peered at her. "Why won't anyone tell me?"

"Cassie!" Nate called from outside.

Cassie and I hurried to the door.

I got there first and slipped down the walkway.

Nate bounded up the few steps as Cassie carried Melody out of the kitchen. He swallowed them in his arms, tears streaming down his ruddy face.

Lucas and Pa stood in the yard, beaming.

~

Nate sat at the head of the table with Melody on his lap while he said grace. He thanked God for Melody's return, but forgot to thank him for the food.

I stifled a giggle. I wasn't about to comment about a prayer. "Where's Mark?" He'd been a part of the search.

Pa set down his water glass. "He wanted to eat with Emily. He said he'd keep an eye on Jenny, too."

Lucas filled everyone in on the argument we witnessed.

I plopped mashed potatoes on my plate. "So, any guesses as to what Brian and Jenny were arguing about?"

Ma shook her head. "Maybe Jenny has a conscience after all and wanted them to give back the baby?"

"Could have been about that." Pa cocked his head. "Where is the other woman, though?"

I ladled venison stew over the potatoes. "Anyone seen her lately?"

Cassie, Nate, and Pa shook their heads.

Lucas swallowed a bite of stew. "Last time I saw her was with you, when you called after them."

"Any idea why they time-traveled here?" Nate asked.

I shrugged. "Richard is the only one I've talked to since we arrived. He told me Allison wanted to prove she could get Todd's machine to work, and his coming with them was an accident."

Cassie choked on her tea and spit out a small amount.

I chuckled, and Lucas doubled his lips under, probably to keep himself from laughing.

"Sorry." Cassie wiped her lips with a linen napkin. "Just a little close to home."

Ma jerked her head at Lucas, her eyes wide and her hand over her mouth.

"It's okay." I touched Ma's arm. "He knows."

"Smart lad." Ma bobbed her head. "I figured it out, too."

Lucas squinted at Ma. "Wait. How'd you know they didn't tell me?"

Ma grinned. "I know them." She pointed to Pa. "This one came here from 2010, thirty-three years ago, and tried to blend in, but I was onto him."

"Ed?" Lucas studied Pa's face. "I didn't know about him." He glanced around the table. "Anyone else?"

Cassie pointed to herself. "Just me...and Jenny."

"And Lydia." Pa nodded at me. "She's been both directions, now."

I tried to smile. "And I aim to go once more."

"After Thanksgiving." Ma patted my shoulder.

"Well, maybe we'll figure out what your friends are up to in the meantime," Nate said.

"They aren't my friends." I leaned against my chair. "I met them a couple of days before they came here. Brian is a relative, though."

Nate scowled. "Dang. I wish you knew more about them."

"Me, too." I dropped my fork, my plate still half-full.

Lucas turned toward Nate. "What's the plan for this afternoon, boss?"

"You can finish the fence mending. I'm going to hang around here." Nate kissed Melody on the top of her head and then winked at Cassie.

"Good man." Pa nodded at Nate, then swiveled toward me. "Lydia, why don't you join me in my shop?"

"Sure." I bounced in my seat, more energetic than I'd felt since I'd gotten up this morning. Maybe since I'd been here.

"That's settled." Ma pushed back from the table. "I guess I'll go home and see what I can get out of Jenny."

Pa smiled at Ma. "Always the sleuth."

Ma winked. "Got to use the brain God gave me."

Everyone else chuckled while I contemplated. Ma was more complex than I'd thought. Maybe I'd misjudged her when I was growing up.

~

Pa entered his shop and peered around the large open room.

"What ya working on, Pa?" I followed him in, adjusting to the dim light. "How long did it take you to stop reaching for a light switch when you walked into a dark room?"

He chuckled. "A while." He pointed to a space in the far corner marked by two worktables. "Keep your voice down. Caleb could come in any minute."

"Are you expecting him today?"

Pa smiled. "Caleb comes over when he wants to. Pretty near every day, now that he has two baby brothers."

I laughed. "Can't say I blame him." I accompanied him to his workspace. "What's so secretive?"

"Something I've been working on this week." He showed me several small plastic gadgets. One looked similar to the fake remote.

I furrowed my brow and patted my pocket, ensuring the real one was there. "I don't understand. We already have a decoy."

"I know, but the one I showed you wasn't the only one. I found these in Jenny's stash while she was in prison. I might be able to get one to work."

"Without electricity?"

He showed me a solar-powered battery charger. "This was with them. If Jenny's looked for them since she got out, she hasn't said anything."

I stood with both hands on my hips. "Are you planning on going back to the twenty-first century? You know you'd have to go to 2020, unless you can take the restraints off Todd's machine."

He scoffed. "It's not for me. It's in case one of your friends gets stuck here." He lowered his head and rubbed the back of his neck. "Or possibly for Caleb."

My eyes widened. If Todd deactivated his machine, Caleb couldn't go forward. "You haven't told him yet, have you?"

"Of course not." He glanced around the barn. "He's just so... He's like you. He'd do much better in the twenty-first century."

I groaned. "I didn't do so hot."

He peered at me. "What are you saying? I thought you were adamant about going back."

"Oh, I am. I don't belong here." I lowered my head. "But I will be getting another job. Something more meaningful."

He leaned against the table and laid the charger down. "Is that why you haven't told us about your work?"

I sighed and sat on an upturned crate. "I was programming video games for my boyfriend's company. We broke up, and now I don't have a job, and I don't have any interest in his games." I studied my boots.

He knelt next to me. "It sounds to me like you followed your heart. Ain't nothing wrong with that."

I rolled my eyes. "You always were a romantic." Suddenly, it hit me that he had ended up here after trying to bail out his girlfriend, Jenny. "Isn't it weird having Jenny live under your roof?"

He snorted. "I'll say. But your ma wouldn't have it any other way. She visited Jenny in jail most days. Petitioned the sheriff to keep her here instead of sending her off to a prison, and even provided most of her meals." He shook his head. "You know your ma when she gets something in her mind."

I smiled and nodded. "One track."

"I love her, but sometimes she tries my patience." He stood and stepped away. "I shouldn't have told you that."

"It's okay. I knew it anyway." I reached out and squeezed his shoulder.

"It's just that you seem so grown up." Pa raked a hand through his salt and pepper hair. "It's strange."

"Well, it's been ten years for me, and only three for you. Time travel is weird, to say the least." My mouth fell open. "Mark is only twenty-two, isn't he? I'm twenty-five."

He shook his head. "Bizarre."

"So." I stood and walked over to his worktable. "Any luck with this?"

He picked up the charger and a remote. "We need plenty of sunlight and several hours to test it. I've been having a hard time finding that combination."

"Hmm." I wanted to help, but at the same time, I didn't really want it to work.

For the first time, I understood how Todd felt about his invention. It was dangerous to have people running around in the wrong time period. So, what gave me the right? I shuddered. I still planned to go back to 2020. It's where I belonged.

~

As I walked the old road through the woods back to Nate's house, memories flooded my mind. I'd run this trail, getting messages to Nate and back to Ma, so many times. The last several months I'd lived here, I'd come to visit Cassie. We even moved into Nate's house for a short period. In 2020, this path didn't exist. All these trees and bushes had been thinned out, and this was now the street behind Todd's house.

I shook my head as I approached Nate's backyard. Why did I feel sad about progress? Instead of wallowing, I should store up memories of my family for my return next week.

Movement behind the barn caught my attention, and I veered to my right to check it out. Lucas strode into the woods directly behind the barn, probably on his way home. I squinted at the bright sun. It was a bit early to call it a day, especially since he'd missed several hours of work. Curious, I followed Lucas, trying to stay far enough behind that he wouldn't notice.

When he'd gotten out of sight, I continued along the path, confident that when I entered the clearing, he'd already be inside his cabin.

"Like me that much, you couldn't stay away, huh?"

I jumped and spun around.

Lucas peered out from behind the largest tree at the edge of the path, a bright smile on his face. He stepped out, then frowned. "I'm sorry. I didn't mean to scare you."

I aimed for a neutral expression, but my heart raced, and I couldn't seem to calm it. "I just—"

"Suspicious?" He ambled to me.

My chin pointed upward. "Um, no. I'm not sure why I followed."

"Well, if you must know." He walked toward his cabin and motioned for me to come with him. "Nate asked me to check out my place for evidence of intrusion."

"Oh. Nobody else has been around Nate's?"

"Nope. They appear to be laying low, now that kidnapping the baby didn't work."

"So why would Nate ask you to come here?"

He slowed as we entered the clearing. "He's still nervous." He flashed a sheepish grin. "He also invited me to supper so I could report back."

It made sense. Nate would want Lucas close for extra protection. "Did he ask you to move in for a few days, too?"

He peered at me with wide-open eyes. "How did you know that?"

"I know Nate. He wants backup. Can't say I blame him."

"Hmm. I turned him down, but maybe I shouldn't have." Lucas approached the door to his cabin and stopped. "I'd invite you in, but it wouldn't be proper."

I laughed but sobered at the scowl on his face. "I'll wander around out here. See if I find anything out of the ordinary."

He nodded and entered the cabin.

I meandered around the perimeter of the small clearing, stopping at a stream that ran behind the dwelling. Lucas had a nice little place here. He'd been a great help to Nate, and he treated me with respect. But who was he, and where was he from? And why couldn't I get him out of my mind long enough to look for clues to the trio's whereabouts? Too bad the twenty-first century didn't seem to produce men like him.

Is that why Cassie had stayed? But she'd been dating Todd when she came here, and Todd's a good man.

No, it wasn't the time period that was the issue. I had fallen for the wrong guy. Austin had been my first real boyfriend, and I'd made so many mistakes. I took a deep breath. From now on, after I returned to the future, I'd use my head more than my heart when evaluating dating prospects.

"Lydia," Lucas called from the front of the cabin.

"Back here!" I headed toward him, but he met me in the side yard. He carried a satchel.

I pointed at the bag. "So, you're moving in for a while?"

"Yes." He stopped a few feet away. "Uh, I guess we'll be neighbors. That is, if you don't mind?"

I shrugged. "Why would I mind? It's not my house, and they didn't invite you to share a room with me."

His cheeks reddened, and he strode toward the path.

I caught up to him. "Did you find anything amiss?"

He tilted his head back and slowed his gait. "I'm not sure—just had a feeling someone had been there—no real proof. Nothing was missing."

I narrowed my eyes. "What do you mean, a feeling?"

He glanced at the cabin. "You know. Things that don't look exactly in the place I left them. But I can't be certain."

I peered at him. "Like somebody picked up something, inspected it, and put it back down, but not in the exact location?"

"Yes!" He gazed at me. "I didn't think anyone would understand that."

How had I figured out what he was trying to say? I strode down the path ahead of Lucas, hiding the flush on my cheeks. Even if he and I were on the same wavelength, I wouldn't allow myself to fall for him.

CHAPTER SEVENTEEN

As Lucas and I approached the kitchen, Nate waited on the walkway steps and nodded at Lucas's satchel. "I'm glad you changed your mind." He frowned and jerked his head at the mudroom door. "We've found something."

I jolted forward. "What?"

Nate turned and walked ahead of us. "Let's go inside first."

Lucas and I exchanged a nervous glance as we entered the dining room.

Cassie sat in her chair holding a sleeping Melody against her shoulder.

Nate cleared his throat. "Cassie, tell them what you found."

She nodded at a paper on the table. "See for yourself."

I picked up the lined notebook paper and read the printing, while Lucas read over my shoulder.

Lucas pointed to the ink. "That wasn't written with a fountain pen."

"More like a ballpoint." The paper shook in my hands. I read aloud, "Hand over the remote and we'll give your baby back. Meet behind your barn at sundown." I furrowed my brow. "This doesn't make sense. We already have Melody."

Cassie shook her head. "I found it under the pillow in the playpen when I went to put her down. I must have missed it earlier."

I plopped onto a chair. "But why would they want to keep her all day?"

"Maybe to make us crazy." Cassie kissed Melody on the head. "It would have worked."

Nate squeezed Cassie's shoulder and peered at Lucas. "I'm so grateful you figured out where they were hiding."

"I just happened to be in the right place. And listening." He pointed up. At first, I had no idea what he meant, but then it dawned on me. He thought God had given him inspiration. Well, whatever, I was glad he'd had it.

"So, now what?" I asked.

Nate motioned toward the parlor. "Lucas, take the room to the right of the stairs." It was the room next to mine. "We'll keep watch at sundown."

"I don't think they'll come." I nodded at the baby. "They know we have Melody already."

Nate sat next to Cassie instead of his normal place at the head of the table. "They could try something else."

I glanced at the doorway, but Lucas had already left the room. "Is that why you wanted Lucas here?"

Nate grimaced. "Partly. I don't think Cassie will let Melody out of her sight, at least until the time-travelers leave."

Cassie raised her eyebrows. "You haven't since you've been home, either."

I couldn't blame them. She wasn't even mine, and I'd been scared. I didn't want to imagine how they'd felt.

"I think Aunt Mattie would be here, too, if she wasn't trying to keep Jenny in check." Cassie pressed her lips together.

"How's Jenny involved?" Lucas stood in the doorway.

Cassie waved her arm. "We're not sure, but she's contacted the travelers." She placed Melody in her cradle next to the table and stood. "I'll go bring supper in. Hope it's not burnt. Lydia, will you help?"

As I passed Nate, he mumbled, "If it is burnt, it won't be the first time."

I stifled a laugh because I couldn't cook with modern appliances. When we entered the kitchen, Cassie hurried to the wood stove to stir the soup. "Pull out that loaf of bread and slice it, please." She pointed to a bread box I'd forgotten existed.

I carried the loaf to the worktable and reached for a knife. "You must be feeling better."

She stayed at the stove. "Why do you say that?"

"You left Melody."

Her lip quivered as she glanced at the doorway. "Nate and Lucas are both there. And we'll be right back." She lifted the pot using two towels and headed outside. I ran to open the back door to the mudroom. How did she manage by herself? Before I could reach it, Nate stood ready to accept the soup pot. Teamwork.

After returning to the kitchen, Cassie helped me place the bread in a basket. "I hope it's enough."

"Soup and bread makes a great supper." I grabbed the metal pitcher out of the icebox. "I'll bring in the milk." One thing I liked about being home was having milk almost direct from the cow.

~

I patted my mouth with my linen napkin. "Best chicken noodle soup I've ever had. I mean that."

Cassie smiled. "You're forgetting your ma's."

I shook my head. "Nope. This was better."

"Good bread, too." Lucas swiped his third piece. Why was I counting?

Nate chuckled, then stopped short. "Do you hear that?"

We all stayed still, except Melody, who chose that moment to wail.

Cassie bent down and picked her up, shushing her. Nate and Lucas hurried into the mudroom. I stood and tried not to make a sound.

Footsteps thudded outside, headed to the front of the house.

Lucas trotted to the foyer with me right behind. He peered out the window near the top of the door, opened it, and stepped onto the porch.

I walked out and stopped next to him.

Allison and Brian stood at the base of the steps, flames leaping from the lit torch in Allison's hand. Richard slunk behind them. Allison wore a gown for the first time. Who had she borrowed it from? What was she up to?

Allison lifted the torch. "Hand over the remote, and I won't set fire to the house. I know how deadly fires can be." She glared at me, as if she knew that was the reason I'd been taken to the future.

I held up both hands. "Why don't you three go back with me? That's why I'm here."

Richard laid a hand on her arm and whispered to her.

She shook her head, her feet planted shoulder-width apart, torch still raised high. Resolute. "We don't trust you."

I mimicked her stance, minus the torch. "Why wouldn't you? What other reason could I have to come here?"

Allison lifted her chin. "Jenny."

I sighed. Nate crept into my peripheral vision and continued around to stand behind them. I focused on Allison, hoping he could get to her before she tired of our conversation. "What did she tell you?"

"That's not important." She held her other hand out, palm up. "The remote."

"I don't have it on me." It was in the drawstring bag in my pocket. Sorry Ma. "Didn't Jenny give you one?"

Allison sneered. "You know it didn't work."

I tilted my head and feigned nonchalance. "If she gave you a remote that didn't work, why do you trust her and not me?"

Brian leaned toward his wife. "That's a good point."

Allison stepped forward. "She says you won't take her back. You know she doesn't belong here, and you do."

"There's a good reason I can't take her back." Or so they tell me. At any rate, if the timeline got messed up, Pa's descendants were at risk. I peered at Brian. "It's in your best interest that she doesn't get control of the time machine and that you go back as soon as possible."

"She told us you'd say that." Allison pulled the torch back, ready to throw it.

I raised my hands. "Wait! The remote is in there. If you set the house on fire, you'll never get home."

She relaxed her arm, and Nate grabbed the torch away from her. He ran to the dirt road and smothered it before

Brian and Richard could catch him.

Emboldened, I strode closer, but stayed on the porch, giving myself the height advantage. "Don't ever try to kidnap Melody or anyone else again."

Allison leered. "It was too easy." She tossed a glance at Richard. "It would have worked if someone had a spine."

Richard glared at her and stepped back. "I told you not to do it. I didn't want any part of it. Frankly, I was relieved when they showed up."

Allison scoffed.

Lucas nodded at Nate. "I just heard the lady confess to kidnapping. Should I go for the sheriff?"

Richard and Brian bolted. Richard ran into Nate, who grabbed Richard's wrists and twisted them behind his back, holding him in a one-handed grip.

Lucas sprinted after Brian and tackled him.

That left Allison for me. But she stood at the base of the steps, chuckling and rolling her eyes. Since she didn't run, I stayed on the porch.

Lucas and Nate tugged the two men in my direction.

Cassie stepped through the front door and held out two lengths of rope. "It's all I could find."

Nate dragged Richard onto the porch and took the rope from Cassie. "Thanks. Please go back in."

"Planning on it." She closed the front door behind her.

Brian struggled against Lucas's hold, but Richard stood still and stared at me as Nate bound his wrists and tied him to the porch rail.

A shrill whistle sounded, and my hands flew to my ears as I swiveled toward the source. Allison. She kept blowing what appeared to be a pewter cylinder—a whistle from this time.

Nate handed off a length of rope to Lucas, jogged to Allison, and snatched the whistle out of her hand.

I let my hands fall to my sides and released my clenched jaw.

Lucas subdued Brian and tied him and Richard together, hands behind their backs.

Nate held Allison's arm in a tight grip. "Lydia, run into town and get the sheriff."

"No need." Allison straightened to her full height and stared into Nate's eyes, a slight smirk on her face.

Hoof beats approached, and the sheriff and two other riders pulled to a stop just off the road.

My jaw dropped. Had she planned this?

Allison pulled away from Nate's grasp. "I told him Lucas had been harassing my friends."

Sheriff Hill dismounted but kept hold of the reins and faced Allison. "You said to meet you at the crossroad, not here." He bobbed his head at Nate. "I didn't expect this had anything to do with you."

Nate stepped toward Sheriff Hill. "She admitted to kidnapping Melody earlier today, and now, she's threatened to burn down my house."

Allison sidled up to the sheriff. "I did no such thing. My friends and I are only sojourning here for a few weeks, visiting our good friends Pastor and Mrs. Kelley." She thrust her arm at Lucas. "This man has been agitating Richard and Brian."

Lucas's face turned beet red. He shuffled from foot to foot, still holding onto Brian, his gaze locked on Nate.

Sheriff Hill wiped his brow. "Seems we have a stand-off here."

"What?" Nate scowled. "You believe these strangers as much as me?"

"According to the law—"

Nate huffed. "They stole two of my horses. They've had them since last week."

The sheriff narrowed his eyes. "Why didn't you report it?"

Nate rubbed his temple. "They were friends of my cousin. I didn't want to get them in trouble at the time."

Sheriff Hill pursed his lips and glanced around the open front yard. "Where are the horses?"

Allison smiled and batted her eyelashes. It would have been more effective if she was attractive. "Have you checked your barn lately?"

Lucas's eyes widened. "I planned to see to the horses after supper. I'll go now." He trotted around the outside of the house.

Nate held up the whistle and turned to the sheriff. "Is this yours?"

Sheriff Hill nodded and accepted it. "She told me Lucas had suggested they meet to hash out their differences, and she didn't feel safe."

Nate pulled the sheriff off to the side. I sidled to the porch rail to hear better.

Allison marched up the porch steps and settled onto the swing as if she owned the place.

"I won't be surprised if my horses are back." Nate's words caught my attention. He focused on the sheriff. "Are they staying with the Kelleys? And how did they ingratiate themselves?"

"You know the Kelleys have that cabin they let missionaries stay in?"

Nate jerked his head back. "That place is decrepit. I didn't think it was still livable."

"Well, the men are staying there, and the woman is staying with the pastor and his wife." Sheriff Hill glanced at Allison. "She claims to be heading west to start a new church, and needed a place to stay for a couple of weeks. They're waiting for a fellow missionary."

Cassie's journals mentioned the Kelleys' soft spot for missionaries headed west.

Lucas jogged into view and nodded at Nate. "All your horses are in their stalls."

I blew a soft raspberry. Allison was smart and manipulative.

Sheriff Hill approached his horse. "Sorry, Nate. Now it's their word against yours, and in the eyes of the law..." He nodded at Brian and Richard. "You need to let them go."

Lucas stomped to the men, his jaw clenched tight. He untied them, dropped the ropes, and balled his hands into fists. He whispered something to them. A warning?

The sheriff mounted his horse and scrutinized us one at a time. "I don't know what exactly is going on, but for your sakes, it needs to stop. Now." He tipped his hat and rode off.

Allison stood and sauntered off the porch toward the side yard, beckoning Richard and Brian. How would they get back into town? She stopped and gazed at me. Her eyes flashed in the fading sunlight. "We'll be back." She turned on her heel and stalked off. Her stooges followed.

I looked at both Nate and Lucas. "Should we go after them?"

Lucas shook his head. "The Jones boy was here with a message from Ed. The Kelleys are visiting Miss Mattie, so I suspect that's where Allison and them are headed." He reached down. "I'll coil up the rope."

"Thanks." Nate heaved a sigh and ushered me to the front door. "Any idea what she's up to?"

"No. I wonder if Jenny knows. Could Allison have a different agenda?" I squinted and cocked my head.

He rubbed the back of his neck. "We need to pray and keep watch."

He could pray. I'd do more than keep watch. Allison had declared war, and I planned to fight.

CHAPTER EIGHTEEN

I stomped into the house, my mind a chaotic jumble of plans.

"Come in here," Cassie called from the small parlor.

Nate entered the parlor while I started upstairs, intent on sorting through my options before listening to anyone else.

"Miss Lydia?" Lucas closed the front door. "Please join us."

I stopped on the second step. How could he already have such power over me? My shoulders lowered. I could make my plans after I listened to theirs. "Oh, all right." I pivoted and trudged through the unpopulated parlor to the dining room.

Melody slept in her cradle, and Cassie had set out tea and small cakes. We sat, one on each side of the table.

"So?" Cassie leaned forward, fingers pressed onto the wood. "What's the plan?"

Nate grinned. "You heard the whole thing, didn't you?"

She nodded. "Most of it."

Narrowing my eyes, I eyed the tea and cakes, then turned to Cassie.

She smiled and flicked her wrist. "It was mostly done.

And Melody went to sleep while I was listening at the door."

Nate poured tea in my cup and his, then set down the pot in front of Lucas. "First thing is to lock up as much as we can."

Lucas filled two cups and handed one to Cassie. "I'll do that. I'll grab a padlock from the tack room before I go home." He chuckled. "Forgot I was staying here. I'll lock my cabin, too."

"Good thinking," Nate said.

Cassie held her teacup in both hands. "Should we hire someone to stand guard?"

Nate rubbed his chin and glanced at the ceiling. "Not sure. Maybe we should pray first."

I stifled an impatient sigh. My reticence wouldn't stop them. At least, he stayed in his chair instead of kneeling like he used to. Maybe he was feeling his age, though he was only thirty-one. All three of them took turns praying for direction, guidance, and safety for all of us. Lucas also prayed for Allison to see the truth and for all of them to come to know Jesus. I held my breath, lest he pray that for me, but he didn't. Why not?

When they finished, I exhaled, relieved and grateful they hadn't expected me to pray. I respected their faith, and they respected my lack of it.

They each stared straight ahead. Apparently, they hadn't heard any answers to their prayers. "Well, first thing is we need to protect the remote. Any ideas where to keep it?"

"Do you have it?" Nate asked.

I tapped my pocket and nodded.

Lucas smirked but then frowned. "You lied to them just now?"

I lifted my chin. "Yes! And I'd do it again."

"All right." Cassie patted the air in front of her. "You could give it to Uncle Ed."

"Jenny's too close to him. That's why I didn't give it to him in the first place." One reason.

Nate slapped his hands on the table. "I think we should hold off. Meet back here for breakfast tomorrow and make plans then."

Cassie smiled. "You always did think better in the morning."

Lucas yawned. "Me, too."

I slumped against my chair. Not being a morning person, I planned to write down my ideas tonight and bring them tomorrow.

"In the meantime." Cassie turned her head toward me. "Why don't you hide the remote somewhere in your room?"

"I will, when I go up." I picked up a cake.

Lucas flashed a smile and joined me, eating his cake in one bite and licking his lips. "Mighty fine, Miss Cassie."

Nate laughed. "That's because Aunt Mattie brought them."

Cassie crossed her eyes and stuck out her tongue.

Nate laughed harder, and Cassie dissolved into giggles.

How could they act so silly at a time like this?

~

Cassie served eggs and sausage to Nate and Lucas, while I carried breakfast plates for Cassie and me.

After saying a quick blessing, Nate rubbed his hands together. "I had a great idea this morning."

Lucas swallowed his first bite. "So did I."

Nate pointed his fork at Lucas. "You first, then."

Lucas set his fork on his plate. "We let it be known, through Jenny, that Lydia plans to stay until the day after Thanksgiving. We'll let Jenny overhear us mention details of what time and place she'll leave from. They'll come to us."

"And we'll be ready." Nate nodded and smiled.

I clenched my jaw. "Why can't I go earlier?"

Cassie leaned over and covered my hand with hers. "Sorry, honey, but your ma already told Jenny you'd be staying until then."

I groaned. Jenny knew how much power Ma wielded.

"It'll be good, though. It'll give us time...." Lucas turned to Nate. "What was your brilliant idea?"

"Oh, it's about the remote." Nate eyed each one of us, a huge grin on his face. "We don't hide it in one place. Establish a rotation and pass it from person to person." He sipped his tea.

"Isn't that risky?" I furrowed my brow. "What if they follow us around?"

Nate set down his cup. "We'll pass it at family gatherings. When Jenny isn't there, of course."

My right hand tightened around the remote in my pocket. How could I let go of my only way home? I squared my shoulders. "I'd feel better keeping it on me."

Nate closed his eyes for a moment, then peered into mine. "This is for your protection. What if one of them finds you alone?"

I leaned forward. "And what if they do that when it's my day to carry it? Or Cassie, when it's her day?"

Nate and Lucas exchanged a glance. Nate cleared his throat. "That's why my original idea was to pass it between

Lucas, your pa, and me." He held up a hand. "But I knew that wouldn't fly. This way, it minimizes the risk."

Lucas nodded. "And on your days and Miss Cassie's, we'll keep an extra eye on each of you."

Once Nate's protective instincts were activated, nothing could change his mind. I suspected the same was true with Lucas. I blew out a breath. "Maybe. It's only going to be passed between the four of us, right?"

"And your pa," Nate said.

I shook my head. "I don't think that's a good idea. Jenny lives there." I sat up straight. "But we could make them think Pa has it. He has a couple of fakes that look real." And one that he might be able to make work. I wasn't sure I liked that idea, but I'd get more information from him later.

"It's settled. Pass the remote to Lucas sometime today, then tomorrow he can pass it to Cassie, and her to me the next day, and so on." Nate pressed his palms to the table and nodded, meeting adjourned.

He and Lucas attacked their plates with gusto, while I exchanged a questioning glance with Cassie.

She cleared her throat. "What about other preparations? You kept talking about time to get ready."

"Oh, well." Nate stopped shoveling food and glanced at Lucas.

"Uh, we've got it covered." Lucas studied his near-empty plate.

I pursed my lips. "So, what is the place and time to be leaked? At least tell me that."

Nate and Lucas took twenty seconds to clean their plates and then sat up straight.

"Okay, just so everyone is on the same page." Nate

pointed from Lucas to himself. "We'll leak that Lydia will call the time machine behind the carriage house at noon the day after Thanksgiving." He peered at me. "Unless there's a better place for it to show up in your time."

I rested my chin on my fist, elbow on the table. That would be on the B&B property but not visible from the house. "It's better than the field where Todd's house will be. You'll make sure those three are on it with me, and Jenny stays here, right?"

"Wait!" Cassie raised her hand and eyed me. "Won't it take two trips?"

I slumped in my chair. "The three-person limit."

"Could Todd have changed it?" Nate asked.

"No. He was resistant to even reactivating it. Allison did that." I snapped my fingers. "I doubt Allison knows about the three-person limit, though. She only had three."

Nate focused on me. "So, we keep to the plan, for now. And at that time, you'll have to make two trips or send someone ahead."

~

The next afternoon, on my way to Ma's, I wrapped my shawl around me tightly as the wind picked up. "Pa." I opened the barn door, hoping he was in his shop out back.

"Here," he called out. "Working on the steam-powered mill."

That meant Caleb was probably with him, and I wouldn't be able to ask about the remote. Could the machine be modified to allow four people? No, it was limited by space. Three was a challenge.

I trudged through the barn and into the shop. Caleb

stood next to Pa, his face shining with eagerness. Maybe staying in this time period would be good for him. He might be an inventor. I scrunched my face. I hadn't heard of any Caleb Gardener in my time, but I didn't know the name of everyone who invented something important.

Caleb greeted me and launched into a lengthy and animated account of how far along they were with the steam-powered motor for the mill.

I exchanged smiles with Pa.

When he could get a word in, Pa set Caleb to work and ushered me out a side door and several yards away. "Lydia, I've been wanting to talk to you."

"Have you tested the remote yet?" I whispered.

"No, but I've charged the battery in it. It wasn't easy to find a patch of sunlight that was hidden enough for nobody to find the charger." He walked through a patch of woods into a clearing. The solar power charger and the remote lay on a tree stump.

"Could we try it now?" I reached for it with a shaky hand.

He took a deep breath. "I'd rather Caleb weren't so close, but—"

"Wait." I thrust my hand up. "It won't work. The only remote that will call the machine is the last one used. Mine."

"Where is it?"

I had to stop and think whose day it was, and we'd only started passing it yesterday. "Lucas has it right now, unless he's already passed it to Cassie." I explained the plan to Pa.

"Not a bad idea." He picked up the remote and disconnected it from the charger. It had a display, so it looked more real than his other one. "This could still work."

He set it to retrieve and pushed the GO button.

I cringed, but nothing happened.

"Hmm." Pa showed me the display, which read: Need location for retrieval.

"Does that mean this could work?" My head spun. Could we figure out the exact location? I held out my palm. "Wait. We already have a working remote that'll call the time machine to it."

Pa nodded, his attention focused on the display. "I'd feel better if we had a contingency plan. Where was the machine when you traveled?"

I pressed my fingers to my temples. "What are you not telling me?"

He rested his hand on my shoulder and peered into my eyes. "Please trust me."

I pursed my lips. Probably Ma had one of her feelings, and Pa was acting on it.

He stepped back. "Well, where was the machine when you left 2020?"

I squinted at the sky, searching my memory. It had been an eventful week. "Todd's garage."

He rubbed his goatee. "I think we'll need latitude and longitude. I have a map and surveyor's gear."

"I'm not sure I could tell you exactly where Todd's garage is, though. It's somewhere in the field off the main road to Nate's."

He held his finger up and checked the remote. "I have another idea. It'll take a while, because I'm going to have to charge this thing every time we use it."

I shook my head. "What are you talking about?"

"We could go over to where Todd's house will be and

try to use the remote from there. We could estimate and then keep moving until we find it."

I waved my arms out to my sides. "It's right out in the open."

"Yeah." He paced in front of the stump. "We might be able to find times when Jenny and your friends are distracted."

"They're not my friends." I turned on my heel and strode through the copse of trees.

Each day, it looked more like I would be going home by myself, but how could I leave three people who belonged in the twenty-first century in the nineteenth? That would be more than irresponsible. At least with me in the future and Jenny back here, there had been balance.

I snapped my fingers. Balance. Was that the key? And how could I achieve that? My spirits soared and then immediately deflated.

There hadn't been balance, not with Ed and Cassie here. For someone who'd experienced time-travel in both directions, I was still clueless about how it worked.

CHAPTER NINETEEN

The next morning, as I finished my fried eggs, the back door creaked open.

Cassie gasped. Nate jumped out of his seat, pushing it backward. Lucas caught Nate's chair, righted it, and took his seat across from me.

Pa sauntered in, and all four of us let out a breath.

"Please announce yourself, Uncle Ed." Nate offered Pa the empty chair next to me. "We're all a bit on edge."

"I guess so." Pa pulled out the chair and sat. "I can't blame you, after Tuesday." He glanced at Melody, who sat in Cassie's lap, eating and spitting runny rice.

"What's up?" Nate resumed his seat at the head of the table.

Pa turned to me. "Your ma took Jenny to a quilting bee at Mrs. Hodges'. I thought you and I could do some experimenting."

Nate leaned forward. "What kind of experimenting?"

"You didn't tell them?" Pa glanced around the table and then faced me.

"We hadn't discussed it, so I wasn't sure you wanted me to." I didn't want them to know about the possible second remote, but I wasn't sure why. Pa would probably tell them, anyway. "You want to try it out now?" I raised an eyebrow. "Actually, this is probably a good time. Cassie might be able to help pinpoint the location."

"Location of what?" Cassie asked.

Pa pulled a toothpick out of his overalls pocket. "Todd's garage. I found another remote that we tried the other day. It wanted a location."

"So, you think if we take it to the spot where the machine is in the future, it might work?" Cassie had always caught on quickly. Well, she'd been an engineer.

"Yeah, but I'm not sure I could find where Todd's garage was. When I landed the second time, I hurried to the house without marking the location." I looked at Cassie, who exchanged a glance with Nate.

"When I traveled, the machine was in the room over the garage." Cassie peered at me. "You probably landed where I landed."

"Maybe between the two of us, we can pinpoint it better." I pressed my fingers on the table. "Do you remember exactly where that was?"

Cassie nodded and wiped Melody's face. "I think so."

"Let's go!" Pa stuck the toothpick in the corner of his mouth as he stood, then walked to Cassie and reached out for Melody.

"I'll take the baby." Nate got there first and grasped the baby in one arm. Melody smiled up at him and wrapped her chubby arm around his muscled one. Instead of nestling into his shoulder, she held her head up and remained bright-eyed as if she knew she was about to go on an adventure.

We marched down the front walkway to the dirt road

that ended in front of the house, then walked down what would in my time be about three houses and veered left into a field. We were pretty far off the road when Cassie stopped and peered at their house. She took a few strides to the side and then a couple of steps back.

"I think this is where I landed." She used her hand as a visor. "I remember the house appearing just like that." She pointed at the front porch.

Pa rubbed his hands together and pulled out the remote. It registered as fully charged.

He pushed the GO button.

All five of us waited in silence. About a minute later, Pa sighed and showed us the remote. It held the same message as yesterday.

"Well, of course it wouldn't work on the first try." Nate nodded at Cassie and then at me. "Could the time machine have been moved?"

Cassie squinted. "Lydia, what part of the garage was it in?"

I shrugged. "The back, near the kitchen door."

"It was next to the window at the front of the house when I used it."

My eyes widened.

"How big was the…garage?" Lucas asked.

I shrugged. "I was never good with spatial measurements."

Cassie bit her lower lip and then paced about ten strides away from the road. "Maybe right here?"

"That's a good estimate." Pa must be thinking back thirty-three years.

"Which side of the room?" Nate asked.

I looked at Cassie. "The machine was in the corner farthest away from the kitchen door."

"Yep. It was in the front corner of the room when I used it. This should be about right."

Pa glanced at the display. "We'll mark it, and then I'll have to charge it again."

Cassie touched his arm. "How are you doing that?"

Pa's face lit up as he produced the charger from his trousers pocket. "Solar power charger." He plugged the remote into it. "Unfortunately, as cloudy as it is, it'll probably take all day."

"Hmm." Nate scratched his chin. "We need to put it somewhere nobody will see it."

It was Cassie's turn to light up. "I know the perfect place. My planter box outside the small parlor window. It gets direct sunlight, and we could tuck it inside so nobody would see it."

Nate looked at Pa. "Try again tomorrow?"

Pa nodded. "If we can keep Jenny occupied. I'll come over as soon as I can in the morning." He hurried across the field, and the rest of us trooped after him.

He placed the charger and remote inside the flower box and squinted at the sun. "It should get sunlight until mid to late afternoon, anyway. Should be enough."

Nate shifted Melody to his other arm. "What happens if we can retrieve the machine? Can we send it back without taking someone to test it?"

I shrugged at Pa. It seemed neither of us had thought of that. "I'll flip through the menu on the remote," Pa said.

Lucas pulled out my remote and handed it to me. The battery on mine had stayed charged so far. I hit the menu button, and an LCD menu appeared. The arrow key on the remote allowed me to scroll through. "It looks like you can with this one." I showed Pa, who bent over to read it.

"Before we use mine, I'll check." Pa straightened up.

"Worse comes to worst, we send one of us to the future and then right back." Lucas rubbed his stubbly chin.

Cassie snorted. "Spoken by someone who hasn't time-traveled."

I grimaced. "Yes. It's not something you want to do often. Believe me."

Lucas pressed his lips together.

Nate handed Melody to Cassie. "On that note, we have work to do today."

"You need me to stay around?" Pa asked.

"Nah." Nate nodded toward the barn. "We'll stay close to home for the next few days."

Pa clapped Nate on the shoulder. "Good man."

As everyone dispersed, I wandered around the field. Why had Nate and Cassie jumped on the bandwagon with this second remote? What was I missing? I slapped my forehead. If Pa insisted on testing his remote, I could make sure the next time, the machine would be in the correct spot.

I scrolled through the remote's menu until I found an option to retrieve it without changing coordinates. I backed up as the mist rolled in. When the machine appeared, my jaw relaxed. I hadn't realized I'd been clenching it. I moved our stone a couple of feet to mark the correct location and found the option to send the machine back. My finger hovered over the button. I could step on the machine and go home right now.

An image of Ma frowning and shaking her head invaded

my mind. My shoulders drooped. I needed to say goodbye before I left. Not only that. She'd be disappointed that I'd stranded three people here. I sent the machine back to the location Todd was monitoring. Would Todd be waiting for me? What would he do when I didn't show up? He'd better stick to our plan and check the hall closet. I'd leave a note now before I forgot.

~

I stood at the worktable in the kitchen, kneading bread dough. My hands worked as if I'd last done it yesterday instead of over ten years ago. Muscle memory allowed my mind to roam into territory I wished it would stay away from. First and foremost, I worried that Pa hadn't been able to distract Jenny. It was now mid-morning, and he'd yet to come and test his remote. Also, I worried that one of us would get anxious and test it without Pa. Me, for instance. Why, though? I had one that worked. Had Pa's enthusiasm rubbed off on me? I'd wait. Pa wanted to be in on it, and with me returning to the future in less than a week, the last thing I wanted to do was disappoint him.

I sighed as I slapped the dough into a rectangular shape and dropped it into the loaf pan.

"Worried?" Cassie carried Melody in and placed her in a padded basket at the other end of the worktable.

"Just anxious to test Pa's remote." I glanced at the door. "Wondering what's keeping him."

She raised her eyebrows, picked up the loaf pan, and headed to the wood stove. "Well, I hope he waits a while longer. Until I get this baked."

I chuckled. "You can always stay here and keep an eye

on the bread."

She placed the bread in the oven and gave me the evil eye. "Right."

I laughed again. "Do you ever think about going back?"

"You mean forward?" She showed me her wry smile.

"Yeah, I guess I do."

She took a deep breath and let it out slowly. "Sometimes. But I'm content here." She ambled to the table and kissed Melody on the top of the head. The baby sighed in her sleep. "When I get frustrated, I pray about it. So far, I feel I'm supposed to stay." She gave me a pointed look. "What about you? Are you thinking of staying?"

"Not for an instant." I stuck my chin up, chest out. "Don't get me wrong. I'm glad I had this chance to visit, but I don't belong here."

She leaned closer. "You were born here."

I stared back at her. "And you weren't."

She nodded and tilted her head. "What about Lucas?"

I clenched my jaw. "What about Lucas?"

She smiled. "I can tell you two have feelings for each other."

"Ha." I rolled my eyes. "No. We've only known each other, what? A week?" I picked up a rag and wiped down the table.

"Mm hmm." Cassie sidled over to the sink in the corner.

I tossed a glance over my shoulder. "I'll admit he's easy on the eye. He's also a good man, the type of person I'll look for. Is that what you want to hear?"

"And I can tell he's interested in you." She kept her back turned and picked up a dish to wash.

I scoffed. "He hasn't given me any indication he's

attracted to me."

"He moved in here to help protect you."

"To protect Melody." I shook my head and scrubbed harder, even though the table was already clean.

She drew out a chuckle. "You don't want to decide whether to stay here or go back."

"I've already decided." I slapped the rag onto a drying rack. "He is geographically unsuitable."

She laughed out loud. "I think you mean, chronologically unsuitable."

"Whatever." I strode to the door and leaned out, hoping Pa would show up. Anything to keep me from thinking about Lucas. He was the last thing I needed right now. It had only been a little over a week since I'd broken up with Austin, though that had been on the rocks for months. Still, even if Lucas was in the right time period, I didn't need a romantic interest now. I needed to get those three rogues back to their correct time and find a good job and a place to live. It was time to start thinking for myself.

"Hey, Miss Lydia." Lucas waved from the edge of the walkway. "Have you seen Ed yet?"

A smile escaped as I shook my head and stepped onto the boards. Why couldn't I keep from smiling when Lucas was nearby?

He took off his wide-brimmed hat and clutched it in his hands as if he needed something to do with them. "Well, I'll do my best to keep Nate from testing the remote." His face lit with a cute, shy smile.

I laughed, and he joined me. "That eager, is he?"

"Yes, ma'am. I can't deny that I am, too." He waved his hat at me and put it back on. "We'll stay close. Probably in the barn." He sauntered off.

"I'll make sure someone comes to get you when Pa shows up," I called.

I turned back toward the kitchen.

"Mm hmm." Cassie carried Melody to me, wearing a knowing smile. "Not attracted at all."

"Oh, hush." I pursed my lips and walked around her into the kitchen in search of something to do.

Cassie chuckled again, and Melody laughed.

Great! Even the baby seemed to read my expressions. Why had I agreed to stay until Friday? This week couldn't be over soon enough.

CHAPTER TWENTY

Nate looked up after saying grace and exchanged a nervous glance with Cassie, then Lucas.

"I'm sure Uncle Ed is fine." Cassie fed Melody a spoonful of sweet potato, but the baby spit it out.

Lucas peered at Nate, his fork still next to his plate. "I can go check on him."

"After dinner." Nate picked up his fork, but let it hover in the air. "Wish I'd gone before."

I didn't have an appetite, either, but this was ridiculous. We either needed to eat or go find Pa. I shoved back from the table.

Nate stood and slid in front of me. "We'll give him a little more time." He sat and bobbed his head toward my chair.

I took a deep breath and scooted my chair under the table, but I wasn't sure I could eat.

Lucas and Nate shoveled in their food as usual.

Cassie chuckled and took a bite of her dinner. Melody gazed at her pa, sweet potato dribbling down her chin.

Before I had finished half of my chicken and dumplings, Nate pushed back from the table. "We can have dessert later."

Lucas stood, and they both hurried out the back door.

"That's if I serve dessert," Cassie called. "They must be eager, putting off apple pie."

I smiled and picked up my half-full plate.

Cassie laid a hand on my arm. "If you don't want the rest, at least keep me company while I finish. Please?"

"Okay." I pushed a dumpling around on my plate, but I couldn't eat any more. "Any idea what's kept Pa?"

Cassie chewed and swallowed. "No."

Horses' hooves approached. I jumped up and ran over to peek out. "It's Pa!" I trotted through the pantry and mudroom out the back door, just in time to see Nate and Lucas running from the barn as Pa reined in Ginger and hopped off.

"Came as soon as I could. Would have gotten a message to you, but the Jones boys were all busy this morning. Mattie had me and Jenny occupied with Thanksgiving plans. She's taken Jenny to town now."

Nate stepped up behind Pa. "We were about to come check on you."

Pa jumped. "Good thing you didn't. 'Twould have been out of the ordinary." Pa tied his horse to the post near the walkway and headed for the window box on the parlor window to retrieve the remote.

All four of us followed, five if you include Melody. Nate took her from her mother and carried her in one arm.

Pa picked up the remote and pressed the ON button. "All charged!" He marched off to the spot I'd marked yesterday and glanced around the open field.

"Well, what are you waiting for?" I hoped nobody

noticed the slight change in the location of the rock.

We caught up to him and circled the marker.

Pa pointed the remote at us. "You might want to stay back a ways. Wouldn't want the machine to pop in on top of one of you."

We backed up a couple of steps, but I wasn't worried. The mist would give us enough warning to get out of the way.

Pa closed his eyes, mumbled what I thought might be a prayer, and then pushed the button. Nothing happened. "We'll have to try—"

I hopped backward as a thick mist rolled in.

Cassie gasped. "I've never seen it from this direction."

When the mist cleared, Todd's machine stood a few feet from Pa. He reached out and folded his hand over the rail next to him.

Lucas approached, his face blanched, and his mouth wide open. "You know, I believed you." He stared at the stainless-steel platform about the size and shape of a treadmill with a railing on either side and a display at one end. "But I didn't really think. . ."

Nate smiled and clapped him on the back. "I understand. I knew Cassie and Pa were from the future, but it didn't seem real until I saw that machine."

"And saw Todd and Lydia leave on it." Cassie draped her hand over his shoulder.

Pa took a deep breath and held up the remote. "Okay, so we know this will call it if we need a backup. I'll send it back now." He pushed a button on the remote.

The machine stayed solid.

"What's going on?" I looked over his shoulder but

couldn't read the controller display.

"Not sure." Pa pushed a button again. Nothing.

I cleared my dry throat. "What does it say?"

He showed me the display. It wanted a time destination.

"Put in the minute after you called it." I tapped my heel.

"I did that." He pushed another button. "Oh, no."

"What?" Nate rushed over.

Pa groaned. "It wants an approximate weight."

"So?" Cassie said.

Pa stood up straight. "I think it means it won't go without taking someone."

"But we're not ready." I sounded whinier than I'd intended.

"It doesn't know that." Pa tapped his forehead.

"Put in zero," Lucas said.

Pa punched the number in. "Nope. We're going to have to send someone or something back." He picked up the rock.

"Wait." I hurried onto the platform and studied the display. An arrow pointed to a button on the screen's edge. When I pressed it, a message scrolled onto the screen. I read it aloud. "I modified this machine so you can't send it back without a person on it. Also, I've programmed a date and time when I know I'll be here. Don't override it, or you'll risk being discovered." My stomach roiled as I stepped off and traded confused glances with Pa and Nate. No way was I about to admit I'd sent this back empty. That had to be why Todd changed it. I lowered my head to hide my wince.

"We'll have to hide it." Nate lifted one end. "Lucas and I could move it." He looked at Pa. "It'll be easy, if we use that hand truck you made last year."

Pa glanced at each of us, the creases in his forehead

prominent. "Who has your remote, Lydia?"

"I do." Nate pulled it out of his pocket and handed it to Pa.

Pa switched it on, but it wouldn't even go to the menu. "I'm sorry." He frowned and handed my remote back to Nate. "I've messed things up. Now it might not work at all."

"Wait," Cassie said. "We can probably operate the machine manually now that it's here. I got here without a remote, and so did Richard and friends."

"Yeah, but that means we need to hide it well and keep a guard on it," Nate said.

"I'll go get the hand truck." Lucas trotted off.

"Where will we put it?" Nate turned to me. "Where in my house would it be safe to appear in your time? The carriage house?"

I shook my head. "Todd's cars are in there." The perfect place popped into my mind, almost with a light bulb over it. "The playroom. It's being used as an attic. Well, they're refurbishing it, but it's mostly storage right now. There's a large enough area in the center of the room near the window seat."

"What about the open stairway?" Cassie asked.

"They put up a door, and walled in the other half."

She scrunched her nose, and I nodded in agreement.

Nate shrugged. "It may not look great, but it's good for our purposes."

We circled the platform and waited for Lucas to return, as if we could shield it from view if anyone happened to approach. The others focused on the machine, but I glanced from the road out front to the trail in the back, jiggling my leg for what seemed an eternity. How would we explain if the Kellys came to visit?

My stomach started to settle when Lucas wheeled the hand truck over. Nate tilted the platform, and Lucas slid the hand truck under it.

When we made it to the back door, Cassie retreated into the kitchen with Melody, but I followed the men upstairs.

They rolled the machine to the staircase, and the three of them hefted it up the two flights and into the playroom. I scooted past them into the room and pointed out the best place to locate it. They set down the machine in the center of the room.

Pa stood and wiped his brow, breathing hard. "It was more awkward than heavy."

Lucas snickered. He hadn't broken a sweat.

Nate pivoted toward the front wall. "We might have to cover the window."

"That could generate attention." Lucas walked over and glanced out. "I'll run down and check if I can see anything." He trotted downstairs.

"Not many folks come in from the front anyway," Pa said.

Nate stood between the machine and the window. "Some do."

Allison and her crew had come in that way with the torch. Or had they? They probably came from the path and walked around to the front.

We stared at the machine until Lucas returned. "I could see there was something here, but couldn't tell what it was." He pointed at the stairway. "I think, if you slide it this way, it'll be fine."

Lucas and Nate muscled it about a foot closer to the

stairs.

I squinted from the top step and tried to remember if anything would be in the way. There shouldn't be unless Chantal had moved something or they started work on the room. I peered at Pa. "It's a bit of a risk."

Nate grimaced. "I can't think of anyplace better."

Lucas tapped the machine's rail. "We'll be able to protect it easier, here."

"I wish we had a door." Nate glanced at me. "How did they rig one?"

I stepped down one stair and stood to one side of the center. "I'm the half-wall. And there's a standard door here." I pointed to the empty space next to me.

Nate raked a hand through his hair. "If we do that, it'll be obvious to anyone who comes upstairs that we're hiding something."

"Agreed." I strode into the room.

"We need to keep Jenny or any of her crew from getting into this house." Pa flung his arm toward the stairwell. "Or at least from coming upstairs."

Nate addressed Lucas. "I think we need to keep the doors locked at all times."

I'd forgotten they had locks.

"Do you have enough keys?" Pa asked.

An image of modern keys popped into my head, but I replaced it with the skeleton keys they used.

"I have two." Nate grinned. "And Aunt Mattie has one."

Pa nodded. "That'll work. I'll get Mattie's and bring it here for Lydia."

Lucas passed me and headed downstairs. "Going back to work."

Pa, Nate, and I followed Lucas at a more leisurely pace. Having the time machine in the house made me nervous, but I wouldn't have to go find it or rely on a remote to call it. If everything worked out, I wouldn't have to ride it home by myself.

Pa stopped in the foyer. "Do you want me to send Mark up to help guard it?"

Nate rubbed his chin. "No. I don't want to draw any attention. I'm glad I already had Lucas move in."

"We could say it was because of the kidnapping." Pa grasped the front doorknob.

Nate squinted. "Just keep an eye on Jenny."

Pa opened the front door.

I tapped his shoulder. "Pa, why ya going out that way?"

He turned and grinned. "Gotta look up through the window myself."

Nate and I laughed, but we followed him outside. I made sure nobody was watching, and we all walked in front of the house and gazed up into the third-story dormer window. I kept moving backward, but never saw anything through that window.

Pa tipped his hat and strode around the house.

I turned to Nate. "Any idea why Ma insisted I stay until the day after Thanksgiving?"

He shrugged. "I know she has some kind of plan, but she won't even tell me."

"Which probably means, Pa doesn't know either." I sighed. Ma and Nate always had a close connection. In the timeline before Pa came back, Ma never married, nor did Nate, and they were the last survivors of the Bridger family.

An involuntary shudder passed through my body.

Nate draped an arm over my shoulder and escorted me to the door. "Try not to worry. I don't know what'll happen, but I'm pretty sure it'll turn out all right."

I studied our feet. "I wish I had that kind of faith."

"You could." His voice, though barely audible, still packed a punch.

I peered up into his face, understanding exactly what he meant. I just didn't feel ready. Didn't know if I ever would.

CHAPTER TWENTY-ONE

Sunday, after church, we congregated in Ma's dining room. Since Jenny hovered at Nate's end of the table, I took the seat next to Pa. Unfortunately, before dinner started, Ma asked to switch places with Jenny so she could help with Melody. That left me directly across from Jenny, something I'd been avoiding for the week and a half I'd been here.

Ma and Lera steered the conversation, with Simon and Pa chiming in once in a while. Cassie and Nate didn't say much, at least to the table at large. I felt content to eat the venison roast and potatoes and listen to the conversation. Jenny stayed unusually quiet, too, until Lera addressed her by name.

"Jenny, who were those three people you were talking to the other day?"

My ears perked up.

"What day?" Jenny looked at Lera, who sat to my right. "Where?"

Lera waved her fork. "On the road to our house, just before the main road. Early in the week. I thought I recognized their horses."

Had Ma put her up to this? Lera didn't appear to know the answer to her question or why the horses seemed familiar.

Jenny flicked her wrist and picked up her fork. "Oh, just some travelers asking directions."

Nate coughed, and Cassie stifled a giggle. Yeah, directions to the twenty-first century. We could've called Jenny out, but none of us wanted to let Simon and Lera know what was going on. That is, if they'd even believe it.

"Hmm." Lera leaned forward. "I was chasing after Simon Jr, and happened to be out there a good while. It normally doesn't take you that long to give directions."

Jenny dropped her fork. "Oh, well. They were missionaries looking for the Kelleys. You know how hard it is to get rid of them. Missionaries, I mean." She grimaced.

Lera flashed her signature sly smile. "I think I saw that same trio last week, too. Don't you think they'd have already found the Kelleys?"

Jenny squirmed and studied her food. "The first time, they were passing through. Maybe they came back to find the pastor?"

"That's odd," Ma said. "Did you know someone stole two of Nate's horses, but they turned up the same day the Kelleys took in that trio?"

Now, my eyes opened wide. What was Ma up to?

Jenny swallowed hard. "What does that have to do with anything?"

"You think they're the thieves?" Simon punched his fist into his hand. "I've had more than one chicken stolen. I thought it was a fox, one time. The other time, I saw a man running."

"I suppose they could be." Jenny leaned back and placed a hand over her heart. "I don't know why you're interrogating me about it."

I smiled and forced myself to relax against the back of my chair. "We aren't. Just asking since you're the one who talked to them."

She shook her head and stuffed a forkful of potatoes in her mouth.

Lera elbowed me, and when I made eye contact with her, she flashed me a conspiratorial grin. The last thing I wanted was to conspire with my former sister-in-law. I loved her, but she had a bit of a wild streak, and as far as I knew, she didn't believe in time travel. We thought she'd accepted that I was cousin Ellen, but now, I wasn't so sure. We'd been getting lax with my identity lately. Even Lucas called me Lydia.

I took a deep breath and plastered a smile on my face. Maybe Lera thought we were getting under Jenny's skin about her aiding and abetting thieves.

"I'll help clean up." I stood and picked up my plate and Pa's.

"I'll let you." Ma smiled and made a bumblebee sound as she held up a spoonful of potatoes to Melody, who sat on her lap.

"I'll help, too." Lera handed her younger son to Simon and stacked hers and Simon's dishes, then followed me out the door. Inside the detached kitchen, she deposited the dishes on the worktable, closed the door behind her, and leaned against it. "I'm not stupid. What's going on? You are Lydia, Mattie's youngest, right?"

My jaw dropped open, and I lowered my head to

conceal it. Too late.

"I knew it!" Lera's eyes gleamed as she lifted my chin. "You've grown. It's been longer in your time, hasn't it?"

A shaky laugh escaped my lips. "What are you talking about?"

She stood straight, hands on hips. "I know Cassie came here from the future. And you went there to heal from your injuries."

I cocked my head at her, my mouth hanging open.

One corner of her mouth quirked upward for a split second, then she pursed her lips and raised her hand. "I get it. You don't want any more people to know than necessary. I haven't told Simon."

"You don't think he suspects Jenny?" I clamped my mouth shut.

"He thinks she's a seer." Her face lit up in triumph, and she clapped her hands together. "She's from your time. That's how she knew what to invest in."

I groaned and slumped into a chair.

"Oh, don't do that. We need to go back in for more dishes." Lera tugged on my sleeve until I stood. "Better yet. You wash and put things away, and I'll bring things out." She picked up a wooden tray and strode back into the house.

I shook my head and walked to the stove to check the wash water we'd started heating before dinner. I never should have underestimated Lera. Cassie and Pa must not have realized how much Lera knew, or they would have told me. Wouldn't they?

~

We left Ma and Pa's house as early as was polite. When

we arrived at Nate and Cassie's, Nate unhitched the team, and Cassie carried Melody into the house.

I followed, but the open kitchen door caught my attention. Who was stealing from them now? "You'd better leave!" I rushed into the kitchen and stopped short.

Lucas sat at the table, his spoon hovering over a soup bowl. The rest of the pot simmered on the stove.

"I'm sorry." I placed my hand over my heart until my pulse slowed to normal.

He grinned. "No problem. I thought to go back to my place, but Cassie said I could eat the soup she had ready for supper."

"You could have come to dinner at Ma's."

"I didn't want to horn in on a family gathering." Lucas heaved a sigh. "I feel bad enough eating dinner every day with Nate and Cassie."

I tilted my head. "Why?"

"It makes me feel like an interloper." He slurped from the large soup spoon while I stood in front of the door, not sure what to do. "You can come in and keep me company, if you like. Leave the door open."

I hesitated. Half of me wanted to run so I wouldn't get attached to him, but the other half was eager to tell him about Jenny's reaction. "I guess I can stay for a few minutes." I took the seat opposite him.

"That's all it will take me to finish." His brown eyes twinkled as he smiled.

"You missed an interesting conversation."

He swallowed. "If it was with Jenny, I'll get over it." He dipped a piece of bread into the soup and took a bite.

I chuckled. "Is that why you didn't come to dinner?"

"One reason. What did I miss?"

"Lera asked her about the three strangers she saw her talking to. She looked a bit like a deer caught in the headlights."

He squinted at me.

"Oh, right. Headlights are bright lights on the front of a car."

He raised an eyebrow.

Of course, he wouldn't know what that was. I blew out a breath. "A car is like a carriage, but it's powered by a motor, instead of pulled by horses."

"Wow!" Lucas's eyes brightened. "I'd like to see that."

"You may. Cars will be around by the early nineteen hundreds." I had a feeling he was hinting about time-traveling, but I wasn't going there. No more time-travelers under my watch. Now I understood how Todd felt.

Lucas set his spoon in the empty bowl and leaned toward me. "Lera's question startled Jenny?"

"Yep. It was almost funny." I leaned back to give myself distance from his stare. "She tried to pass it off as giving directions."

"Of course she would." He puckered his lips and averted his gaze. "I might go wandering around this afternoon. Maybe happen to pass the Kelleys' old cabin."

I pressed my palms onto the table. "Where Richard and Brian are staying?"

He nodded. "That's the one."

"It's your day off. Don't do this on my account."

He stood, picked up his bowl, and walked to the sink. "I like to go riding on my day off. Normally, I go to the creek and pray." He washed his bowl with the water Cassie had left from breakfast, then glanced over his shoulder. "Would you like to come with me?"

"Yes." Only to look for Brian and Richard. If I could talk to them alone, I might be able to take the two of them out of here. "But just the riding part."

"Lucas, you don't have to do your dishes." Cassie stood in the doorway, holding Melody. "We'll get them after supper. It's bad enough having to eat the same soup for both meals."

"No." Lucas dried his bowl. "That's mighty fine venison soup, Miss Cassie."

Cassie's face broke into a huge smile. She didn't get many compliments on her cooking. At least she hadn't when I'd been here. "Thank you, Lucas." She fixed her gaze on me. "Lydia, can you come with me? I need help changing Melody."

"Uh." I turned to Lucas.

"I can wait a while," he said.

Cassie raised her eyebrows and headed back into the house. I followed. When we reached the small parlor, Cassie motioned for me to sit in a wingback chair while she sat on the sofa. "You and Lucas?"

"We're going riding this afternoon. I'm hoping to spot Brian or Richard without Allison. That's all."

She flashed a knowing smile as she patted Melody's back against her shoulder.

"I thought you needed to change her."

"I already did." Her smile widened.

I groaned. "What did you want to talk to me about?"

Cassie shifted Melody to her other shoulder. "I'm curious. What did Lera want?"

"She's never been subtle, has she?"

Cassie laughed. "Lera is a lot of things, but subtle isn't one of them. Did she know more about the trio than she let on?"

I took a deep breath and let it out. Might as well get it over with. "Only that they're time-travelers. And she knows you and Jenny are, too. Not sure she knows about Pa."

Cassie winced.

My breath caught. "Wait. You knew?"

She sighed. "Your pa and I didn't think it was something you needed to know. We never talk about it with Lera."

I put my hands on my hips. "How did she find out?"

"Well, for someone who is still learning how to read, Lera isn't dumb."

I'd forgotten Lera couldn't read. She'd hidden it well, and Cassie was the one who'd figured it out. "Are you teaching her?"

She grinned and bounced Melody on her knee. "Mm hmm. Well, I taught her along with Caleb. It was good motivation for him. Lera and Caleb can read at a fifth-grade level, which is average even for the twenty-first century."

My shoulders sagged. "I know." Maybe I'd volunteer as a reading tutor after I established myself in a new job. Before I could add meaning to my life, I needed to get the trio back to the right century. Why had I agreed to wait until Friday?

~

When I entered the barn, Lucas had Codger bridled and saddled, and had begun saddling Mr. Ed for me.

"So." Lucas buckled the saddle under Mr. Ed. "Are you going to tell me more about the future?"

"No." I crossed my arms over my chest.

"Why not?" He handed me Mr. Ed's reins.

"Because it's not fair, to you or anyone else, to know what's coming."

He waved his arm as he spoke. "I meant about everyday things. Like cars and such."

"I shouldn't have told you that." I placed my left foot in the leather stirrup and let him help me onto Mr. Ed, thankful I'd changed into Cassie's riding breeches.

He mounted Codger and looked at me. "Which way do you think we should go?"

"Do you know where the Kelleys' cabin is?"

He nodded. "I'd like to find their original hideout first, then we'll go there."

"Why? They moved four days ago at the latest."

Lucas squinted into the sun. "That move was quick. They could've left something behind. And they might wander back there."

I wasn't convinced, but the more time I spent riding, the more chances I'd have of catching Brian by himself. "Do you have an idea where the hideout was?"

"I might." He rode Codger toward the front of the house.

I followed, coming up beside him. "Are you going to tell me where we're going?"

He grinned. "It wouldn't be fair to you or everyone else to know what's coming in the future."

"Not the same thing, and you know it." I shook my head and tried not to smile.

We walked the horses in silence for a while.

"All right. I thought we should head to Highland's place."

How could I have forgotten? Ma's little spies had spotted them in a barn near there.

Lucas picked up speed and headed for the main road.

"Not taking the shortcut?" I called.

"Thought we'd take that on the way back."

I squeezed my heels into Mr. Ed's flanks, and he broke into a trot. Lucas was taking it easy, probably to keep from missing anything, since we were on the hunt. How I wish we were hunting game and not people. I concentrated on what we were doing and tried not to let my mind wander. The rhythm of Mr. Ed's gait, the breeze on my face, and the earthy odor from a nearby stream kept me grounded in the present. In my peripheral vision, fields and trees were not as distant as they would be in the future.

Lucas detoured around the town and slowed when we rejoined the main road near the turnoff to Highland's place. "Someone's been here recently." He pointed to wheel tracks in the mud.

"Probably Lera and Simon on their way home from Ma's." I bobbed my head toward the main road. "Simon complained of his chickens being stolen, so—"

"The hideout could be close." Lucas gazed across the road and ahead. "I'm not sure what's up that way. Could it be a barn?"

I veered in the direction he pointed. Lucas trotted ahead of me and slowed when we came to a slight break in the tree line. He started in, holding branches for me like he did when we'd gone to visit the Oldhams. After about half an hour, he stopped and held his open hand out to me.

I listened, and in addition to the birds chirping, small animals skittering, and a gurgling stream, I heard a low-pitched murmur. I caught my breath. Was that a voice?

Lucas touched his finger to his lips. We stayed as still as possible on horseback. It was a voice, but only one, and it sounded like it was mumbling. Lucas slid off the saddle and tiptoed toward the sound. He took another step, then stopped behind a tree and peered around it.

Too bad I wouldn't be able to get down as quietly as he had, despite the riding breeches.

Lucas strode away from the tree and out of sight. I craned my neck to see, but too many trees stood in my way. My heart pounded and my shoulders tensed. I'd give Lucas five minutes.

After about thirty seconds, I dismounted, grabbed both Mr. Ed's and Codger's reins, tied them to some trees, then ran in the direction Lucas had gone. When I entered the clearing, Lucas was talking to a grizzled old man.

"Can you tell me the last time you saw them?" Lucas asked.

The man lifted his head and rubbed his scraggly gray beard between a gnarled thumb and forefinger. "I reckon it was less than a week ago. I shooed them over yonder." He pointed across the clearing behind his shack.

"Thank you." Lucas glanced at me. "May we ride through here?"

"Of course. And if you find them, scare them off farther. They're stealing my game."

"They're hunting?" I leaned forward, eyes wide.

"No!" The man waved his hands toward a lean-to several yards from the shack. "They stole game I'd killed. After I'd skinned it."

I exhaled. "That makes more sense."

"City folks." The guy spit and stamped on the ground.

"Yes." Lucas strode to the horses, and I followed.

We rode through the clearing and down a path behind the shack. This woodland was thicker than the last, and I feared we'd get lost. "I hope you have a better sense of direction than I do."

Lucas glanced back at me with a smile. "I have a compass."

"That's good to know." Not that I knew how to use one. I'd have to trust him for that.

We'd ridden through thick forest for about ten minutes when we came to a small clearing with a lean-to made of pine boughs against the only remaining wall of a dilapidated structure. Small stones encircled the remnants of a fire.

Lucas slipped out of his saddle, tied Codger to a tree, and approached me.

I slid into his arms, feeling a rush when his hands circled my waist, but disappointment when my feet touched the ground and he stepped away.

Lucas pointed to a piece of stationery skewered on a stick near the lean-to. "This could be where they were staying."

"That's Ma's stationery." Instead of pulling it off, I picked up the stick and read the note. "Meet me at dawn tomorrow. Same place." Lucas held out his hand, and I gave it to him. "This was their hideout. It's probably Jenny's handwriting. It's not Ma's."

He looked up at me from the note, his brow furrowed. "Why would you think it was?"

I smirked. "Wouldn't put it past Ma to try and flush them out."

He nodded. "Yeah. I've got the feeling she's up to something regarding these travelers."

"I'd be surprised if she wasn't." Memories of Ma flooded into my mind. "She's probably trying to figure out how to get them saved."

He guffawed. "That she is." He sobered and peered at me. "You know she feels she failed you. She told me that."

I scoffed. "Lord knows she tried. It's just that... I don't know." I let my hands fall to my side and wandered around the small clearing.

"It doesn't make sense?"

I whirled to face him. "Yes! That's it." But a niggling fear prickled my skin. Was it really?

"Does time travel make sense?"

I snorted. "Of course not."

"Does all of this?" He swept his hand across the sky. "Does all this coming into existence by itself make sense?" He flexed his hand into a fist, then opened it. "Does the complexity of our bodies make sense?"

I pursed my lips and folded my arms across my chest. "You're on a roll, aren't you?"

He chuckled. "You see. I felt the same way you do." He raised one hand. "Well, maybe not the same, but similar. I just didn't believe in fairy tales."

"Exactly. That's what the whole Jesus thing sounds like!" I dropped my hands to my sides and looked up at him.

His gaze pierced mine. "Your Ma started asking me about all these things I've taken for granted. And she told me about how Jesus had changed her life and Ed's. And Nate's, and Cassie's."

I pivoted away, wrapping my arms around my waist.

He gently placed a hand on my shoulder. "You grew up with her and witnessed the change in Cassie at least, and still, you won't believe?"

"It's not that I won't." I broke away from him. "I can't."

"Mm hmm." He stayed quiet, and I snuck a peek to see him poking through the few objects under the lean-to and around the area.

I ambled over to him. "This was mighty rough living for them."

"This would be rough living for me." Lucas slid the note off the stick.

Thankfully, he must have decided to let the evangelism rest. I have to admit, it sounded more plausible coming from him than from Ma. Why was that?

Lucas pocketed the stationery and dropped the stick. "We'd better get going before it gets dark." He strode toward the woods where we'd left our horses.

"What about going to the Kelleys' cabin?"

He glanced up at the sky and picked up his pace. "Storm's coming. We need to hurry. Should have brought a lantern. Looks like we're taking the main roads back."

I sighed. No point in trying to change his mind. "Unless we can make it to the shortcut before it starts to get dark." I followed him and let him help me up onto Mr. Ed. Lucas untied the horses, mounted Codger, and then led the way back to the old-timer's shack.

The old man waved. "See 'em?"

"No, but we found where they were staying," Lucas said. "I don't think they'll be back."

"If they steal anything else, I might go smoke them out." The man grunted and sat on a crate.

Lucas pulled his compass out and checked it before we rode off. If I had come out here on my own, I probably wouldn't have made it back to Cassie and Nate's tonight. With or without the trio, I planned to travel home by the end of the week.

CHAPTER TWENTY-TWO

When Cassie asked me to take some bread and pies over to Lera's for Thanksgiving tomorrow, I jumped at the chance. For three days, I'd been stuck babysitting and doing household chores while Cassie baked for the feast at Lera's. Nate had sent Lucas out each day searching for Richard or Brian, but he hadn't seen them without Allison or one of the Kelleys.

Now, Lucas harnessed Lucy to the small carriage while Nate helped me load the goodies into it. Nate tucked the last pie behind the seat. "Lucas, accompany Lydia, will you?"

"I am perfectly capable of driving myself." I jumped onto the seat and grabbed Lucy's reins.

"I know that." Nate motioned for Lucas to climb up with me. "I just worry about those three attacking you."

I heaved a sigh. They wouldn't hurt me, but I didn't have the energy to convince him.

Lucas settled next to me and patted his pistol stuck in his waistband.

I glanced at it. "Do you really think you'll need that?"

"I hope not, but I like to be prepared." He waved at Nate as we started out. "Been carrying one most of the time of late. So has Nate."

"The kidnapping spooked him." It didn't need to be a question.

Lucas nodded. "Yes, ma'am."

I drove the carriage toward the shortcut.

He stayed quiet while I drove. I hit a few ruts and had a hard time keeping the horse going at a steady clip. Lucas hadn't spoken to me much since Sunday. Maybe he'd been sulking because I wouldn't fill him in on the future, but a peek at his handsome face indicated he wasn't so much sulking as contemplating. He had his brow furrowed, but not in a way that made him look mad. His open eyes and his chin tilted up made him appear alert. What was he thinking? I couldn't bring myself to ask. I hated it when people asked me that question. Besides, I didn't want to get to know him any more than I already had. I'd be leaving the day after tomorrow.

"Can you stop for a second?" Lucas pointed at a fallen tree.

I pulled on the reins, and the horse stopped. "Guess I can." I flashed a big, toothy grin.

He hopped off, holding his hand up to tell me to stay put. I scowled as he jogged to the tree, knelt, and inspected it. It wasn't a large tree, so anything could have happened, but we hadn't had any big storms lately, only gentle rain, the kind farmers love.

Lucas stood and scanned the area, then walked back to the carriage, his forehead more creased than before.

"What's up?"

"Don't know." He hopped on. "We'd better get going. Cassie will want you back soon."

I snapped the reins, probably harder than necessary. "Aren't you going to tell me what you found?"

"When I figure it out." He spoke in a neutral tone, contrasting with my irritation.

"Well, explain what you saw, and maybe I can help." I watched him out of my peripheral vision while trying to keep an eye on the path. Unless I was mistaken, we were close to the main road.

He rubbed his temple. "I'm pretty sure someone pulled that tree down. But I can't figure out why. It would have taken someone extremely strong or equipped with the right kind of tool."

I squinted. "An animal couldn't have done it?"

He shook his head. "I don't think so. Well, we do have bears, but I haven't seen or heard of any around lately." He rubbed the back of his neck. "Might be nothing. It's just that I felt a bit of a shiver when we approached it."

I narrowed my eyes. "Like a sixth sense or something? I didn't think you believed in stuff like that."

"You mean stuff you can't explain?"

"Yeah, the supernatural." We entered the main road, which was packed harder, and I sped Lucy up a little.

He grinned. "That would be you who doesn't believe in the supernatural. I believe in God and the Bible, which includes angels and demons, so yes, I believe in the supernatural."

"Oh." I couldn't think of anything else to say, and apparently, neither could he.

We stayed silent until we turned onto the tree-lined road leading to Lera's house. As always, it reminded me of Twelve Oaks from *Gone with the Wind*. The house used to be that grand, but not anymore. After the fire, they built a much simpler home.

"That tree." Lucas caught me by surprise. "It was about halfway between Nate's house and the main road, right?"

"Yes. Why?"

"Maybe they were trying to make a hideout there, or…" He pinched his chin. "I don't know. It's just strange. And the only strange people I know around here are those three."

"And Jenny." I lowered my voice. "And me."

"No." He said it quickly, then faced me and placed his hand on mine on top of the reins. Our eyes met. "*You* are not strange. Not to me."

I took a deep breath and focused on the road. "Well, I should be."

"Why?" He tilted his head toward me.

"Because I don't belong here." I tightened my hold on the reins.

"You were born here." His voice was soft.

"Yes, but I left. I spent ten years there. I belong there now. I always did. Pa told me I was born ahead of my time." I gasped as the revelation hit. This is the first time I understood what he meant. He knew I'd go to the future.

Lucas' eyes flashed. "What makes you think I belong here, then?"

My jaw dropped. "You're not saying?" I shook my head. "You wouldn't be asking me about the future if you were from there."

He tipped his head back and laughed. "You thought I was?" He laughed again. "No. I was born here, too." He pressed his lips together. "I don't feel like I belong here, though. I might want to go to the future."

"Okay." That was the last thing I'd ever expected. "You seem to fit in well here."

"Only because of Nate and Cassie." He lowered his head as we approached Lera's. "Before them, I didn't have anyone."

I hadn't thought of why he was there by himself. Hadn't wanted to. I stopped the horses near Lera's back door, but stayed in my seat and peered at him.

"I was the youngest son of five." He took his hat off and twirled it in his hands. "After my parents died, my family fell apart. My brothers divided the farm, and well, there wasn't much left for me. I decided to set out and find my own fortune."

"That was brave."

He sighed. "If it wasn't for Nate, I probably wouldn't be alive right now." He raised his index finger. "No. If it wasn't for God and Nate. But God also used Cassie and Miss Mattie to bring me to Himself."

I blinked, wanting to know more about Lucas but not God. "Why do you think you don't belong in this time period?"

"Lydia!" Lera bounded out of the house. "Just the person I need to see."

"I'll tell you later," Lucas whispered. I couldn't help but think he looked relieved at the interruption.

I hopped down and headed to the back of the carriage to get the baked goods.

Lera rushed over. "Don't unload the pies! We can't have Thanksgiving dinner here."

"What?" I gaped at her. "Does Ma know?"

"She sent word to me!" She flailed her arms.

I reared back. "That doesn't make sense."

Lera pointed to the youngest Jones boy as he mounted one of Pa's old horses. "Your ma said Cassie had agreed to host, and for you to take back the bread and pies I've already finished."

"What was the reason?" I had no idea what Ma had up her sleeve.

"She's too far behind with her cooking and wouldn't be able to get it all the way over here in time."

I scoffed. It couldn't be her real reason. "You'd think she'd have let Cassie know before I left."

Lera shrugged and strode to her kitchen. Lucas extended his arm out and waited for me to go in front of him, then he followed us into Lera's kitchen, where her cook set a fourth pie onto the worktable.

Lera motioned toward the cook. "Lydia, I don't think you've met Gayla, have you?"

"No, I haven't."

"Pleased to meet you, ma'am." The slim, middle-aged black woman curtsied.

"Same." I curtsied back.

Lera scowled but recovered quickly. "Well, let's get these loaded in your wagon."

Each of us, including Gayla, took a baked dish and walked out to the carriage. Lera wore an apron, so I assumed she'd done some of the work. Ma had told me they'd downsized their staff, only hiring a groundskeeper, a maid, and the cook in addition to the part-time nanny. They used to have at least twelve on staff, but then they'd had a much bigger house.

Gayla set down her dish and hurried back to the kitchen.

Lucas loaded his, then took Lera's from her and placed it in the now crowded area behind the seat. Because he seemed to have them arranged so they wouldn't break, I handed him the one I held.

Lera stepped back. "We'll see you tomorrow. I'll be there bright and early to help."

"Are you bringing any of your staff?" I asked.

"No. They have tomorrow off." She headed into her kitchen, then whirled around and gazed at Lucas. "Besides, it wouldn't be a family meal if we had staff to wait on us."

Lucas had been invited, but I didn't like the way Lera looked at him, as if he were an interloper. He wasn't any more of one than she'd been. "It won't be just a family meal, anyway. Jenny will be there."

Lera chuckled. "I'd almost forgotten." She leaned in and whispered, "I try to forget she's around."

"I understand." One corner of my lips quirked upward. At one time, Lera had thought she'd lost Simon to Jenny.

Lucas helped me onto the carriage, not that I needed any assistance, but I enjoyed the attention. He let me drive again. Did he aim to stay alert in case we were ambushed by the time-travelers?

At the end of the long driveway, Lucas broke the silence. "I think you should take the long way this time."

I turned to him and cocked my head.

He glanced behind the seat. "We don't have much padding between the dishes."

I nodded and continued to the main road, concentrating on not hitting any potholes. My friends complained about the highways in Washington. They didn't know bad roads.

"Do you think it was a coincidence that your ma's

message didn't get to Cassie until after we left?" Lucas sounded thoughtful.

I shrugged. "Hadn't thought about it. But I don't buy her excuse at all."

"I wondered about that." He scanned the open fields. "Why would your ma want the dinner moved to Cassie's?"

"I have no idea. And that worries me." I pursed my lips. He chuckled.

We rode in silence for a while. I almost asked him what he was about to say when Lera interrupted us, but changed my mind. I wasn't sure I wanted to know.

When we got close to town, Lucas chatted about the livery being taken over by the son-in-law of the original owner and other things going on in town. I half-listened until he mentioned someone nominating Nate for the town council.

"I can see that." I glanced at him.

He smiled. "Finally, I said something that registered."

I straightened up and almost snapped the reins, but we were in the middle of Main Street. Speeding up wouldn't do. "I'm sorry I haven't been doting on your every word." Why did I feel so annoyed?

He chuckled, his eyes twinkling. "Didn't mean anything by it. I know you have a lot on your mind."

"So why were you prattling on?" I glimpsed a familiar figure with blonde ringlets crossing the street.

"I don't know. Maybe to keep myself from thinking too much."

I snorted, forgetting how close Jenny was.

She stopped in the middle of the street right in front of us. I yanked the reins to halt in time. She raised her chin, one hand resting on her day dress. "What are you doing out here?"

I wanted to yell at her to move, but Lucas touched my arm. How could he know me so well already?

Lucas tipped his hat. "We're bringing dishes from Miss Lera's."

I stared daggers at her. "Why aren't you helping Ma?"

"I'm running an errand for her." She sauntered across the road toward the mercantile. "See you tomorrow," she called in a sing-song voice.

"She's probably meeting Brian and them," I muttered under my breath as I snapped the reins.

"Too bad we need to get the food delivered."

I peered at him and could almost see the gears turning in his head. "We might be able to delay a few minutes. What do you have in mind?"

"Pull over behind the livery." He pointed to the building across the street from the mercantile. "If she sees us, we'll say we were checking the horse's shoes."

I drove around the building and stopped the rig. Lucas helped me down, and I waited while he tied the reins to a rail. He waved to a young man who must be the new owner. "Is it all right if I leave this here? We'll only be a few minutes."

"No problem," the man called back. "Need any work done?"

"Not at the moment." Lucas ushered me across the street, and we slowed when we came to the mercantile.

I glanced around, trying not to make it look obvious. "Don't see anyone."

"I doubt they'd meet out here." He ushered me down an

alley two stores away from the mercantile. Why didn't I think of that?

At the back of the building, he stopped and peered around the corner, then positioned me in front of him and stood behind me.

I snapped my fingers. "Bingo."

CHAPTER TWENTY-THREE

"What?" Lucas whispered.

I nodded at Jenny and Allison. "Too bad we can't hear them."

"No. What does bingo mean?" He shifted and brushed my back with his chest.

I stepped forward to put some space between us. "Oh, it's just an expression. I'm not sure I can explain."

"Something I'd have to live in the future to understand." He pressed into me again.

"Would you cut it out?" I couldn't move farther forward without risking Jenny seeing me.

He sighed. "I have no idea what you mean."

I cringed. "I mean backup."

He complied. "Sorry. I just wanted to see better."

Jenny's face was angled away from us. Allison stood with a rigid posture and glared down at Jenny. Was Jenny stringing her along somehow? Like she'd done to Cassie?

"I wonder where the two men are," Lucas said.

I whirled around, paranoid they were behind us.

Lucas locked eyes with me. His arms encircled me with an inch gap between us. My chest tightened as we froze for several seconds. His brown eyes brimmed with warmth. Was he holding his breath, too? He closed his arms, embracing me. My skin tingled.

I pushed him back and sidestepped him. "I was making sure Richard and Brian aren't here."

He cleared his throat. "Of course."

I pivoted toward Allison and Jenny, who separated and stormed off in different directions, almost like they were going to their corners in a boxing match. "I'm going in." I strode forward, but a strong hand clasped my arm.

"Think first," Lucas whispered. "The sheriff's office is close by. Allison could have another whistle."

Dang, he was right. We'd agreed with Pa and Ma to lure them to the farm, rather than confront them in town. My insides twisted into a knot, wanting to force Allison and her stooges onto the time machine. But I wouldn't risk more trouble for Nate or Lucas. Against my better judgment, I stopped and leaned against him. "Okay."

He turned me around, held onto my shoulder, and gazed at my face. Was that longing in his expression?

Even if it was, I couldn't encourage him. I strode back down the alley. "I don't think we're going to find out anything more."

When we reached the street, he placed a hand on my shoulder. "Stop. Look first."

I peered around the corner of the building and looked both ways as far as I could see. "They're not in sight." I started to move, but he held me fast.

"Wait. I want to apologize for what happened back there."

I took a deep breath, still angled away from him. "I'm

sorry, too. If I misled you."

"Good." He walked into the street. "Glad that's cleared up."

I had to jog back to the buggy to keep up with him. This time, he didn't help me up, but he grabbed the reins and drove us back to Nate's. I didn't bother to complain. Let him sulk if he wanted to.

"So, any ideas what they're up to?" Lucas asked.

I glanced around at the near-empty fields we passed about a mile outside of town. "Jenny has some scheme to gain control of the time machine, but I have no idea what." Why had she waited so long to make her move?

He gazed straight ahead, his strong jaw clenched. "My thinking is that Allison has her own ideas, and the two don't mesh."

I nodded. "Makes sense. I wish I knew more about Allison." I peeked at him. "She does seem to be the leader of the three, doesn't she?"

"That's my guess." He continued facing straight ahead, all business now.

I sat back, crossed my arms over my chest, and tried to conjure a plan. But how could I figure out what to do when I had no idea what Allison's motives were?

After several minutes of silence, Lucas nudged my shoulder. "Did you interact with Allison at all before they jumped here?"

I racked my brain. "I spoke to her husband, Brian, quite a bit, but Allison was hardly ever in the room."

He raised one eyebrow. "Maybe Brian gave you some kind of clue?"

I snorted. "If I'd had any idea they were planning to use

the time machine, I'd have paid closer attention."

"What do you remember?" He glanced at me, then turned to the horse. Since nothing out of the ordinary was happening, I suspected he intended to give me time to think.

To the best of my ability, I replayed all my interactions with Brian, but Allison hadn't been there for most of them. They'd eaten breakfast and dinner together, but that was about it. She'd faded into the background, which was probably intentional. I had seen her with Richard in passing once.

A picture flashed into my mind. "Wait!"

"What?" Lucas swiveled his head toward me, his eyes wide with expectation.

"The one time Allison acted affectionate with Brian was after she'd noticed me come into the room. Other than that, she treated him like a colleague. She spent more time with Richard." I glanced at Lucas, who focused on the road ahead. "Could Allison be posing as Brian's wife?"

"Hmm." Lucas closed his eyes for a second. "Remember anything else? What about Richard?"

"I spent more time with Brian." An image of Richard waving the ad printouts surfaced in my mind. "He was into the history of this place."

"He acts more like a spectator," Lucas said.

"Yep. He didn't believe in time-travel. I think he was at the house to find those journals. I'm almost positive they have one, they haven't shown me." The one for this year. But that would be different now, wouldn't it? Is that why it had been missing? I shook my head. No, it couldn't be. We hadn't traveled to the future yet.

"What are you not telling me?" Lucas stared at me, his

eyes narrowed.

I pointed ahead. "Watch the road, will you?"

He snapped his head to face forward. "Well?"

I sighed. "Nothing important. Just trying to process all this time-travel stuff."

"It makes your head hurt, too?" He crossed his eyes, a goofy grin on his face.

"Yeah, a bit." I pursed my lips. "Sometimes I wish I hadn't learned about it." Why did I say that? I would have died. Ma would say I'd be in hell. I shuddered. When I was younger, I would have laughed it off. Lucas appeared to be concentrating on the road ahead, but his mouth moved. "Did you say something?"

He startled. "Oh, what?"

"I thought you were talking to me."

He grinned. "I was talking to God."

"Oh." I folded my hands in my lap and studied the floorboards. Why did it seem so easy for everyone around me to accept a higher power in their life? And why was I starting to envy them?

~

As I helped set the table, I admired the elegant place cards Cassie had made and already set out. They added formality to the occasion, but more importantly for me, they let me avoid sitting near Jenny. While setting the flatware, I lingered at each place long enough to read the names. The current arrangement placed Jenny across from Ma and next to Pa, who was at one end of the table. My place card was near the other end between Lera and Lucas, who had the seat catty-corner from Nate and across from Cassie. I would rather have switched places with Lucas, but this was all right. On second thought, it wouldn't be a bad idea to keep better tabs on Jenny. To that end, I hurried around the table and switched Caleb's card with Jenny's. Caleb would want to sit next to Pa, anyway, and that would put Jenny slightly closer on the opposite side from me. Satisfied, I strode out of the dining room toward the kitchen.

I stopped on the walkway just outside the kitchen door. The noise level indicated there were at least three, and possibly four, women in the small space. The door opened, but nobody came out, so I peered inside, catching a whiff of turkey mingled with cornbread stuffing and cranberries. Chaos might be an understatement to describe the scene. Lera took a hot casserole out of the oven while Ma had to scoot out of her way to continue stirring something on the woodstove. Emily tended to a pot hanging over the fire in the fireplace, and Jenny stood at the worktable, sticking spoons into serving dishes and placing them on trays. Jenny glowered at me. I tried to suppress my smile, but from her continued piercing glare, I probably didn't succeed.

"Anything I can do?" I called in.

"Yes," Ma said. "Take those trays into the dining room."

I stepped one foot into the room but didn't dare go any further. "Jenny, can you bring them to me?"

"Why should I?" She drove a spoon into the mashed potatoes.

"Because one more person won't fit in there."

"Oh, all right." She picked up a tray and stalked to the door. "I've got a better idea. I'll take this in, and you go pick up the other one."

It made sense, so I stepped aside, allowed her to leave,

and weaved between Ma and Lera to the worktable. I placed two small dishes of condiments in the remaining space on the silver tray. Cassie was pulling out all the stops for this dinner. Where was Cassie? Instead of asking, I picked up the tray and carried it to the dining room, expecting Jenny to be returning. When I got there, her tray was on the sideboard, but Jenny wasn't anywhere to be seen. With a heavy sigh, I trudged back to the kitchen.

"She got away, didn't she?" Lera wore a smug smile.

Emily giggled as she passed me, carrying another silver tray laden with food.

"Yes." I grimaced.

"Don't worry." Lera brought a finished pumpkin pie over to the worktable. "You're out of practice dealing with her."

"I guess." I surveyed the room. "How much more food are we taking in?"

"Oh, just those two trays." Ma bobbed her head toward the worktable as she brought a large roasted turkey over. "And this." She stood to her full height, all of five feet, and held her head high.

I whistled in appreciation. "It smells delicious!"

Ma winked. "I hope it tastes as good as it looks."

"I'm sure it will." Lera picked up one tray and led the way into the house. I lifted the other and followed while Ma carried the main course.

When we entered the dining room, I was surprised to see everyone gathered and standing behind their labeled seats. Maybe Jenny had rounded everyone up. She could have told one of us.

"I see everyone found their name cards." Lera set her

tray on the sideboard, and Ma placed the turkey in front of Pa.

Cassie caught my eye, then flicked her gaze at Caleb, standing next to Pa and Jenny on the other side of him. I gave a brief nod and a shrug. I'd explain later.

"Before I carve." Pa folded his hands together. "I'd like to say the blessing."

I set my tray on the sideboard and hurried to stand behind my seat. Lucas reached over and clasped my hand, which unnerved me until Lera reached for my other hand. Lucas's hand felt unusually warm. I shook that off as I listened to Pa say grace.

Pa thanked God for his blessings, which he said were mostly everyone standing around the table. That surprised me because Jenny, Lucas, and Simon were here. Well, I could see Lucas being a blessing, but the other two?

Then he thanked God for the good harvest and the food. It was one of the shortest blessings I'd ever heard him deliver. Was it because it was the first time I'd ever really listened?

Everyone chorused, "Amen." Chairs shuffled as we took our seats, and Pa carved the turkey.

Ma went to the sideboard, picked up one dish at a time, and passed it down the table. When the dish had finished making the rounds, she took what she wanted and then set it back on the sideboard. I had forgotten this routine, getting used to all the dishes being on the table, or everyone filling their plates smorgasbord style. Ma had to be tired, but I knew not to try and take over for her. Cassie and Lera each kept an eye on her while also attending to their neighbors. Melody sat in Cassie's lap, and baby Andrew sat in Lera's, so to help

Ma, they'd have had to hand off a baby first.

After all the food had been passed, Ma brought her plate to the table. Everyone chatted, mostly about the food. Contented moans emanated from around the table. Not surprising because everything was delicious, especially the turkey and dressing.

Ma clinked her glass until everyone stopped chatting. "I think it would be nice for each person to tell what they're thankful for. I'll start."

I stifled a groan. How could I have let this sneak up on me? She used to do this every year.

"I am thankful to have everyone here, especially Lydia."

I forced a tight smile.

Simon went next, so it would be my turn soon. What would I say? My mind went blank. No, it was so full of thoughts and emotions, I couldn't pick one out. Lera squeezed my hand, letting me know she had finished.

"I'm thankful for..." I hesitated and glanced around the table. "Being able to see you all again." Lucas brushed my hand with his, and I peered at him. "And meeting you." Our eyes met. He wore a gorgeous smile, lighting up his whole face.

"My turn." Lucas leaned forward. "I am grateful to be included like family. And to have the opportunity to meet such a lovely lady."

I snorted, and everyone else laughed.

Lucas squeezed my hand slightly.

I pulled my hand away and picked up my fork. He'd shown his romantic feelings for me, but I'd been pushing mine away. Now, I indulged in a daydream about me and Lucas as a couple. He was kind, thoughtful, and hardworking. Too bad he didn't live in the correct century. Nate, Cassie, Emily, and Mark spoke briefly, but I let their words wash over me.

Jenny tapped the table. "My turn. I'm thankful for the opportunity to accompany Lydia on her journey."

My muscles tightened into knots as I snapped my head toward her.

She locked gazes with me, a smirk on her face.

CHAPTER TWENTY-FOUR

My mouth hung open for a second before I caught myself. "What are you talking about?"

Jenny nodded at Ma. "Miss Mattie told me you were leaving tomorrow and you would welcome the company."

I leaned forward and shot a glare at Ma. My jaw was clenched so tight, I couldn't speak. That was probably good, since I'd yell at Ma.

"I'm sorry." Ma leaned back, hiding behind Lera and Simon, but her voice sounded smooth and in control. "I told you I thought Lydia would enjoy the company. I didn't get a chance to talk to her about it yet." She'd probably planned this, but why?

I squirmed in my seat. "We'll talk about it later."

"Caleb." Pa winked at his grandson. "That leaves you and me. What are you thankful for?"

"Turkey!" Caleb held up a drumstick. Everyone laughed. Caleb knew how to lighten the mood.

"That leaves me." Pa glanced around the table. "I am thankful for family, but I already thanked God for that. I'm also thankful for assurances from the Almighty. Promises that God doesn't change and won't ever leave us." He peered at Jenny. "No one can counter God's will."

Was Pa referring to Jenny wanting to change the timeline?

Jenny cleared her throat and smiled at Pa. "I hope I understand that one day."

"I hope you do too." Pa smiled back at her.

Lucas leaned in and whispered, "Do you believe what your Pa just said?"

"I'd like to," I whispered back.

Nate asked Lucas a question, redirecting his attention. I tried to tune into their conversation, but Jenny distracted me.

"I'm sorry, Miss Mattie." Jenny glanced at me. "I should have made sure you'd cleared it with Lydia before I mentioned it." Her face lit up. "I'm just so excited."

"It's okay," Ma said. "You two will work it out, I'm certain."

Lera steered the conversation to a new topic, and I tuned out.

Lucas kept quiet. Even having known him for only a short time, I guessed he was probably keeping track of the conversation and would help me remember it later. Somehow, his presence both relaxed and invigorated me.

"Lydia." Jenny broke into my reverie.

"Yes?" I pursed my lips, not bothering to hide my contempt.

"Simon asked where you've been."

Simon leaned forward and pivoted his head toward me. "And how you grew up so fast."

I leaned back, hiding my deer-in-the-headlights reaction. "Uh." I should have listened to Ma's explanation.

"Oh, she's been away at her sister's house.

Convalescing," Ma said.

"Right." Simon cleared his throat. "When was the last time Sarah visited?"

"She hasn't." Ma's speech sounded clipped. "Not since she got married. She says it's too long of a buggy ride for her babies."

"Well, she does have three now, right?" Cassie asked.

"She's been busy." I tsked under my breath. She'd only been married about four years.

Jenny grinned. "Is that why you aged so much? Helping her with all those babies?"

I gritted my teeth.

Emily leaned forward to look at Jenny. "If you had serious injuries like Lydia's, you probably would have aged too."

I reared back, surprised. It was the first time Emily had ever stood up for me. It was also the first time she'd spoken to the group, other than when she'd been put on the spot. I nodded at her to thank her. Lera took over the conversation again, and I couldn't get a word in after that. No problem there. I should thank Lera and Simon for drawing Caleb, Mark, and Emily out and letting me sit and eat in peace.

When most of the plates were empty, Ma stood. "I hope everyone has saved room for pie."

I groaned as did most everyone except Caleb.

"Really?" Ma asked. "I guess we can have dessert later, then."

"Can I have mine now?" Caleb pushed back from the table, his eyes shining.

Ma chuckled. "Just as soon as we get the table cleared."

I scooted my chair back and stood.

Lucas grabbed my plate. "Since the ladies cooked and served, I propose we men clean up."

Mark drew back, stunned, but Pa and Nate stood and nodded.

"Ladies." Nate lifted Melody off Cassie's lap. "Why don't you go into the parlor?"

"Now, Nate." Ma picked up her plate, but Pa took it from her.

"Let us do this." Pa leaned toward her, his voice low.

Ma let go with a huff and marched to the parlor. I chuckled and followed her. Cassie took Melody back, and Lera carried her youngest. I stopped short, remembering Simon Jr. was still in the high chair. When I turned to get him, Emily already held him on her hip.

"Thanks," I said.

"Oh, well, I always take care of Jr. here."

"No, thanks for what you said earlier. It meant a lot to me."

She grinned. "Sisters have to stick together." We strolled to the parlor, but she stopped before we got to the door. "Besides, I can't stand her. She thinks she's better than everyone else, even though she spent three years in jail." She shook her head. "I just don't understand some people."

"Neither do I." I thought I had Emily pegged, but I guess three years can make a difference.

I squinted as Emily and I entered the vacant sitting room.

"They must be in the large parlor." Emily strolled through the room. "This one will be too small when the men join us."

She led the way to the large parlor on the other side of

the house. I stopped in the doorway. They must have moved the furniture around while I'd been busy the last few days.

"You never come in here, do you?" Cassie stood in the middle of the room and grinned at me. Someone had arranged four sofas and four chairs in two groupings, one on either end of the long room, but open toward each other. I'd never seen so much furniture in this room. Full bookcases lined the interior wall between the two fireplaces, which weren't in use. The temperature was moderate for late November.

"Where did all this furniture come from?" The more ornate pieces near the front of the room looked familiar, but the furniture at the back had cleaner lines and was much more modern. I hurried over to the plush upholstered sofa. "Did Pa make this?"

Cassie smiled wide. "Yep. I designed it, though."

"We've left that grouping for the men when they finish." Ma sat on one of the wingback chairs in the first section.

Jenny sat in the chair opposite Ma and bobbed her head toward Cassie. "You're going to give yourself away."

Cassie walked over to her, patting Melody on the back. "How so?"

"You know." Jenny sat up straight and cleared her throat.

"Why don't you enlighten me?" Cassie took a seat on the settee, catty-corner from Jenny.

Jenny glanced at Emily and Lera, each holding one of Lera's sons. Lera sat on the sofa nearest Ma, and Emily stood behind the second sofa. "Maybe later."

Lera put her baby down on a blanket on the sofa. "If you're holding back because of me and Emily, don't bother."

"What?" I stared at Lera.

"We both know Jenny and Cassie are from the future." Lera wore a smug smile. "I think Mark and Simon are the only ones who don't know."

I blinked. "What about Caleb?"

Lera laughed. "He's the one who told me. I didn't believe him at first, but later it made sense."

"Wait." Cassie held up her hand. "You figured it out after the fire."

Lera shook her head. "No. Caleb told me earlier that day. I didn't believe it until Lydia vanished."

Jenny laughed, but it sounded forced and hollow. "You guys crack me up. You really believe that?"

"Nice try." I sat on the second sofa, across from Jenny. "Okay, so here it is. You are not going with me when I leave."

"Not so fast." Ma raised one hand toward each of us. "I have a plan."

I clenched my jaw. "And why wouldn't you run it by me first?" I nearly bit my tongue to avoid uttering several swear words.

"Now, hear me out." She kept one hand raised and looked from me to Jenny. "You two need to get those other three travelers back to their time, correct?"

I glared at Jenny. "They wouldn't have come here if not for her."

Jenny scowled. "What are you talking about?"

"They came because of that ad you put in the paper. The upside-down one for Nate's business."

She flicked her wrist. "Oh, that. It was meant for you. I wanted you to bring the time machine back."

"So you could go erase the past." I jumped up, nearly spitting out my words.

She took a deep breath and stood. "No. I just want to go home. To my own time, anyway."

"Mm, hmm." I closed the gap and faced her. "What are you going to do when you get there?"

She shrugged. "Well, I don't belong here."

"You could." Ma peered at Jenny. "If you wanted to."

"I don't want to," Jenny whispered.

I touched Jenny's shoulder. "What's going on with Allison?"

"How would I know?" She stepped away.

"I saw you arguing with her. She must want something."

She shook her head and pursed her lips. What wasn't she telling me?

"Don't you want to hear my plan?" Ma straightened and lifted her chin.

I perched on the edge of the sofa. She motioned for Jenny to sit, and she obliged.

Ma also commanded Emily, Lera, and Cassie's attention. She gazed at me. "So, there's three of them and a limit of three on the time machine, right?"

I nodded.

"You send the three of them back without the remote." Ma clapped her hands on her lap. "You call the time machine back, and they can't do anything about it."

Jenny leaned forward. "But what if they get control of it after we return to the future?"

I scoffed. "I think Ma's plan is for us to stay here."

"Next plan." Jenny huffed.

Emily laid her hand on my arm. "You really want to go

to a place where you don't have any family?"

"Yes." I didn't have to think about it, but she couldn't know how much different and easier life was in the twenty-first century.

"How?" Emily looked directly into my eyes, tears forming in hers.

I exchanged a glance with Cassie, hoping she would help me explain, but she pressed her lips together and focused on Ma. *Here goes.* I took a deep breath. "I've lived in the future for ten years and have gotten used to life there. I have friends, if not family. Also, I can work at any job I want. I'm free to be myself. I don't have that here."

Emily tilted her head. "How come I feel free to be myself here, and you don't?"

"I don't know." I exhaled. How could Emily understand my reasons when they were beginning to sound shallow to me?

"Let's get back to the plan," Jenny said.

Ma smiled. "I've sent messages to Allison and them at the Kelleys'." Her eyes twinkled. Even though we'd rejected her plan, she was enjoying this. "And I happen to have a good guess at where they are right now."

"Where?" Jenny and I said in unison.

Ma beamed. "At my house. I sent the youngest Jones boy with an invitation to tea at four o'clock."

I glanced at the mantle clock, which showed about fifteen minutes before four.

"Aunt Mattie, why would you invite them if you knew you'd be here?" Cassie squinted at Ma.

Ma turned to me. "Take Nate and Lucas with you. They'll help you corral the futurists and send them back."

My eyes went wide. "Ma, I can't summon the machine. I'll have to go get—"

Jenny jumped up, fists at her sides. "Why did you act like you were going back? Are we stuck here?"

"I'll still be able to go." I hopped off the sofa and ran to the kitchen.

Jenny caught me in the back hallway. "Where's the time machine? Is it here?"

CHAPTER TWENTY-FIVE

Nate, Lucas, and I race-walked the back road from Nate's and entered the side yard at Ma and Pa's.

I nodded at the quiet home. "I hope they're still here."

"And that they'll go along with the plan." Nate strode down the side yard.

I didn't hold out much hope for that, but it was time to confront them. What had Ma written in her note that made her certain they'd be here?

We rounded the corner at the front of the house. Allison and Brian sat in the swing at the end of the porch, and Richard paced.

Nate stepped in front of Lucas and me.

Richard stopped at the edge of the porch and glared at all three of us. "Where's Mattie Gardner?"

"At my place." Nate stood on the paving stones and addressed Richard. "She told us you'd be here. Why do you want to see her?"

Allison and Brian stood. She sauntered to the railing and looked down her nose at us. "Mattie said she could help us."

"I'm sure she can." Nate gestured toward the trail. "Why don't you come with us, and we can get you home?"

Richard started down the steps.

"Wait!" Allison raised her hands. "Mrs. Gardner needs to tell us what she knows, first."

I narrowed my eyes and tried to see Nate's face, but he kept it trained on Allison.

"I'm sure she will. Come with us." Nate walked toward the porch.

Allison stood still, both hands on the railing. "Why did she invite us here, if she'd be at your place?"

"That is an excellent question." Nate landed one foot on the first step. "I never could figure out Aunt Mattie."

I sidled in, trying to catch Allison off guard. "What information do you want?"

Brian stepped forward. "What the original timeline—"

"Hush, Brian." Allison clutched his arm. "Bring Mattie here."

Nate slapped the newel post. "Well, Miss Allison, that is easier said than done. When Aunt Mattie has her mind made up, don't nobody change it." He tipped his hat and turned away.

"Wait." Richard rushed to Nate. "Who has control of the time machine?"

Allison jerked her head at Lucas, her eyes wide. "Richard! What are you talking about?"

"Oh, stuff it, Allison." Richard marched down the paving stones. "They all know." He stopped and peered into my eyes. "Take me back, okay?"

I nodded. Maybe this would be easier than I thought.

"Not so fast!" Allison pulled out a pistol and pointed it at Richard. Nate and Lucas slid in front of him, holding their arms out. It seemed to be an instinctive move. I cowered behind, but Richard strode around them and faced Allison.

"It's over, Allison. You've proved time-travel possible. Let's just go home."

Allison took a deep breath and pointed the gun at Lucas. "It's not over until I say it's over."

Lucas didn't flinch even with a pistol pointed at him. As I studied the gun, I recognized it from this decade, or close, so its aim might not be all that accurate.

Nate held his palms up. "Put that down before someone gets hurt."

Allison waved the gun at Lucas. "Go get Mattie, now!"

"What could she possibly know that you don't?" Lucas's voice stayed steady.

Brian slid forward. "She wrote that—"

Allison pointed the gun at Brian. "No more until she gets here!"

Brian furrowed his brow and sidled away from her.

She trembled slightly, her gaze darted from Brian to Richard to the three of us, but she kept the gun trained on Brian. That confirmed my suspicion that he probably wasn't her husband.

Nate approached the railing. "It appears we're at an impasse. You won't come with us, and Aunt Mattie won't come here."

"The time machine is at Nate's." It slipped out of my mouth before I could stop it. "I can take you home from there."

"I'll go with you." Richard closed the gap between us.

"Fine!" Allison poked the gun into Brian's chest. "You go. Whatever happens to him will be on your head."

Richard trudged back toward Brian.

Brian pointed from Richard to us. "Go."

"No, man." Richard sat down on the edge of the porch, his long legs reaching past the three steps to the ground.

While Allison watched Richard and Brian, Nate slid closer to her at the rail. I held my breath and glanced at Lucas.

Lucas strolled toward Richard and exaggerated his shrug. "I guess we'll just have to tell Mrs. Gardner we failed."

Allison turned toward Lucas, and Nate grabbed the pistol. Boom! Crack. A limb fell from a large oak and landed next to the porch. Nate jumped back and unloaded the gun with shaky hands.

I held my hand over my heart and exhaled. My heartbeat settled after ascertaining that the only victim was the tree.

Allison planted her feet and crossed her arms over her chest. "So, are you going to haul me off to jail like you did Jenny?"

"No, ma'am." Nate pocketed the bullets and handed me the pistol. "I didn't put Jenny in jail."

Allison glared at Nate. "Well, your kind did."

Nate narrowed his eyes. "What did she tell you about that?"

Allison huffed. "That they put her there because they didn't understand her. Because she claimed to be from the future, and they didn't believe her."

"Huh." Nate peered at me.

"Well?" Allison called. "Aren't you going to explain?"

Nate shrugged. "Would you believe me?"

Brian stepped away from Allison. "I might."

"She went to jail because she was convicted of theft.

They couldn't find enough evidence to convict her of manslaughter."

Brian gasped. "Who do they think she killed?"

Allison grabbed his arm. "It's a lie, so what does it matter?"

My face heated, and I lurched toward her, pointing the gun as if it were still loaded. "John. My brother!"

Allison swiped the pistol as Lucas slid between us. He pivoted to face me and ushered me down the walkway. "Nate still has the bullets."

Nate tipped his hat. "If you want to go to the future, you know where to find us." He strode around the house the way we came, and Lucas and I followed.

When we entered the wooded road, footsteps thudded behind us, and I glanced back. Richard and Brian plodded down the trail, but Allison wasn't with them.

Halfway to Nate's, Brian and Richard caught up.

Richard huffed and puffed as he walked next to me. "Can you please take us home?"

"Yes." I continued at a good clip. "If you tell me what Allison wants."

"Information." Brian flanked me. "About the original timeline."

Nate glanced back at Brian. "How would Aunt Mattie know that?"

Brian shrugged. "She said she had some documents."

I squinted at Nate. "Pa!"

"Ed!" Nate said at the same time. "He must have brought something with him that first time."

"Why wouldn't he have told us before, though?" I joined Nate, leaving Lucas behind with Richard and Brian.

"We'll have to ask him that."

I chewed on my lip as we rushed to Nate's house. I glanced behind us several times, but I never caught a glimpse of Allison. What was she up to?

At the house, Nate opened the back door and let us in. I raced through to the large parlor. "Pa!"

"He's outside with Caleb and Simon." Lera glanced up at me and sipped her tea as if it were a normal Thanksgiving Day.

Ma had the decency to set down her cup and frown. She motioned for me to sit in the chair next to her, but I stayed on my feet.

"Maybe you can tell me." I tried to keep my voice calm. "What information did you promise Allison?"

Ma glanced at Nate, Lucas, Brian, and Richard, who stood near the open double doors. "Is she here?"

"No. She insisted you come to her."

Ma smiled. "I thought as much."

I stamped my foot. "What is going on?"

"Patience, dear." Ma patted the seat on the sofa next to her.

I let out a strangled scream. "Just tell me."

Ma sighed, leaned over to her needlework bag, and pulled out several crinkled and stapled sheets of paper. Instead of handing it to me, she held it up. "This was in a coat pocket in your father's trunk when we first got married. He'd had it folded so small it could be hidden in a hand. I wasn't even sure he remembered he'd brought it."

I reached for it. "What is it?"

She glanced at Lera. "I need to show it to Lera first."

"Why?" Lera's eyes widened, and she cocked her head

at Ma.

"Because it's your family tree. As it was before Ed came." Ma held out the papers to Lera.

Lera closed her eyes and swallowed. "It was different. I didn't marry John first, because he didn't exist." It came out in a whisper.

"What does it have to do with Allison?" I paced in front of Ma and Lera.

Lera shook her head. "I'm fine with what is. I don't want to know. Lydia can see it."

"Thank you!" I snatched it out of Ma's hand.

She turned her head from side to side. "Tsk. Tsk. When did you get so impatient?"

"Always been that way." Pa stood in the doorway. "What's this?"

"You don't remember?" Ma took the paper from me and showed it to Pa.

"Oh, that." Pa held his hand up as if he would push it away. "It doesn't matter anymore."

"But this is what Allison is looking for." I peered at him. "How'd it get here?"

Pa waved his hand to Ma. "Jenny had been researching her family. In addition to proving time-travel, she hoped to meet some of them. She left that on the copier at work, and I grabbed it and put it in my jacket pocket. I wanted to ask her about it. Must have been there when I traveled."

Ma handed me the printout. As I flipped through it, their conversation faded to background noise.

The sheets contained a list of marriages and births going back two hundred years from 2010. I flipped to the page where Lera was listed. She was born in 1842 and married

Simon in 1862. I read through until I saw Jenny's birth in 1983. Jenny was a descendant of Simon and Lera's first son, also Simon Jr., but born in 1864. In the timeline I knew, Lera married John in 1861, had Caleb in 1862, and married Simon in 1870. I understood how Ed messed that up. Everything after Simon and Lera was probably different. None of those children were born. But why would Allison care? And how would she even know?

~

"What's it doing here?" Richard pointed to the time machine as the rest of the family, minus Caleb, Mark, and Simon, trooped up the stairs to the playroom.

"We moved it here." Pa tapped the rail. Nobody asked for an explanation, and none of us supplied one.

Brian hurried to it and stopped short of the platform. "Can we use it now?"

I strode over to him. "Don't you want to stay and make sure your wife gets back?"

He scoffed. "Haven't you figured out she's not my wife?"

I chuckled. "Just confirming. How did you get involved with her?"

Brian scowled and nodded at Richard. "She approached us in the library when we were researching my family, right after Richard posted online about the book."

Richard approached. "She told us this bizarre story about a time machine associated with the B&B. I wanted to brush her off but—"

Brian grasped the time-machine rail. "That piqued my interest. Because of my grandmother."

"Then she offered to pay us to include her on our weekend at the B&B." Richard shrugged. "I didn't believe her, so I figured why not?" He grimaced.

I cocked my head. "But why did you cooperate with her when you got here? I would have taken you home right away."

Richard pressed his lips together and locked eyes with Brian.

Brian rubbed his temple. "We might as well tell them now. Allison brought that pistol with her. We didn't know about it until a couple of minutes after we arrived, when you popped in and out right away."

"We were halfway to you, but she waved her weapon." Richard shook his head. "Kept threatening us the whole time we were here."

Lucas entered my peripheral vision and rubbed his chin. "I wondered where she got that gun. It looked similar to mine."

I groaned. "Why did I let her snatch it? I think it was from this decade, or maybe the 1880s."

Pa rubbed his temple. "It could be in the wrong timeline."

"We need to get the pistol." Lucas pointed his hat at Nate.

"Or send it back with her." I waved my arm over the machine as if it were a game-show prize. "First things first."

Brian grinned. "Well, it's been an adventure."

"One I don't want to repeat. Let's get moving." Richard rubbed his hands together and hopped onto the platform. "Can we go back to the time right after we left?"

I shook my head. "You can't go back until after I left.

Fortunately, Todd should be waiting." I gasped. "But they'll stay in this room. Todd's waiting in the garage of his house."

"I don't care where we end up." Richard clutched one of the rails. "I just want to get back to 2020."

"Me, too." Brian joined Richard on the platform.

It would carry three, so I could go with them, but a niggling fear held me back. Allison. I couldn't trust her here with Jenny. Would the machine pop back, or would my remote start to work? Todd could deactivate the machine. My breath hitched. "Pa, do you think we should send the two of them back by themselves?"

His brow creased. "You'd risk getting stuck here." He rubbed his stubble. "Wish I understood how this dang thing works."

I closed my eyes. Staying in 1873 was the last thing I wanted, but it would keep Allison and Jenny here, too. I peered at Pa. "Let's send them. And then if I can get the machine back, I can take Allison later." I palmed my remote in my pocket.

Ma smiled, and Pa nodded.

Lucas gazed at me. Was that an expression of respect?

I reached over the rail to the display and powered up the machine. It was set to the time Todd had reprogrammed when I'd sent it by itself. I backed away from the machine and nodded to Richard and Brian. Part of me longed to go, but for my conscience's sake, I'd take the risk, which somehow didn't feel as high as I would have thought last week.

Brian and Richard held onto both rails and faced the control panel. I reached over the rail and pressed the button. Nothing changed. After a moment, I slumped, about to admit defeat, when a mist rolled into the room.

"What's going on?" Lera emerged from the crowd.

"It's working!" Richard's tone sounded like a muffled shout.

Moments later, the mist cleared, and the machine was gone. Lera and Emily gasped. Ma gazed up at Pa, a smile on her face.

Pa pulled Ma in close. "Give it a few minutes and then try to call it back."

Nate left Cassie's side and strode to Pa. "Shouldn't she wait until she needs it?"

"No. This way, I'll know whether I can get it back or not." I programmed my remote and called the machine back from half an hour after they should have arrived to give them time to get off.

The machine appeared in another dense mist. But when the mist cleared, Jamal, a white-knuckled grip on the handrail, stared wide-eyed from the platform.

CHAPTER TWENTY-SIX

My expression probably mirrored Jamal's. "What are you doing here?"

Nate tapped my shoulder. "Who's this?"

"Chantal's brother. I'll explain later," I whispered.

Jamal blinked, rubbed his eyes, and glanced around the room. "What's going on?"

I reached out to him and led him off the platform to the window seat. "It's a long story."

He plopped down with a grimace.

I sat next to him. "Tell me what happened."

"Those two guys showed up." He glanced out the window and blinked.

"Richard and Brian?"

He nodded. "They just appeared in this room, with that." He pointed to the machine.

My face flushed. "You were there?"

"Yeah. I was doing some work for Chantal."

"Who's Chantal?" Pa stood a few feet away, along with Nate and Lucas.

"Jamal's sister." I flicked my wrist, irritated at the interruption. "So, what actually happened?"

"Did the mist appear?" Lucas asked.

I glared at him, Nate, and Pa until they moved back and joined Ma, Cassie, Lera, and Emily, who all stood near the doorway, eyes glued to Jamal.

"Yes." Jamal rubbed the back of his neck. "The mist freaked me out, but Brian and Richard freaked me out more." He rubbed his hands on his thighs. "They told me they'd traveled in time, and you'd followed them. Todd had told us you'd gone to Seattle to pack."

"I had no idea you'd be in this room." If Todd hadn't changed the time, he wouldn't have been. I blew out a breath. "So, what then?"

"They demanded their things." He pointed to the corner. "Their suitcases were packed and sitting right over there. They took them and left."

I touched his shoulder. "And then?"

He tapped his heel. "I tried to make sense of everything. I was examining the control panel when the mist rolled in again. I didn't have time to jump off." He shook his head. "No, that isn't it. I couldn't jump off. It's like there was a force holding me on." He peered at me. "So, now what?"

I stood and gestured at the machine. "We send you back and you don't tell anyone, other than Todd. Let Todd know where the machine is and tell him to keep it guarded until I get back."

Jamal nodded and hurried to the platform.

Lucas mumbled something I couldn't understand as I followed Jamal.

I started to program the remote, but Pa laid a hand on my arm. "Wait. Which remote did you use?"

I showed him the one I'd brought with me. "Yours is

back in the window box."

"Good." Pa flashed a sheepish grin. "I wish I hadn't played around with it. It confused us."

That gave me an idea, but first, I needed to send Jamal home. I dialed in a minute after he'd left—"

"Wait!" Jamal clasped my forearm. "Could I use this machine later if I need it?"

I squinted. "Why would you want to?"

He cleared his throat. "I have a negative situation. I may need to escape." He ambled off the platform and widened his eyes. "Could I stay a while? Or go back to a later date?"

That must be the trouble Chantal had been worried about. I swallowed hard and pointed to the machine. "No. Todd would have my hide. He wants to destroy this thing as soon as I get everyone back."

Nate, Lucas, and Pa crowded around us.

Jamal lowered his head and stepped onto the machine. "Fine."

I put my finger to my lips. "And don't tell anyone. Especially Chantal."

He scoffed. "Do you think I'm insane?"

I shrugged and activated the remote, bracing myself.

The mist rolled in, and I jumped back.

"Dang." Pa gagged. "It's almost as bad to be here when it travels as to be on it."

I chuckled as the fog cleared, leaving empty space where the machine had been.

"So, you're leaving it in the future?" Lucas asked.

I nodded.

"We've proved we can get it back," Pa said.

"I want to try something." I trotted to the entrance. Ma,

Emily, and Cassie moved out of my way, and Lera started to follow me. "I'll be back in a second." I hurried downstairs to the small parlor, opened the window, fished out Pa's remote, and jogged back upstairs. It had power, so I programmed it and recalled the time machine, but even after five minutes, nothing happened.

Pa exhaled and reached for the remote. "Good. I'll get rid of this."

"No!" I pocketed it. It looked just different enough, I could tell it was the fake, but Jenny wouldn't be able to. "This could come in handy. I might let Jenny think she has the real remote."

Nate sat on the window seat and gazed out. "But she'll find out soon enough it doesn't work."

"Still, I think I'll hang onto it." Somehow, this remote was the key.

Nate slapped his thighs and stood. "Now that the excitement is over, let's get back to the festivities."

Pa and Nate ushered the women out of the playroom, leaving me and Lucas straggling behind.

I studied his face. "What was that you mumbled when Jamal was here?"

He grinned. "I said, I would have wanted to explore for a while." He held his elbow out for me to grasp. "Would you like to accompany me on a walk?"

"Sure." I batted my eyelashes at him. "Are you going to tell me your ulterior motive?"

"To spend time with you." He smiled and led me downstairs.

"Mm hmm." From the foyer, I glanced into the large parlor where everyone else chatted. Nobody would miss us.

Lucas held the front door open for me as I walked out and stopped on the porch. "You just want to find out more information about the future."

He closed the door and poked his index finger into his chest. "Me?"

"Yes. I can see the eagerness on your face. You want to go there, don't you?"

"I have to admit, the prospect intrigues me." He furrowed his brow and led me to the stream. "But I really want to talk about something I saw in you. Up in that room."

I narrowed my eyes at him. "What?"

He faced the sky as we veered down the stream bank, then peered at me. "I was proud of you when you risked being stuck here to send Brian and Richard back."

I shrugged and patted the working remote, which was in my pocket along with Pa's.

He touched my shoulder. "When you decided to keep the fake remote, you didn't quite know why, did you?"

I snorted. "I thought it might work, but now I'm glad it won't."

He slowed his pace. "But you knew you needed it, anyway, didn't you? A gut feeling."

I squinted despite the cloudy day. "How did you know?"

"Didn't for sure, but I had that gut feeling, too. And I'd been praying about it."

I rolled my eyes. "Here we go."

"No, hear me out." He stopped and placed his hands on my upper arms. "Please."

I took a deep breath and let it out. "Okay."

"I believe that God is involved here. He's been giving me messages, and I think He wants to give them to you, too.

You just can't hear Him yet."

I scoffed, but stayed in his grasp and gazed at him.

His brown eyes bore into mine. "I also think He's going to use you to keep the timeline the way it is."

My fists landed on my hips as I backed away. "If you know so much, why is Allison so bent on changing it?"

He shook his head. "That, I don't know. But I do believe God has a plan for you. Just as he has a plan for me and for all of us."

I sighed and closed my eyes. "I'll think about it, Lucas."

"You know what to do." His voice softened. "Pray about it."

Lucas accompanied me but stayed quiet as we strolled along the stream. We'd walked out without donning coats, and I'd forgotten a hat. No real need to protect my eyes on this cloudy day. I shivered with each gust of wind.

After a long while, I voiced my thoughts. "I believe I always rejected the idea of surrendering my life to God because I already had so many authority figures." I glanced at Lucas." And when I went to the future, I took the opportunity to be my own boss."

I expected Lucas to ask how that worked out for me, but he kept his mouth shut. Surprising.

~

Lucas swept his hand toward the darkening sky. "Maybe we should head back."

I dragged my feet, but went along because he was right. We'd meandered away from Nate's for an hour. Most of that time had been spent in silence, but not the kind where I'm trying to figure out what to say. My mind couldn't focus on any one thing for more than a couple of seconds. It flitted from our previous conversation about faith, to my family, to Allison and Jenny, and what their motives could be, to the man walking beside me. Okay, so Lucas commanded most of my thought space during that walk. Part of me wanted to see if I would stay attracted to him when I got to know him better, but the sane part needed to finish my task and return to my life in 2020.

I heaved a sigh and looked up at Lucas.

"Make any decisions?" He glanced at me.

"No." A raindrop plopped on my head. I jogged toward the house, though we were still pretty far away. If the rain picked up, we'd be soaked, jog or not. "My thoughts are all over the place."

He kept pace with me. "I'll keep praying."

My breath hitched. "Is that what you've been doing this whole time?" I tried to stop, but he clasped my hand and continued our steady slog.

The rain fell harder, and I shivered. It was probably just as well I wasn't wearing a coat because my heavy wrap would be a burden, slowing me down. What else was weighing me down? My negative attitude?

Funny how jogging in a driving rain could make me focus on the most important thing. I'd been wandering, running away, and now I ran to something, someone. "God," I whispered in my spirit. "I give in. I've known the truth about you from the time I was little, but I was stubborn. I wanted to run my own life. Now I realize how short-sighted I was. Forgive me, please."

The storm increased in intensity, and we picked up our speed. Running seemed effortless. I felt lighter somehow.

When we reached the cover of Nate's porch, we stopped, both leaning over and huffing to catch our breath. I laughed before I could talk.

"What?" Lucas straightened.

"That was fun." I laughed again, and Lucas joined me. Then he stopped and stared at me, as if he could peer into my soul.

He leaned in and whispered, "Do you have something to tell me?"

I lowered my head. "I prayed."

He picked me up and twirled me around, a huge grin on his face. "I knew it. I knew you were close."

"Put me down!" I banged on his shoulder with one hand while I held on for dear life with the other.

"Never!" He kept his grip on my waist and twirled me again. Finally, my feet touched the wooden porch, but he pulled me into a tight hug.

I leaned my head on his soggy shirt, warm despite the damp chill in the air. What was I doing? I pushed away, turned, and stopped short of the front door. Lera and Ma would be livid if we dripped all over the foyer and stairs. "We need to get into some dry clothes and then make a plan." I grasped Lucas's hand and hurried around the outside to the laundry room.

"Yes, ma'am." He chuckled and kept pace with me.

I shook my head, but a small grin escaped my lips. How? How could I feel such joy with my life in such a mess?

"I'm with you."

I stopped short, my hand on the laundry room door. "Why did you say that?"

"I didn't say anything." Lucas pushed the door, and we

both nearly fell inside.

My foot landed hard, and I grasped a shelf to steady myself. "You said, 'I'm with you,' which went perfectly with what I was thinking at the time."

He raised his eyebrows and stared at me, a slow grin spreading across his lips. "It wasn't me."

"Then who?" My own eyes widened as it dawned on me.

Lucas pointed at the ceiling.

I shook my head. "Really?"

He nodded. "God's always with us." He cleared his throat and gazed at me. "Well, now he's with you, too." A wide smile spread across his lips.

"Huh." I grabbed a couple of towels off the shelf. "I guess."

"Where have you two been?" Lera stood under the covered walkway next to the laundry room. "Oh! Go up and get some dry clothes."

Lucas and I laughed, dried off as much as possible, and raced through the back hallway to the stairs.

"Come to the large parlor, quick," Lera called. "We've got news!"

~

After drying off with a coarse cotton towel and changing into Cassie's gray suit, I entered the large parlor. It seemed empty with only Ma and Lera relaxing around a tea table.

Lucas entered behind me. "I can go find Nate and Ed, if you ladies want to be alone."

"No." Lera patted the seat on the sofa next to her and

pointed to the wingback chair catty-corner to it. "Sit. Both of you."

Ma's eyes shone. "We have something to tell you."

I hesitated and then walked to the sofa. "Where's everyone else?"

Ma clicked her tongue. "Mark and Emily went to her family's house."

Lera vibrated with energy, her eyes bright. "Cassie's upstairs with Melody. Caleb and the men are out in the barn."

"Maybe I should join them." Lucas stood in front of the wingback chair.

Lera flashed her wicked grin. "Don't you want to hear our news?"

I motioned for Lucas to sit. "Clearly, she wants to tell us." Someone wasn't accounted for. "Wait, where's Jenny?"

Lera scoffed. "That's what I'm trying to tell you." She took a deep breath. "Allison showed up while you were gone. She caused a commotion out back, and Jenny went to try to get her to leave, or so she said."

I raised an eyebrow. "But?"

"Let her tell it." Ma leaned forward.

I scowled at Ma and swiveled my head toward Lera.

"Well, I just happened to go to the kitchen to fetch some tea." The glint in Lera's eye betrayed her. "And I overheard most of their conversation."

"Oh, it was just a coincidence, huh?" I pursed my lips, then relaxed into a grin.

Lera winked. "Don't you want to hear it?"

"I do." Lucas shifted forward in his chair.

Lera looked at me, and I circled my index finger for her to go on.

"Anyway. It seems Allison has been trying to get Jenny to steal the remote for the time machine." She peered at Lucas.

"It's all right. He knows."

She glanced at Ma. "Mattie told me. It's just…"

"What?" I shifted in my seat. "You wanted him here."

"Yes." She glanced at her lap and shrugged. "I feel strange talking about this all of a sudden."

"Why? Because you're not supposed to know? I feel strange talking about it with you, too." I grinned and nodded. "Go on."

Lera's eyes sparkled. "Jenny tried to put Allison off, and Allison accused her of wanting to keep her here. Then Jenny accused Allison of the same thing."

"I've seen them arguing." It made sense, but I didn't understand why Jenny hadn't attempted to steal the remote yet. "Did you hear anything else?"

"That's the best part." Ma smiled.

"Let me tell it." Lera glanced at Ma. "I heard it."

I stood and paced. "Someone tell me." I stopped and stared down at Lera.

"Sit, first." She sat rigid with her chin in the air.

With a sigh, I perched on the edge of the sofa. "So?"

"Jenny is waiting for you to decide to stay here." She bobbed her head toward Lucas. "So she can steal the remote and strand you here."

I stifled the urge to curse and instead took a deep breath. "Did she say why?"

"She doesn't want interference with the time machine."

I snorted. "She'll get that from Todd."

Lera raised her index finger. "Allison brought up Todd's

name, and Jenny dismissed her. She said she could handle him."

I clenched my jaw. "Is that all you heard?"

"It's all I could make sense of." Lera furrowed her brow. "Who's Todd?"

"He invented the time machine and took me to the future."

Lera half stood and sat again. "The black man who warned us about the fire?"

"Yes. Did they say anything else?"

Lera stared at the fireplace and shook her head.

"Why don't you write down everything you remember?" My hand flew to my mouth. Lera couldn't write. "I'm sorry."

"It's all right." She patted my arm. "I could now, but it would take me a while. Cassie started to take dictation, but she had to change Melody's diaper. She glanced at the parlor door. "She should be back by now."

I strolled to the small writing desk near the window and spied a pen and inkwell sitting next to a piece of Cassie's stationery.

Lucas reached it before I could. He brought it over and read, "I messed up. I need to make it right." He waved the page. "That's all that's here. Who said that?"

"Jenny." Lera squinted. "I'm not sure what she meant."

I took a deep breath and let the words sink in. "It's what I've feared all along."

"Yep." Cassie stood just inside the pocket door. "She wants to go back to 2010 before Ed came. That would undo everything."

Lera gasped, her eyes wide. "But that means I wouldn't have married John!" She stood and stared at Cassie. "Caleb wouldn't…" She glanced at Mattie and then collapsed onto the couch. "Lydia, Sarah, Mark, and Melody wouldn't exist." Her face contorted in horror.

I laid my hand on Lera's arm. "Nor would your other two. You'd have different children."

"This is what you were hinting at earlier," Lera whispered.

"We don't think it's possible." Ma leaned over and gently squeezed Lera's shoulder. "God allowed Ed to change things for a reason."

Lera gulped and nodded.

Even as a new believer, I understood a few things, so I spoke up. "But we don't know for sure. Who can know the mind of God?"

"True." Cassie sat next to me. "Aunt Mattie and I have a peace about this, though."

"That doesn't mean we shouldn't try and stop her." I locked gazes with Lera. "We will stop her."

Lera sat up and held her head high. "With the Lord's help, she won't succeed."

CHAPTER TWENTY-SEVEN

Lucas placed Cassie's notes on the writing desk. "Do Nate and Ed know about this?"

Lera shook her head. "Not yet. They've been with Simon and my boys. I've never told Simon about any of this." She covered her face with her hands, elbows resting on her thighs.

Cassie knelt next to her. "Don't worry about it. He probably wouldn't believe you if you told him."

"But he might." Lera flicked away a tear and sat up straight. "After all, he knew something was up with Jenny and all her market predictions."

Cassie turned toward Lucas. "She made Simon a fortune, telling him which stocks to buy and other investments."

"Yeah, knowledge of the future could come in handy that way." Lucas nodded at me. "So, what now?"

I shrugged and looked at Ma and Cassie.

Ma slid out of her chair to her knees. "I say we pray first."

Lucas knelt and reached out to me. "Lydia can join us now."

I flashed him a scowl as I knelt, but before I could glance at Ma, she engulfed me in a bear hug. "Finally, my precious girl!" She squeezed me tight for a moment and then leaned back and wiped a tear from her smiling face. "At least one good thing has come from all this. She clasped her hands together and gazed at the ceiling. "Thank you, Jesus!"

"Amen!" Cassie and Lera chorused.

I chuckled and shook my head. "So, we're all on our knees."

"I'll start." Ma scooted back. We clasped hands in a circle, and she thanked God again for my salvation, and continued with a prayer for help in dealing with Jenny and Allison. "Please, Father, soften the hearts of Richard, Allison, Brian, and Jenny. Bring them to a saving knowledge of You."

It wouldn't have occurred to me to pray for them. How had I not seen the goodness in my mother, before?

Lera said a short prayer, followed by Lucas, and Cassie.

When it was my turn, I took a breath and gathered my thoughts, but Nate's voice pierced the air. "Lord, please grant us Your favor and bring us success, if it's in Your will."

"Amen," Pa said.

I exhaled, and my shoulders lowered. Someday, I'd pray in public.

"When did you two get here?" Ma glanced up at Pa and Nate, who stood behind Cassie.

"Early enough to know what you were praying about." Nate extended a hand to help Ma up. "Care to fill us in on the details?"

Lera peered around Nate. "Where's Simon?"

"In the small parlor with all the boys." Pa smirked. "He's

expecting us back with toys soon, so make it quick."

Lera paraphrased her story, then Nate hurried out of the room.

"I'll give him the rest of the details later," Cassie said.

Lucas stood in the center of the room and glanced at each of us. "Anyone else hear any clear guidance?"

We shook our heads.

"Wait!" Ma raised her hand. "You did?"

Lucas puffed out his chest and smiled wide. "Yep!"

"So, spill!" Lera strode over to him, hands on hips.

He stepped back and held his hand up. "I only got part of it." He narrowed his eyes at me.

I shrugged. "I got nothing."

"One step at a time," Ma said.

Lucas nodded at Ma. "Invite Allison over for tea tomorrow."

Ma tilted her head. "But the machine is here."

"No, it's not." I held up the remote, checking to make sure I had the right one. "Remember, I can summon it with this."

Lucas detailed his plan.

Ma clapped her hands together. "You are too devious."

"Not me." Lucas pointed upwards.

Even if the plan was from God, why would He give that particular message to Lucas? It was odd that Lera wouldn't have thought of it. Hers was the devious mind. I glanced in her direction and grinned at her wide eyes and gaping mouth.

"Why, Lucas, I'm impressed!" Lera strode toward him. "If I wasn't already married, I'd be smitten."

Pa chuckled. "She means to say that she likes the way you think."

Lucas sputtered, "It wasn't me."

"Well." Ma patted Lucas on the chest. "It's a good plan."

~

Jenny set the china teacups and saucers on one silver tray. "So, who is this special guest Miss Mattie invited?"

I placed the scones and teacakes on the other tray and flashed her my innocent expression. "Do you think Ma would tell me?"

She pursed her lips and placed one hand on her hip. "You always did know more than you let on."

I cocked my head and shrugged. "We'll find out in a few minutes." I arranged the teacakes and scones on the plates and carried my tray to the parlor with Jenny behind me.

"Really, I don't understand these people." Jenny set her tray on the intricately inlaid round table next to one of the small sofas. "We just had that big Thanksgiving dinner yesterday. Why invite someone over to tea today?"

I smirked as I set my tray on the rectangular cherry table in front of the sofa. "They are more fellowship-oriented in this time than we are. And they don't have social media."

Jenny leaned closer. "Is Facebook still around?"

I nodded. "It's getting bigger, with the older demographic anyway. Lots of clout."

She cleared her throat and smoothed her apron. "I'm sorry. I shouldn't think about those things."

I rolled my eyes and headed toward the pantry. "I already know you want to go back, or forward, I guess."

She took a deep breath. "Wait."

I stopped, still facing away from her.

"I wanted to talk to you about that."

I whirled around and studied her expression. Her eyes gleamed, and she held herself erect. Her face was open, accepting. In other words, she didn't look much like the Jenny I remembered. I narrowed my eyes and closed the gap. She didn't flinch. If this were a game of chicken, she would win.

I took a deep breath and let it out. "I can take you back any time. But you have to promise not to ever mess with the time machine again." A memory from the day before flashed into my mind. "Wait. Lera heard you say that you wanted to strand me here. You didn't want interference with the machine."

She bit her lip and studied the floor. "I lied." She raised her head and gazed at me. "I wanted that woman to think that. To keep her off guard. She's the one who wants to control the machine."

My stomach knotted. "How am I supposed to believe you now?" Chaos reigned in my mind. I needed to talk to Lucas about this. No. Cassie or Ma. Why had I thought of Lucas first?

"Lydia." Jenny touched my shoulder. "You know what going back without control of the time machine means for me, don't you?"

"Yes. You'll have to start over." I didn't really care, or I hadn't until yesterday. A sigh escaped my lips. "I can help you. And Todd and Chantal probably will let you stay at the B&B until you can establish an identity."

She cocked her head. I explained who Chantal was and that Nate's house was being used as a bed and breakfast. She nodded. Was she considering it?

"Of course." I flicked my wrist. "We still need to deal

with Allison."

She blinked. "The other time traveler?"

A grin spread on my face. "You didn't know her name? You've been arguing with her enough."

"You've been spying!" Jenny stepped back, her eyes bright. "I'm impressed."

I chuckled and shook my head. What was keeping Ma?

Hoof beats and carriage wheels stole my attention, and I ran outside as Lera and Cassie, in Lera's carriage, entered the side yard from the road to Nate's. Now, we needed the guest of honor. I hoped Ma had gotten the message to her in time.

Cassie climbed out of the carriage, and I ran over to her. "Where's Melody?"

"Caleb's babysitting." Lera wore a proud smile as she appeared from the other side of the carriage. "Simon has my two at home."

"Don't you have a nanny?" They had downsized, but Simon was still rich.

"Yes. That just means I don't have to worry as much." Lera winked at Cassie.

"I'm not worried." Cassie beamed. "Caleb's good with Melody. He has lots of practice with babies at home."

Lera laughed. "Our nanny is only part-time, and she doesn't help Caleb." She sobered and gazed over my shoulder. I turned around.

The youngest Jones boy approached the front porch, driving Pa's small carriage. Allison sat behind him, wearing a dark green gown she must have borrowed from Mrs. Kelley.

"Where's Ma?" I glanced toward the kitchen.

The front door opened and closed. "Welcome," Ma called from the porch.

Lera, Cassie, and I hurried to the front of the house. I glanced back to see that the carriage horse was tethered. Lera must have done that quickly.

Ma and Jenny stood on the porch, and Allison climbed from the carriage with the help of the youngest Jones boy.

"Looks like it's show time," Cassie whispered in my ear. "You ready?"

Patting the remote in my pocket, I nodded. "You?"

Cassie held up her drawstring bag. "I'm still not sure why we're here and not at our house."

"Lucas thinks it's to keep Todd from hampering us, until we get everyone back to where they belong."

Cassie leaned in. "Are you sure you don't belong here?"

I took a deep breath. "Yes." I would redeem my life in the future by doing something worthwhile. Maybe I'd find a man like Lucas.

We followed Ma, Lera, Allison, and a gaping Jenny into the house.

Jenny held me back just inside the front door. "What are you up to?"

I huffed. "We're trying to get her back to her own time."

"Be careful." Jenny swallowed and pursed her lips. "She's dangerous."

I clamped my mouth shut to keep from saying, *Look who's talking.* Instead, I nodded. "Noted."

"Jenny, dear." Ma used her company voice. "Would you get the teapots from the kitchen, please?" She ushered Allison to her best wingback chair. "I've made black tea and green tea. They should be thoroughly steeped by now."

"You needn't have gone to the trouble." Allison flashed a scowl in my direction. "I only came to talk to her."

"Oh?" Ma feigned ignorance. "You know Lydia?"

"Yes." She grimaced, showing teeth. Was that supposed to be a smile?

"Well, that's nice." Ma glanced at the front door as she sat in the upholstered chair across from Allison. "You two can reminisce while we have our tea. Won't that be fun?"

"Yes, I think it will." Cassie perched on the sofa with a sly smile on her face.

Lera clapped her hands together. "How do you two know each other?"

I sat next to Cassie and nodded at Allison.

"Er." Allison cleared her throat. "We met on a weekend trip."

"Oh? Do tell." Ma had that twinkle in her eye. She was enjoying this. Even though she was a devout Christian and truly wished the best for everyone, she loved putting people on the spot and watching them squirm. I wasn't sure she'd admit it, though.

"Oh, well." Allison smoothed her plain forest-green skirt. "I just want a word in private. It concerns someone else we both met that weekend."

"We won't tell." Ma glanced at Cassie and Lera. "Will we girls?"

They both shook their heads, and Lera made a motion as if locking her lips. Like anyone who knew her would believe that.

"Tea time." Jenny brought in the teapots and set them on the tray with the cups, leaving the small towels wrapped around the handles.

Ma bobbed her head at Jenny. "Please, pour."

Jenny sighed. "Which one?"

"The green tea is in the white one, and the black tea is in the flowered one." Ma pointed to each in turn.

Cassie pointed to the white teapot. "Green for me, please."

Jenny poured all our tea, switching from one pot to the other. Why was she going along with this? She had to be biding her time. Was she trying to stay on Ma's good side in case everything went sour?

~

Ma, Lera, and Cassie kept the conversation going while sipping tea and tasting cakes and scones. Jenny and Allison became more antsy as the time wore on. Nate, Pa, and Lucas were outside waiting as we'd planned. I waited, thankful we'd all said a prayer together yesterday, and Nate, Cassie, Lucas, and I had prayed this morning. Funny, just a few days ago, I wouldn't have thought much about it, but now, it comforted me.

"Well." Allison stood and smoothed out her skirt. "Thank you for tea. It was nice to get to know you." She curtsied toward Ma and glanced at me.

"I'll see you to the door." I followed her out of the room, and Jenny accompanied us. Cassie was the person I needed, though. I opened the front door for Allison and ushered her out to the porch. "What did you want to talk to me about?"

"Like you don't know." She scoffed and marched down the stairs. "What did you do with Richard and Brian?"

Was she more worried about Richard? "I sent them back. That's what they wanted."

She stamped her foot. "The fools. We weren't finished."

"Apparently, they thought you were." I followed her to the paving stones and glanced behind me. Cassie had just reached the doorway.

Allison stood with one hand on her hip. "I'll be finished when I get control of the machine."

"You figured out how to use it." I walked to the side of the house where we'd planned to locate the time machine. That should place it near the woods at the back of the starter-home subdivision in the future. "You could figure out how to control it when you get back."

She caught up to me. "But you already know."

I stopped at our marker stone and took a deep breath. "I promised I wouldn't give up the secret."

"Where is it?" Allison turned in a circle. "You led me here for a reason."

With Cassie a few yards behind me, I pulled out the remote and made a show of pushing the button. "Move over to your left."

A mist swirled in, and Allison scurried away from it. When the fog cleared, the time machine sat in its place.

"A remote!" Allison jogged toward me, eyes on the gadget. Before she reached me, the remote was snatched out of my hand. Jenny ran to the machine with the stolen controller.

"Stop her!" Cassie trotted to me.

I sprinted toward Jenny on the machine, but she was too fast. The mist rolled in, leaving Allison and me just outside of it. Allison started to enter, but I held her back. "Don't. We don't know what will happen if you're not on the platform." More importantly, why did it leave? Could Todd have programmed it to pop back to the future if it detected weight?

"But she's going to ruin everything!" Allison pushed me.

I stepped back to avoid falling. "How do you know?"

"She'll keep control of the machine and leave us stranded here." She waved her arm at the empty space where the machine had been. "She started all this. Changed the timeline and now she's decided to keep it like it is."

Good news for us. "How do you believe her?" I touched her arm, but she pulled away and stared at the empty space. Nate and Lucas stood near the barn. Cassie was still behind me, and I didn't know where Ma and Pa were. Thankfully, everyone stayed quiet.

"I just do, that's all." She lifted her chin. "I wanted to change it back."

I scoffed. "Even if you knew about time-travel, you wouldn't remember the reality Jenny knew."

She turned to me, eyes flashing. "But I did. Through hypnosis." Her eyes widened, and she clasped her hand over her mouth.

I jerked forward. "What did you remember?"

She sighed and dropped her arms. "I had a husband. He was a descendant of Simon and Lera's oldest. The one who wasn't born in the new timeline." She wiped away a tear. Was it real? "He was my soul mate. I won't find anyone close to him in this new timeline."

I furrowed my brow. "Why do you believe Jenny won't fix things for you?"

She huffed and jabbed her arm at the spot where the machine sat. "We're stuck here. Even if she does fix things, it won't affect me." She furrowed her brow. "Why aren't you upset?"

"What do you mean?" I cocked my head. Oh. She thought Jenny had the real remote. I grinned and held my hand out to Cassie, who strode over and placed it in my hand. "Just a bit of subterfuge."

Allison's eyes widened again, and she reached toward me. I drew the remote away from her.

"You mean she called it?" She pointed at Cassie, who nodded. Allison giggled, then broke into a louder laugh. "Jenny thinks she has the right one? Why did it leave, then?"

Cassie flashed a sheepish grin. "I pressed the GO button again. It was an accident."

Alison snorted. "How long before she figures it out?"

A fog rolled in.

I pointed to the mist. "Probably not long."

This time, the machine popped back, probably because Jenny didn't have the controller.

I pivoted toward Cassie to shield the remote from Allison so I could program it for a couple of days after Jenny would have returned, giving her time to leave before we showed up. Then I peered at Allison. "Are you ready to go home?"

Allison shook her head. "Where's Mattie?"

Ma strode from the back door, and Pa jogged over from the barn.

Allison extended her hand to Ma. "I need that printout you promised me."

Ma and Pa exchanged a glance. Pa shrugged. "I don't see how it'll hurt."

"I thought you might insist." Ma reached into her bag and fished out that crumpled, stapled paper with Lera's original family tree.

Allison grabbed it and strode onto the platform. "Now, I'm ready."

I joined her. "Why is that so important?"

She clasped the paper over her heart and showed us a wistful smile. "I wanted a record of my true love."

My stomach soured, and I grimaced. I didn't buy it for a second. She planned to change the timeline back. I clutched the remote tighter. No way would I let her touch it, and as soon as we returned, I'd give it to Todd. Now was a great time to deactivate the machine.

"Wait!" Cassie stumbled over to me. "You're not even going to say goodbye?"

What was I thinking? Well, I wasn't. I stepped off the platform and pocketed the remote. I'd hoped to avoid the teary farewells, especially with Allison here, but how could I? I would probably never see them again. A tear escaped the corner of my eye, and I sniffed.

Ma handed me a clean handkerchief. "I knew you'd go today." She smiled through her tears. "I've had time to prepare, and I'm still not ready." She patted my shoulder. "But you are. I'm so thankful you're a believer now. I can let you go, knowing I'll see you again." She smothered me in a hug. "Sorry, I couldn't get Mark or Caleb here, and Lera says goodbye. She didn't want to cry in front of everyone."

I hadn't thought Lera was that sentimental. I grinned through my tears and squeezed Ma one last time before she let me go.

Pa hugged me tight and released me. "God speed, Lydia." He sounded so choked up that he could barely get three words out.

"I'll continue to write." Cassie gave me a quick hug.

Nate kissed me on the cheek and gave me a bear hug. "You take care."

Lucas stood near the platform, his gaze glued on Allison. I approached him slowly. What could I say with everyone else present? "Lucas." I swallowed hard. "I'm so happy I got to know you at least a little."

"Me, too, Lydia." His gaze still on Allison, he held out his hand as if to shake mine, then pulled me into a hug. "Watch her," he whispered in my ear.

I nodded, pulled the remote out of my pocket, and joined Allison on the platform. Before I could push the button, she grabbed the remote. Lucas jumped up and reached for it. I slid between Lucas and Allison while the mist swirled in, and my family's shouting receded. As the machine shook, keeping us locked on with a force I'd never get used to, we struggled in slow motion. I tried to grab the remote, but every move was a chore, and I couldn't see through the fog. Did Allison have it or did Lucas? I prayed Lucas had it. When my stomach settled and the mist cleared, about a hundred pairs of eyes stared at us. I gulped and froze.

CHAPTER TWENTY-EIGHT

Okay, so there weren't a hundred people, but at least a dozen park goers stood, mouths agape. We'd missed our mark, having landed farther from the woods than planned.

Lucas held up the remote.

I exhaled, relieved.

He stepped off the platform and offered his elbow to escort me off.

As Allison froze on the platform, I smiled, curled my hand around Lucas's crooked arm, and walked into the park.

"Great stunt, Lucas!" I patted him on the shoulder and made eye contact with the nosiest woman on the edge of the playground. "Performance art."

She raised one eyebrow and backed away from me as we passed. Lucas led me off the field and into a sparse patch of trees. I caught my breath as Allison ran toward us, her hands shielding her face.

She stopped short. "Where are we?"

"I think we're right where we were. This is what became of Mattie's yard. The more pertinent question is when." It was too warm for February when I thought we'd arrive. I reached toward Lucas for the remote.

"Did you see that guy with the scarf around the lower half of his face?" Lucas pointed at a middle-aged man race-walking on a trail that wound around the park. "It's hot. Why would he cover his face?"

I shrugged, concerned more about what the remote readout would say. Of course, the display was blank. I shook it and banged on it, but nothing. "What happened?"

"What are you saying?" Allison swooped in and swiped the remote out of my hand, pushing the buttons wildly. "It's broken?" She scowled at me and then at Lucas.

I raised both hands to prove they were empty. "One of you had it when we jumped."

"I grabbed it as she pressed the GO button." Lucas pointed at Allison.

Allison glared at him. "I didn't trust you."

"I wasn't on the machine when you stole it." Lucas used his steely tone.

Allison turned away and slipped the remote into her pocket. "I guess we need to figure out what day it is."

She wanted control of the time machine. If she tried to fix it, I had to stop her. Todd was right. This machine was dangerous. Wait. Maybe the machine would work manually. I jogged to it, Lucas and Allison right behind me. A few people still milled around the park at a distance. "Help me move this." I bobbed my head toward a copse of trees.

The three of us lifted the machine and carried it into the woods. I stepped onto it.

"What are you doing?" Allison pulled on my arm.

I snagged it away and hit the ON button. The display stayed dark. I tapped it a few times.

Allison sneered. "What did you think would happen?"

"It might've worked without the remote." I slumped against the railing.

She cackled. "You'd go back just to keep me from getting my hands on this." She patted the edge of the control panel.

"No." The real reason was to send Lucas home, but I couldn't say that because he crept up behind Allison.

"I can still figure out how to control that machine." She held up the remote and waved it back and forth.

Lucas grabbed it out of her hand.

She whirled around and lunged for him.

He jumped back and stuck the remote in his trousers pocket.

Allison faced me and huffed. "Now what?"

That was a good question. Not only did I not know exactly how far in the future we'd come, but I didn't have a way to send Lucas back to where he belonged.

Lucas touched my shoulder. "Find Todd?"

I snapped my head in his direction to see the grin on his face.

Before I could ask him how he knew about Todd, he held his hands up and leaned back. "Hey. I listen."

"Okay." I strode into the field, orienting myself to the landscape. "That street should lead us to the main road into Todd's subdivision. We'll have to take the long way, though, so it'll be a couple of miles." I pointed to a road at the front of the park.

Though the sun peeked over the horizon, over a dozen people were in the park. Walking through in our nineteenth-century clothing, we drew the attention of everyone. I stuck my chin in the air and ignored the gawking. At least I tried to.

When I elongated my stride, Lucas snickered. "A bit self-conscious?"

Allison hurried behind us. "Easy for you to say. You're not quite as conspicuous. Let's get to Todd's fast."

Lucas wore work clothes and a cowboy-style hat, so he blended in better than Allison and I did in our full skirts and Victorian jackets. Like Cassie, I wasn't wearing a hoop, just a full slip.

"I'm with you two, though." Lucas chuckled as he kept pace with us.

I pulled out the handkerchief Ma had given me to wipe my brow. "It must be summer. We jumped at least five months. Maybe longer."

"Hope it's still 2020," Allison said.

When we exited the park into the starter-home neighborhood, Lucas gaped.

"Don't slow down." I pulled on his arm. "I'll explain everything later."

"Wow!" Lucas kept pace with us, but rubbernecked at houses, cars, bicycles, and a teenager walking down the street, talking on a cell phone. His mind was probably swirling, too.

Finally, we reached the street where Nate's house sat at the end of the cul-de-sac. I heaved a sigh of relief to see the bed and breakfast sign still out front.

Allison broke into a run, a feat in that dress. At least if it hadn't been too long, she and I would find our 2020 clothes at Chantal's.

Lucas and I hurried to Nate's house. Allison stood at the front door. Why hadn't she gone in?

"What's up?" I climbed the porch steps.

Allison stood, hands on hips, and huffed. "She won't let me in."

"Chantal?" I cocked my head.

"Lydia?" Chantal stood behind the screen door wearing a piece of cloth over her nose and mouth. "What on earth? What happened to you? We've been worried sick."

I squinted at her. "Can't explain, right now. Are our things still here?"

"Yes. Wait here." She hurried to her desk.

Lucas and I glanced at each other and shrugged.

Chantal returned and handed us rectangular pieces of cloth with elastic hoops on the ends. "Put these on before you come in. I can't believe you didn't know that. Where have you been?"

I pulled the elastic over my ears and followed Chantal inside. Lucas and Allison entered behind me. A sign on the desk read: Masks required in public spaces. Meals will be served in private rooms.

I pointed to the sign. "What's this all about?" My voice sounded muffled, and sweat already dampened my mask.

Chantal stuck a hand on her hip. "COVID. Where have you been?"

Allison stepped around me. "Is that the virus that started in China late last year?"

"Yes. It's like you two lost several months." Chantal pointed to Lucas. "Who's this?"

I froze. "Uh."

"Lucas Sullivan." He put out his hand to shake.

Chantal stuck her hands in the air. "We don't shake hands anymore." She opened her laptop and looked up at me.

"Your room is available if you want it. I can get your things out of storage."

I glanced at Lucas. "Is there a room for him?"

Chantal nodded and clicked her mouse.

"What about mine?" Allison leaned on the desk.

Chantal clicked her tongue. "I can get you your things, but I don't have a room for you. You still owe me from your last visit."

Allison thumped her knuckles on the desk. "Didn't Brian pay you?"

"He paid half. That was four months ago."

My breath hitched. We lost four months?

Allison's eyes blazed, and her jaw tightened. "Fine. Get my things and I'll settle the bill."

I stifled a giggle.

Chantal nodded at me. "Follow me." She pointed at Allison. "Wait here. I'll bring your bags down." Chantal led the way upstairs, and Lucas and I followed. She opened the door near the top of the stairs. "Lucas, you can stay here."

I blinked. "Where's Jamal?"

She pursed her lips. "The fool went back to Atlanta last week. Against my advice."

Lucas glanced at me, then peered into the room and whistled. "Looks similar."

I cleared my throat and caught his attention, then I gave my head a small shake.

Lucas smiled at Chantal. "Thank you for taking me in. As soon as possible, I'll pay for the room."

Chantal shrugged. "I have plenty of work around here, if you want to work for room and board, for the immediate future."

Lucas's eyes sparkled. "Yes, ma'am."

Chantal nodded and ushered me down the hall to the room I had occupied in all three time periods. "You can stay here until Friday. Then you can move in with me and Todd. This room is rented for the weekend."

I hugged her. "Thank you for everything."

She gave me an extra squeeze and released me. "You will tell me where you've been, right? Or rather, when?"

I gasped.

She snapped her fingers. "I knew it. Todd's contraption is a time machine."

I winced. "Yes." Why would I think she'd be unable to figure it out when so many others had? "You said, I have until Friday? How long is that?"

She chuckled. "Today is Wednesday, July 29."

I clasped the doorknob and glanced down the hallway.

Lucas stood in front of his room, a lock of sandy hair drooped over his forehead, and wonder shone in his expressive eyes.

I flushed. Should I move in with Todd and Chantal today? No. It was only two days, and Chantal might need time to get her guest room ready. Also, Todd might be able to send Lucas back. But would Lucas go? I shuddered. What a mess.

~

Chantal had called Todd at work and filled him in on our arrival. He'd leave as soon as possible, but that could be anytime. While we waited, Lucas and I strolled around outside the B&B. It felt good to take the masks off. He wore an old t-shirt of Todd's, which he'd donned over his suspenders, allowing him to blend in. I had changed into my jeans and a t-shirt, my jeans plastered to my thighs in this heat. If I couldn't get some shopping done soon, these jeans were destined to become cut-offs.

Lucas gazed at me. "Where do you think Allison went?"

I shrugged. "Back to Atlanta? That's where she lived, I think." I fingered the broken remote that I'd, for some unknown reason, stuck in my jeans pocket after changing. "I wouldn't be upset to never see her again."

A new black Audi pulled up and parked on the cul-de-sac. Todd climbed out.

We headed toward him, but he shook his head and marched to the wooded area away from the house, motioning for us to follow. "Where's Jenny?" Todd stared into my eyes, one hand on my upper arm.

"I don't know." I pulled my arm away. "She used the machine to come here, but she had the wrong remote with her. It popped back to us."

He rubbed his temple. "Last Thursday, around nine at night, someone reported a UFO in the park near the next subdivision."

"That's where we landed!" I glanced at Lucas. "It had to be Jenny."

Todd groaned and bobbed his head at Lucas. "Who's this?"

"Lucas. He works for—I mean, worked for Nate."

"Send him back."

"Can't." I dipped my head and scuffed my foot on the ground. "The remote broke. Can't get a display on the machine either." I fished the broken remote out of my pocket and handed it to him.

"How did that happen?" Todd inspected the remote and tapped it against his palm.

"Allison." Lucas cleared his throat. "She tried to steal it, and I stopped her."

"They must have broken it en route." I peered at Todd. "Can you fix it?"

He shook his head, his eyes narrowed, and his mouth pursed. Then he lifted his chin and studied Lucas. "You'll have to stay."

Lucas straightened to his full height and nodded. "Thought as much."

I lunged at Todd. "No. Wait. He doesn't belong here."

Todd pulled away from me and heaved a sigh. "I made a promise to destroy that machine as soon as you got back. And not meddle in time-travel again."

I tilted my head. "Who asked you to do that?"

Todd glanced at the sky, then flashed a small smile. "God. But my boss agrees."

Lucas nodded, a slight grin on his face. Had he wanted this all along?

Todd strode to the Audi. "Time to make good on that promise."

Lucas caught up to him. "We moved the machine, but we'll show you where."

Todd opened the driver's door. "Get in."

I jogged over and got in the back, expecting Lucas to follow me, but he took the front passenger seat. Too bad I couldn't watch his face when Todd drove.

After he put the car in gear, Todd glanced at me in the rear-view. "How did you end up in that park?"

I flushed. "We were in Mattie's side yard."

Before I could tell Lucas about the seatbelt, Todd sped off down the street, going a bit too fast for a residential area. Lucas held onto the armrest on the door, his back rigid. The alarm blaring, I showed Lucas the belt. After he pulled it out, I locked it in place and leaned back.

When we pulled into the small parking lot near the playground, Lucas glanced over his shoulder and grinned. "When can I learn to operate one of these?"

Todd opened his door and got out, so I followed him around and met Lucas on the other side. "You'll have to wait." I didn't want to go into the details of getting a permit and an ID.

Todd glanced around the park. "Where is it?"

"In the woods. On the other side of the playground." I followed Todd as he stalked off. The three of us could probably carry the thing, but it would be awkward and draw attention. How would he get the machine into the Audi?

Todd strode to the control panel and pushed a couple of buttons. The display illuminated.

Lucas and I gasped.

I scanned the screen. "Can you send him back?" Lucas squeezed my hand. He didn't want to go back. At least not yet.

"I wish I could." Todd wiped his brow. "A lot has been going on at work. Allison's boss has been asking questions. He wants to take over the time machine, and my boss wants the whole thing to end. I've put them both off, waiting for you." He blew out a breath. "I'd need to fix this, and that would delay getting rid of it." He closed his eyes and gripped the handrails, revealing white knuckles. After a moment, he gazed at Lucas. "If it was just that..."

Lucas nodded. "It's also your promise to God. I understand." He gazed at me for a moment, then raised his face to the sky and took a deep breath. "I'll stay willingly."

My stomach did a weird flip. Was Lucas staying for me? Did I want that?

Todd reached over the rail and shook Lucas's hand. "I can help you with an identity." He pushed a few more buttons. A sequence of numbers flashed in descending order, and Todd hopped off the machine. When the numbers on the display hit zero, the machine collapsed with a pop. I wouldn't call it an explosion, more like an implosion. All the parts lay in a heap.

Applause sounded from behind me. The lady from earlier emerged from behind a tree. "Impressive. Bizarre, but impressive." She stopped clapping and walked away.

Todd scowled and raised his eyebrows.

"I told her it was performance art."

Todd laughed, and Lucas and I joined in.

Todd picked up one of the larger pieces, motioning for us to do the same. "We need to clean this up. I should have done this years ago."

It took us three trips, but we got all the pieces into Todd's trunk. We drove to a junkyard before going home.

By the time we made it back to the B&B, I was exhausted and hungry, but we had a plan to get an ID for Lucas. Todd's boss would come through one last time.

We donned our masks before we walked in the door. Todd ushered us straight to the kitchen, where he told us we could remove the masks. We sat down to dinner already on the table.

"Thank you so much for this." I patted Chantal's arm.

"You're welcome." She handed me a platter of fish, but then pulled it back. "That is, if you fill me in on all the details."

Todd motioned for Chantal to let go. "Fine."

I nodded and accepted the platter.

Chantal said grace. I joined in silently, thanking God for a new start, the chance to see my family again, and say goodbye properly. I vowed to continue that journal so I could sort out all my feelings about my family. Did I make the wrong choice, coming back?

Lucas squeezed my hand, and my eyes shot open.

Chantal chuckled. "Glad to see you were also praying. I finished before you did."

I cleared my throat. "Lots to pray about."

Chantal nodded. "Always. Now, tell me what's going on."

As we filled Chantal in on time-travel and explained everything that happened, she sat still, her gaze transfixed.

When Todd finished, she leaned back. "So much makes sense now."

"Really?" I squinted. "It's so strange."

She flicked her wrist. "Yes, but even from the beginning. You being the only survivor from that car crash, and your injuries didn't seem to match. It didn't make sense to me then." She sat up straight. "And Brian and Richard, suddenly appearing in the house, without masks, or any idea about COVID. You, missing for five months without explanation." She wagged her finger at Todd. "I knew she wouldn't leave and not tell us, unless she couldn't for some reason."

"What about the note I left in the closet?"

Todd lowered his head. "I got it. But it only explained a short delay."

I rubbed the back of my neck. "Yeah. The arrival time must have messed up when Jenny traveled."

Chantal blew out a breath. "An unidentified object appeared and disappeared in the park last week. Was that Jenny?"

I nodded.

"And today, you and Lucas showed up wearing period clothing." Chantal shook her head. "It's hard to believe, but with all the evidence, I do."

Todd covered her hand with his. "I'm sorry I didn't tell you sooner."

She clasped his hand in both of hers and smiled. "Thank you for telling me now. I'm glad there won't be this big secret between us." She broke into a huge grin. "Because we have an important job to do together."

Todd cocked his head.

She pulled one hand away and pressed it to her flat stomach. "Starting in about seven months, we'll be raising a child."

Todd jumped out of his chair, his eyes wide, and a smile growing on his lips. He let out a whoop. "Really? You're not kidding?"

Chantal reached into her pocket and pulled out an ultrasound picture. "Proof."

Todd picked her up off her chair and twirled her around.

"Whoa. Don't throw your back out, Daddy." Chantal laughed.

I couldn't wipe the smile off my face if I tried. Good for them. It was obviously what they wanted.

~

Ding ding. I blinked against the sun streaming between the curtain panels and pushed myself onto my elbows. What was that sound? Ding ding. I groaned and eyed my phone, which lay on the nightstand, probably fully charged by now. This was the first time in weeks I'd heard my text notification. I hadn't missed it.

I sat up, unplugged my phone, and squinted at it. Then, I dropped it onto the bed. A hundred and fifteen text messages. I peeked at it again. Most from the same account—Austin.

My stomach growled. I needed sustenance before going through all those messages. Thankfully, I'd spent last evening catching up with Todd and Chantal on what I'd missed and filling them in on my last two weeks. When I went to bed, I plugged my dead phone in. God knew I needed that unplugged time.

I dragged myself out of bed, dressed in my skinny jeans and a white tee, and headed downstairs to raid the kitchen. On my way out the door, I glimpsed the closet at the back of the house. Could the rest of Cassie's journals be there now? I trotted around the staircase to the back hallway. Several journals lay on the shelves in the attic closet. I sorted through them. "Yes!" The missing one from 1873 - 1874 was there, as was the one from 1875. I stuffed them under my arm and rifled through the rest, just earlier volumes and the family Bible. Later, I'd check the shelves in both parlors. There had to be more. I carried the journals to the kitchen.

Lucas sat at the counter, scarfing down pancakes and bacon. He swallowed and smiled. "Morning. Chantal let us sleep in. She left breakfast for us." He motioned to the two stainless-steel steam trays at the end of the counter and a plate next to them.

"Good morning." I set the journals on the counter and helped myself to two pancakes and several strips of bacon. "I'll have to thank her later."

"Here's the syrup." He slid a small pitcher to me as I sat on the adjacent stool.

"Thanks, I'm starved." I poured syrup and cut my pancake.

His brows went up.

"Right." I set down my fork, clasped my hands, and prayed silently.

He nodded at me. "I'm surprised you put that much food on your plate."

"I guess my stomach isn't as knotted." I smiled and took a bite. "Mm. I hope so, anyway."

He helped himself to more bacon.

"There're more pancakes."

He shook his head. "I've already had a stack."

"Good to know your appetite hasn't diminished."

He laughed. "If that happens, you'll know something's wrong." He pointed to the journals. "May I?"

I nodded. "You'll find your name in them."

He picked up the top one and flipped through it. "Yours too."

I choked on bacon, but managed to swallow it. "I'm fine."

"Sorry. I shouldn't have said it that way. Cassie refers to Cousin Ellen visiting long enough to escort some criminals posing as missionaries out of town." He snickered.

"What'd she write about you?"

He read silently, his expression changing from a confused squint to the widest open-mouthed grin I'd seen on him. Lucas laughed so long, he snorted and couldn't speak.

I snatched the journal away and read:

Our hired hand, Lucas, was so smitten with Cousin Ellen that he accompanied her out west. Of course, he told us he felt led to go as protection from the criminal element she had with her.

He stopped laughing when I frowned at him. "What's so funny?" My shoulders tensed. Why did his reaction bother me? Did I want it to be true?

Lucas cleared his throat. "You don't..." His Adam's apple bobbed up and down. "It surprised me, is all."

I continued reading silently.

Lucas fidgeted as he finished his bacon. "Are you going to tell me what happened?"

"In the spring of 1874, Nate hired someone to replace you. By summer, Mark and Emily were expecting. In the autumn, Pa got to use his steam-powered mill." I shrugged. "Some excitement, but not from time-travelers."

"Good." Lucas sipped coffee.

"Lydia, your notifications are going crazy." Chantal strode into the kitchen and held my phone out for me.

I rolled my eyes as I accepted it and opened my messages.

"What's that?" Lucas's eyes widened as he peered at my phone.

Austin's latest text caught my attention. I hopped off the stool and strode down the center hallway to the front porch. As I left, Chantal was trying to explain smartphones to

Lucas.

Despite the heat, I plopped onto the porch swing. I should at least skim all these messages before replying. In the first few, Austin apologized for our New Year's Eve argument, then he wanted to know when I'd be back. His texts referred to voicemails and got more and more unhinged. I blew out a breath. Of course, he thought I'd ghosted him. Well, I had, but not intentionally. Still, I couldn't tell him where I'd been, and I didn't know why we'd been gone five months in this time, and only a little over two weeks in the past.

Dear Lord, what should I tell him? My thumbs trembled as I typed out a message. "I'm sorry. I didn't mean to ghost you, but I haven't had my phone for five months." I hit 'send' and my hands shook harder. In California, it was seven-thirty in the morning. How soon would he see this?"

I leaned back, praying for the right words if he replied. Ding, ding. That was quick.

"Call me. I need to see your face to know it's you."

That was fair. I took a deep breath and placed the video call. As it connected, I pasted on a sheepish smile. "Hi, Austin. I just got your texts this morning—really."

His nose filled the screen, then he pulled the phone back to reveal his face and a snatch of my bedroom wallpaper at the apartment. "It is you. You had me worried sick. Why were you away from your phone so long?"

I paused as my mind reeled. "I went away without it. To do some soul searching." It wasn't an outright lie. "Austin. I've decided I won't be coming back. Is Rene still living with you?"

He nodded, his face blank.

"I'll have her pack up my stuff and ship it."

"What about us?" Austin pleaded.

"We've been over for nearly a year, Austin." I leaned against the back of the swing and sighed. "Maybe longer. I should never have worked for you."

He sat up straight. "Yeah. I shouldn't have offered. Listen, I have a buddy out here you could work for. Maybe our relationship would work—"

"I'm done with Seattle." I sat up straight, proud of myself for not budging.

The screen blurred as he jumped off the bed. "You've met someone else!"

"That's not—"

"Ugh. And I passed up a date with Bianca, waiting for you."

"Why would you do that?" My face heated. "I told you we were through." A year ago, Austin's attraction to Bianca, a friend's sister, had irritated me. Today, it encouraged me. "Ask her out."

His face filled the screen, jaw clenched and eyes narrowed. "Maybe I will."

"Good. I wish you all the best." I spoke the truth.

"Wait. Really?" He wore his puppy dog face.

"Really, Austin." I shook my head and hovered my thumb over the end icon.

"Fine." Austin gritted his teeth. "Don't come crawling back." He clicked off.

I stifled a smirk. Maybe it's for the best this way. Let him have the last word. My shoulders relaxed.

My ring tone played, and my shoulders tensed again until I checked the caller ID. Why would Chantal call me? I answered.

Lucas's smiling face filled up the screen. "I can see you. This is amazing."

I smirked. "Yep. But you could walk through the house and see me."

Chantal leaned into view. "The only way to explain was to show him."

Lucas filled up the screen again. "Will you teach me everything I need to learn to live here?"

I sighed. "Yes, but it'll take a while."

Chantal appeared on screen again. "In the meantime, I'll teach you how to clean bathrooms." She ended the call.

I chuckled as I stood, unstuck my jeans from the back of my thighs, and headed into the house to finish breakfast.

~

After Lucas and Chantal finished cleaning the guest rooms, I brought my laptop to the kitchen and set it up on the butcher block table.

Lucas poured coffee for both of us and joined me. "What's that?"

"Your first lesson." I plugged in the mouse and opened an Internet browser. "I wanted to check on Brian and Richard." Lucas watched over my shoulder as I pulled up a search engine and typed in Richard's name. It came up in a class listing for GA State. "He's teaching at the college." The second hit for him was an article about a book he was researching with a partner, Brian.

Lucas pointed at the screen. "They're writing a book?"

"Looks like it." I typed Brian's name in and found a LinkedIn page. He was still employed at a law firm in

Atlanta. "They seem to be doing fine. And the book they're writing is fiction, so I don't think they'll be talking about their experience."

Lucas sat back and grinned. "Nobody would take them seriously if they claimed it was true."

I nodded. On a whim, I typed in Jenny Highland. A few articles came up, but none related our Jenny.

Lucas cocked his head. "Who are you looking for now?"

"Jenny, but she appears to be off the grid."

"Huh?"

"She's either using a different name or not doing anything that would be reported on." I gave Lucas a crash course in social media.

He leaned back. "I think I'll stay off the grid, too."

"Good plan." He was a quick learner. I closed the laptop and studied him. He sipped his black coffee and stared off into space, an unreadable expression on his face. "Are you okay getting stuck here?"

He startled and gazed at me, a smile forming on his lips. "I will be. With God's help." He took a deep breath. "I'm of two minds about it. I'll miss Nate and Cassie, and even your ma." One corner of his mouth quirked upward. "I'll also miss working in the fields. And I've reminded myself over and over since yesterday that I wouldn't have had Codger all that much longer anyway."

Of course, he missed his horse. "Why not?"

He snorted. "Why do you think his name was Codger? He was old. Not even sure how old." He clasped my hand on the table and gazed into my eyes. "Thank you for asking. I'm glad you're here. Staying in this house is familiar, sort of. The same but different. One of the few things that is."

"Living in this time is an adjustment." I blew out a breath. "With this COVID thing, it's that way for everyone right now."

"Lydia…" He rubbed my hand with his thumb, but I jerked it away. He leaned back. "I'd better get back to work. Thanks again."

I tensed. What was he planning to say? I may never find out, now.

~

The next morning, I zipped my small suitcase, ready to wheel it down the street to temporary lodging at Todd's. He and Chantal had agreed to store the rest of my stuff when it arrived from Seattle.

I let out a breath as I picked up my small case from the bed and plopped it on the floor by the door.

"Lydia," Lucas called.

"Here." I strode into the hallway. "You can get into my room to clean it."

"I'll carry this downstairs for you." Lucas picked up the case.

I chuckled, raised the handle, and pulled it on the wheels.

He took it from me, but when he got to the staircase, he lifted it and carried it down without collapsing the handle. I giggled all the way downstairs behind him.

Outside on the large porch, he stopped. "I could wheel it down the street for you."

I smiled. "No need. Don't you have work to do?"

He nodded. "I have time."

"It's fine." Why did this feel like goodbye? I'd be right

down the street, at least for a while. And neither of us had plans to leave the area.

"Do you have any leads on a job, yet?" He still held the handle of my case.

"Todd set up a couple of interviews for me next week." I shifted my weight. "I'll be around here for a while. In fact, I'll probably be eating dinner with you most nights."

He shook his head. "It's going to take some getting used to. Eating dinner in the evening and lunch at midday. The portions they call lunch portions." He scoffed. "I'll need two. Especially if I get construction work."

He'd have more changes to worry about than that. Was he bringing up something minuscule to keep from dwelling on the big stuff? I'd be here to help him, but I had a lot to adjust to, also. "Well, I'd better..." I motioned toward Todd's.

"Lydia." Lucas touched my shoulder. "Would you?" He shuffled his feet. "Accompany me on a walk this evening?"

I tilted my head. "Yes?"

He grinned. "I think the term Chantal uses is date, but I can't invite you out to dinner, not without wages."

I smiled. "Yes, I'd like to go out with you, get to know you better. You're a great friend."

He slumped. "I'm aimin' for more than friends."

My breath caught. "Really?"

He snorted. "Why do you think I came here?"

"Uh." I flailed my arm. "You said you didn't belong back there, and you were always so curious about the future."

"That may have been a reason to visit, but why do you think I didn't press to go back?"

I pressed my lips together and side-eyed him. "You respected Todd's conviction?"

He placed his hands on my shoulders and lowered his head toward me. "I love you."

Air whooshed out of me, and my pulse rate sped up. I tilted my head back and gazed into his warm brown eyes. "Oh." Why couldn't I say anything else? Like, how special he made me feel, and how wonderful he was. Instead, I circled his neck in a hug, then planted a soft kiss on his lips. He responded, deepening the kiss.

A throat cleared, and we jolted away. My cheeks burned like lava.

"Uh, Lucas, that room isn't cleaning itself."

Lucas smiled at me, then turned to Chantal. "Yes, ma'am." He glanced back as he entered the house. "See you this evening."

I waved as he disappeared.

Chantal giggled and hugged me. "I knew that boy was smitten with you. He's a great catch, too."

I heaved a sigh. "It's so soon, though."

"Sometimes, it doesn't take a lot of time to know." She ushered me inside. "I'll be praying, and I know he will. He and I had a long talk about that." She squeezed my shoulder. "He told me the good news about you, too. We expect you to accompany us to church."

I rolled my eyes. "Actually, I'm looking forward to it." I stopped next to her desk. "Wait, why did you bring me back in here?"

She waved her hand toward the large parlor. "While cleaning in there, I found some journals. Thought you might be interested."

"Thanks." I strode into the room and located the stack. There were some of Nate's mom's and a teenager from the fifties, but only what I'd already seen. Melody's journals weren't even here. I scanned the rest of the shelves. Nothing. I trudged into the foyer where Chantal sat in front of her laptop. "Any other journals anywhere?"

She shook her head. "Just in there and the closet upstairs."

"I was afraid of that." I ambled outside, carried my case off the porch, and wheeled it toward Todd's.

The last journal of Cassie's was 1875. I stopped in the middle of the sidewalk and grabbed that journal from the pocket of my overnight bag. My hands shook as I flipped the pages. The entry about thinking she saw Jenny was still there, on the last filled-in page. I shuddered. We still had no idea where Jenny was. At least she couldn't use Todd's time machine. I wish I could've seen her face when she found out Todd's machine had been destroyed. I groaned. That didn't mean Jenny or Allison wouldn't make a new one.

I squeezed my eyes shut and soaked in the early morning sunshine. "Dear Lord, please take care of my family. Don't let Jenny or Allison succeed in their time-travel quest." I opened my eyes and strolled down the street, a smile on my face.

I planned to concentrate on the present and future, thankful I had a family with Todd, Chantal, and now Lucas.

With God, maybe this new life would work out after all.

If you'd like to stay updated on news about book three in the New Hope Trilogy and receive a free short story, sign up for my newsletter at:
https://pamelagbaker.com/?page_id=20.

Acknowledgements:
Chasing Time was born from a conversation with Julie Gwinn when I pitched its prequel, *Message Sent Through Time*, as a stand-alone. She encouraged me to write at least two more in the series. After praying about it, ideas for two more books popped into my head. The writing process took considerably longer.

Thank you, Gary Baker and Jim Franz, for your help with the developmental edit, and my two critique groups, ACFW Scribes and Word Weavers Macon-Bibb Chapter, for your encouragement and advice in improving the manuscript. Thanks also to Winged Publications for taking a chance on me, and the great covers, editing, and formatting.

All praise and thanks go to God for the gift of stories and mentors to teach and hone my skills.

www.ingramcontent.com/pod-product-compliance
Lightning Source LLC
Chambersburg PA
CBHW070607300726

48975CB00006B/1744